Cameron's Landing

Cameron's Landing

ANNE STUART

DOUBLEDAY & COMPANY, INC.
GARDEN CITY, NEW YORK
1977

All of the characters in this book
are fictitious, and any resemblance
to actual persons, living or dead,
is purely coincidental.

Library of Congress Cataloging in Publication Data

Stuart, Anne.
Cameron's Landing.

I. Title.
PZ4.S9245Cam   [PS3569.T78] 813'.5'4
ISBN: 0-385-12077-X
Library of Congress Catalog Card Number 76-50792

For Richie,
who is the finest man of this and every other generation.

Cameron's Landing

Chapter I

It was a very old man rowing the small, well-made dory. He tied up at the dock, climbed out very slowly, and took stock of me through his rheumy old eyes.

"You'll be the girl for Cameron's Landing," he said briefly, his eyes not quite meeting mine. "We've been expecting you." He reached down and shouldered the trunk with strength surprising in a man so old. "We'd best be going. It's getting on toward supper, you know." His voice was accusing. "Wouldn't do to be late for supper."

I could think of nothing to say. "Yes," I murmured inanely. He deposited the trunk neatly in the stern of the boat, then turned to help me climb in.

"Mind where you step," he cautioned sullenly. "It's damp in here."

"Thank you, Mr. . . . ?" I let it trail meaningfully as I seated myself on one of the rough plank seats, tucking my long legs beneath me.

"You might as well call me John. Everyone else does," he said morosely. Without waiting for reply he cast off and we rowed in silence. He made strong, smooth sweeps through the icy blue water of late spring, and once more I was impressed with the deceptive strength of him.

"Is something wrong?" I questioned hesitantly.

"Wrong?" he barked. "Why should anything be wrong? Don't tell me you're one of these overimaginative females who jump at their own shadows. You won't be on Cameron's Landing for long if you are." That idea seemed to please him, for he cackled merrily. "Though whose idea it was to bring an inlander here I don't know. We don't need outsiders around here; we can take care of our own when we're in trouble," he snapped.

"And are you in trouble?" I questioned casually.

"No!" he spat back at me. "Stop asking questions that don't concern you."

I was getting exasperated. The man was clearly bordering on the senile, and it was useless to argue with the sly logic of the old. "All right," I said firmly. "I don't want to fight with you. I'm here to earn my living, nothing more."

He considered this for a moment, then cackled again. "That's what they all say. We'll see, girly, we'll see. You may not be too bad, at that. All the same, you'd better watch out. There's ghosties on this island. They might like to trip a young lady like yourself and toss you into the water by the rocks. Surrounded by cliffs on three sides, this island is. And how would you like that, my girl?"

"Not a bit," I answered coolly. "I'll keep an eye out for ghosties and troublemaking old men, don't you worry."

This pleased him, for he grinned a toothless grin as the boat reached the sandy shore. A horse and wagon were tethered in front of what was obviously a combination boathouse and stables.

"There's our elegant transportation, girly. As you can see, the Camerons do not share your lofty opinion of yourself. You get the kitchen cart, not the family carriage." This seeming slight amused him even more, for a wheezing chuckle escaped him before I turned in full fury.

"You're a nasty old man!" I said roundly, fairly fuming with indignation. "I've come almost two hundred miles from my father's farm in Vermont to take a job with people I've scarcely heard of and I'm met by a mean, demented old loon who's doing his best to scare me out of my wits. Well, I won't be scared!" My own fierceness surprised me. "I've come this far and I'm going to stay!"

"Hoity-toity," he muttered, unimpressed. "You may have second thoughts after you've spent a few nights here."

Ignoring this, I scrambled out of the dory and onto dry land again. I was now in the Camerons' domain, totally dependent on their whims. And whims they had in plenty, if I were to believe all that I had read about them in the society pages of the Boston and New York newspapers my father had subscribed to.

It was a deceptively tranquil place. The sea was strong in my nostrils, and that, combined with the damp spring smell of awakening earth, brought a small ache of loneliness. The trees were taller here on this island, and the white birches grew in abundance. I sighed, and looked at the ancient figure of Old John, sincerely hoping his ideas of ghosties and danger were only figments of a senile imagination. From an island there was only one avenue of escape, and I had never seen the ocean before this afternoon.

The sun was setting as we drove through the tall pines and birch trees that bordered the rutted dirt road. The smell of the pine needles mingled with the air and I felt a sudden wave of determination. It was a strange and lovely place in the late spring twilight, and I could belong here if I tried. And try I must.

The road turned a sharp corner, and suddenly we were upon the house. I stared up at it in amazement not unmixed with apprehension. It was gigantic, more like a castle than a private home. It was made from heavy stone, and I could just imagine the barges bringing the materials across that narrow strait, day after day until this edifice was finished. The cost must have been enormous, even back then, but that was in keeping with all that I had heard of the illustrious Camerons. They had made their fortune in the China trade, and had husbanded it wisely, so that none of the descendants need do anything but spend their generous inheritance.

We drove straight to the back of the mansion, past extensive stables and outbuildings. "This'll be your entrance," Old John wheezed, putting me in my place. "A part-time governess-companion ain't considered to be exactly of the quality level."

"Naturally," I agreed calmly, seething inwardly. This business of working for a living was going to be harder than I had imagined back in the gentle atmosphere of my father's house. Being a Vermonter and a Scot, I found any form of subservience hard to bear. Well, this was one of the things I would have to accustom myself to, I warned my rising temper.

"It's a dour house," I mentioned, unable to free myself from my feelings of foreboding at the sight of that dark pile of masonry with its leaded casement windows.

"That it is, missy," he said with new respect in his voice. "Some don't see it right off, those that aren't gifted with 'the sight.'"

"More damned than gifted," I murmured thoughtlessly, looking upward at the looming building.

"Eh . . . ?" Something was troubling Old John. "What would your name be, miss?"

"Lorna MacDougall," I answered in surprise. "Didn't they tell you?"

"Eh, they don't tell Old John nothing," he muttered. "I'm sorry, miss, if I seemed a bit rough. I didn't understand that you were a Scot too. That makes a difference."

"Does it?" I asked dryly. "Why?"

"This is Cameron land. They're as Scottish as you can be, and all who work here are Scots too, with the exception of that Thora Monroe, who brought you here. And in some ways she's not a bad woman either," he reflected. "But you're welcome here, Miss Lorna. Maybe one with the sight might make a difference to this troubled house."

"Don't tell anyone about that, would you?" I asked hastily. "It's more a trouble than a blessing, and I prefer to forget about it."

He shook his grizzled head sorrowfully. "That's as may be, miss. But you won't be allowed to forget it, not here at Cameron's Landing. You may need it to survive."

With this gloomy pronouncement he brought the wagon to a halt and leapt with surprising agility to the ground. Tying the horse to a hitching post, he was around to my side and helping me down with newfound courtesy before I could pull my scattered thoughts together. A door opened in the black mass of stone and light poured out into the twilight.

"Is that you, John?" a rough, scarcely feminine voice called out. "Have you brought her?"

"That I have, Thora. We'll be there in a shake," he called back, pulling my heavy trunk from the back of the wagon effortlessly and starting toward the light. "Follow me, miss."

I did so, picking my way over the muddy ground. The light inside the door was blinding for a moment, and a blast of heat overwhelmed me. It hadn't been more than mildly brisk outside, but this warmth more than made up for it. Slowly my eyes became accustomed to the light, and I focused on a skinny, severe-looking middle-aged woman in housekeeper's black bombazine. She looked quite fierce, and I nearly trembled as I held out a hand. "Miss Monroe?"

She smiled, and all severity left her bony face. "Heavens, call me Thora, dear. So you're Ian MacDougall's daughter? You poor little thing."

I nodded, bemused by her terming me a poor little thing. I stood close to six feet in stout leather brogues, and I quite towered above the housekeeper. She rambled on. "I was so sorry to hear about your father's accident, my dear. It must go hard on him to be bedridden, an active, charming man like he was. And your sweet mother's holding up just fine, I'm sure. I suppose they'll miss you terrible—those ten brothers and sisters of yours . . ."

"Nine," I interposed hastily.

"Well, nine, whatever." She waved off an extra child or two as something of no consequence. As I suppose it was, to her. "So now you're here to help make ends meet for your poor beleaguered household. It's pleased I was to get your mother's letter asking if we needed someone, for I've missed my friends and kin in the thirty-five years I've been here. I'm glad you could come to us for a bit, instead of finding yourself a husband and a family of your own right off, as you could have easily done, a pretty little thing like you. However, you look like you've got a good head on your shoulders and I'm sure you've plenty of time for weddings and birthings to come." She gave a deep sigh, presumably for her own lost weddings and birthings, and then beamed upon me like a proud mother.

"I guess so." I was at a loss for an answer in the face of this hearty little woman. I had no doubts at that time as to the sincerity of her welcome, and the kitchen exuded a pleasant, easygoing atmosphere that seemed to give the lie to my previous misgivings about the Cameron mansion.

"You must be terribly tired after your trip. Come and meet the girls and then I'll show you where you can wash up before you meet the old lady." She turned her ramrod-straight back and called loudly, "Katie, Nancy, get off your lazy bottoms and come over here."

My eyes followed the direction of her order and saw two young girls in starched uniforms curled comfortably in chairs around the scarred oak table. The two of them, with surprisingly similar motions, uncurled themselves and came forward to be presented. Katie was the older and bolder of the two, with thick black hair and a sensuous, curving mouth. Nancy was plumper and jollier, yet both of their greetings were innocently friendly. I envied them their unconscious provocativeness, yet I couldn't really wish I had been blessed with it. Life would have been difficult in the extreme were I constantly exposed to the importunities of men. As it was, my height had sufficiently discouraged most men, and my education, unusual for a woman in those times, frightened the rest.

"Beautiful hair you have, Lorna," Katie sighed, touching her own raven locks with patent dissatisfaction. "I always wanted to have red hair."

"Not if you were born with it," I assured her wryly.

"Maybe." She was skeptical. "You're going to be the little ones' governess?"

"I'm not sure," I began, as Thora answered at the same time.

"Now, Katie, we'll have to see what the old lady says." She turned to me. "I'll show you to my room where you can have a bit of a wash before supper. I'm afraid I can't show you to your own quarters yet— they haven't been decided upon."

"Really?" I questioned. It seemed rather late to make a decision like that one.

"The old lady said to wait." Thora made a moue of disdain. "She wants to interview you and see . . . well, see where she thinks you belong in the social structure of the Castle. That's what we call this place, behind the Camerons' backs, of course."

I nodded. "It's an apt name." I brushed at my travel-stained skirts. "I *would* like a wash," I added gratefully. "Where the spring mud has dried it's become dust already and I feel absolutely filthy."

"Well, you're so lovely and proper-looking, no one would think it," Thora reassured me, opening a door at the far end of the kitchen. "You can wash in here—I like to be near the center of things," she explained, noting my surprise at the proximity of her rooms to the kitchen. "Nancy, girl, bring Lorna some warm water so she can make herself presentable for Lady Margaret."

"*Lady* Margaret?" I questioned.

"The daughter of a Scottish peer before she married Josiah Cameron," Thora explained, her voice a shade disrespectful. "And she seldom lets anyone forget it."

I found myself in a small dressing room off Thora Monroe's scrupulously neat bedroom. Taking a comb out of my reticule, I started to work on my tangled auburn head before Nancy brought me a steaming basin of water. I thanked her absently, busily trying to arrange my mussed hair without having to replait the waist-length locks. Finally I decided the effect was neat enough, and commenced washing some of the travel dirt from my skin, noting with satisfaction the pale, heart-shaped face and green eyes which shone from beneath surprisingly black brows and lashes, and decided I looked as proper as could be managed in these less than ideal conditions. I would have liked to change into a more suitable working dress than my fashionable green traveling costume. Somehow in that handsome dress I looked a little too much like a defiant, headstrong young lady and not enough like the meek little working girl I was supposed to be. I didn't think the formidable Lady Margaret was going to be too pleased with my appearance.

I was totally unprepared for her reaction. After a welcome meal of chicken stew and sour-dough biscuits I went before the mistress, as they called her, my knees shaking, my palms sweaty with fright. Suppose she disapproved of me, said I wouldn't do at all? Suppose she ordered me back to Vermont immediately, without a trial period?

My family depended on me. My father had been a lawyer and a gentleman farmer, and, though he had abundant charm, he was none too successful at either occupation. When he had fallen down the steep flight of stairs in our old farmhouse and broken his back, the doctors' bills had taken what little money he had saved. We'd made it through the winter, but just barely, and I swore I wouldn't have to watch my large family go hungry again. Lady Margaret paid outrageously well, a suspicious circumstance in itself that I chose to ignore, and I would send every single penny home to my harassed mother to spend, for she was as careful as my father was improvident. My two eldest brothers had taken on work as hired hands for one of our neighbors, but I would be making twice what they could bring home. No, this job was too good to lose, and I would have to control my hasty temper and my pride, like it or not.

A short while later I found myself in a huge, cold, dimly lit room. At the far end was a meager fire, and what seemed to my unfortunately myopic eyes a bundle of blue rags. "Well, don't you stand there, girl. Come here!" An imperious, faintly British voice sounded from the rags, and I firmly checked my first impulse to scurry forward. I moved down the length of the room at a slow, stately pace, at least with a sufficient show of outward calm. If I were to remain here, and I must, it would have to be at least partly on my own terms. I came to stand before her, and my eyes took in the whole of her tiny form, from her autocratic silvered head to the thin, blue-veined hand grasping an ornate, silver-headed walking stick with unnecessary force. She looked me up and down with her faded blue eyes as I examined her. She had the tired, pain-creased expression of an invalid, and I rightly suspected that she was a victim of painful rheumatism. As she spoke, I realized with surprise that she wasn't quite as ancient as she had first appeared, perhaps in her early seventies.

"You're the new girl that housekeeper had brought here?" she snapped.

"I am Lorna MacDougall," I answered with comparable queenliness.

"Lorna MacDougall, eh?" She peered through the gloom. "Come closer, girl, and let me take a look at you. Sit here." She gestured to an ornate footstool by her feet. I seated my lengthy frame as gracefully as possible, my eyes never leaving hers in an unconscious test of strength. Hers wavered first, and she looked away angrily.

"Haven't you been told a good servant keeps her eyes lowered in front of her employer?" she demanded waspishly.

Now was the time of decision. "I am not a servant." I made the statement calmly, assuredly.

She laughed then, and her laugh was surprisingly young and full-throated for one of her feeble appearance. "My father had red hair, just like yours," she announced, "and a temper to match. I loved my father very much, but don't expect me to be partial to you because of that."

"No, ma'am," I answered docilely, surprised that my boldness had been accepted.

"So you've come to Cameron's Landing, Lorna MacDougall. To find your fortune, perhaps?" Her narrow blue eyes peered at me through the gloom of the drafty room.

"No, my lady. To get away from my family," I lied. I wasn't about to expose my need to her. I had a suspicion she'd use it cruelly.

She laughed again, this time without humor. "My family isn't any better, my dear. One of them may be a murderer."

Chapter II

A slight chill ran through me. My instincts had not been mistaken after all; something was wrong with this house. I kept my expression blank.

The old lady was watching me carefully. "Well, at least you don't try to contradict me when I tell you that. One of us here on the island killed my husband. Maybe one of my own children. And I mean to find out who did, no matter what the consequences," she added in a hushed, furiously determined voice. "What do you say to that, Lorna MacDougall?"

"I'd say that might be a dangerous occupation for an old woman," I answered, surprised at my own temerity.

"But not for a young one, eh?" She leaned back with a sigh of satisfaction. "I was hoping you'd feel that way, my dear. Because that is exactly what you've been brought here to do. To find who is the snake in this earthly paradise. You'll have certain ordinary duties, ones that I'll devise for you so no one will suspect my real purpose, but in your spare time you will be my spy. You will be my feet and my eyes and my ears; you will be able to go places that this tired old body of mine can no longer go. Do you agree to this?" She peered at me through the gloom. "If not, I can just as easily send you back to Vermont and find someone a little more willing."

"I didn't say I was unwilling," I answered her mildly. "I don't quite see how I could help you, however. Surely the local constable is more proficient in the investigations of . . . murders?" I couldn't quite believe that melodramatic word.

"You would think so, wouldn't you?" she snapped, grasping her cane with one claw-like hand and tapping it nervously on the cold stone floor. "They botched the entire thing completely—a bigger pack of fools I have never seen. They were here for days on end, accusing everyone with their wretched insinuations and proving absolutely nothing. Whereas you, my dear girl, will have all the advantages they lacked."

"Such as?" I questioned skeptically. I had a feeling of being taken over against my will, and I didn't relish the sensation. Besides, the abruptness of this bizarre conversation made it seem curiously unreal.

"Such as a modicum of intelligence! Such as living here, a trusted member of the household, so that the murderer will never suspect your real purpose here."

"And what if I find the killer?" I said reasonably. "Don't you think I might be in danger from him? After all, if he really killed your husband then he probably won't hesitate to kill again. No," I rose decisively, "I don't think I can help you."

"Yes, you will!" she screamed shrilly, her wrinkled face mottled with rage. "You will do as I say or you will leave here and return to your wretched cow farm or whatever it is."

"Certainly, ma'am." I started toward the door, sternly ignoring the flash of guilt and dismay that swept over me as I thought of returning home empty-handed, another mouth to feed. But I wouldn't humble myself before this miserable old tyrant—surely there were other jobs.

"Lorna." Her voice, suddenly weak and quavery, caught me as my hand touched the brass doorknob. "Come back, girl. I . . . I'm sorry I lost my temper with you. Please come back." This new weakness on the old lady's part surprised me. I moved back to her side, thankful for another chance, yet all the time watching her with suspicion.

"Lorna," she whispered, and the sound was that of a sick, sad old woman. "Please help me, my dear. Josiah was often a cruel man; harsh, I suppose, but he was all I ever loved in this world. Someone on this island murdered him, perhaps even one of his own children. The suspicion is tearing this family apart. I must find out who did it and have him punished, or we'll never have any peace. Please, my child. I haven't much time left anyway, but I want to die knowing who in my own family I can trust." Tears were running down her wrinkled, autocratic old face, and I felt pity stir within me and build in intensity. Her earnestness was that of a deathbed wish, and who was I to deny her? Still, a reluctance and a sense of foreboding that I have learned not to ignore warred within me, and I asked one last question.

"But why me? Surely there are others more qualified, more involved?"

"I am a woman of strong opinions," she informed me in a slightly firmer voice. "The moment you walked in the door, looking so much like my dear father, I knew you would be the one to help me. Once I make up my mind I don't often change it. And you must admit," she gathered strength, "that the pay is more than generous, even if the work I'm asking you to undertake might prove to be slightly . . . hazardous. As a matter of fact, the pay is princely. With a bonus of, say, a thousand dollars when you find the murderer? That would do you very nicely, wouldn't it, my dear? Why, you could move to New York or Boston and be very comfortable for a long while. Long enough to find yourself a rich husband. Come, come, here I'm offering you life on a silver platter, and you stand about quibbling! Will you or won't you?"

I thought of the farm, of the difference my salary would make, and the incredible advantages of a thousand dollars. "All right," I agreed slowly, reluctantly, my mind still unable to ignore the presentiment of disaster that seemed to loom over me. "I'll help you."

"Have I your word?" Her voice grew feeble again.

"You have my word," I affirmed, and immediately new life flooded back into Lady Margaret's wasted frame. She sat upright with vigor and rubbed her bony, be-ringed hands together.

"Then we must make plans. The children will be here in a few days—you'd best be fully prepared. I think for our purposes you will serve as governess for Allison's dear little children when they're visiting, and companion to me. Is there anything else you'd like to do to keep busy? I'd rather you didn't do housework—you should retain a modicum of social standing. Perhaps you'd like to do a bit of gardening?"

I shook my head ruefully. "I'm afraid I'm useless with plants. I seem to carry a blight in my fingers—my father never would let me work on our garden. If I might . . ." I hesitated. "If I might possibly help with the horses? That would get me out to places where I might hear things I wouldn't otherwise. And I love animals."

"Well, I don't know," she said doubtfully. "It doesn't seem quite lady-like, somehow."

"Oh, it wouldn't be," I assured her cheerfully. "But truly, I think it would be the most useful thing I could do. One hears a lot of gossip around a stable. And John needs me—he's getting old and there's no one around to help him."

"You know a lot about this household for someone who has been here for a few hours," she grumbled. "It's not for want of money that we have so little help. The townspeople won't come out here, ever since Josiah died. They believe it's haunted or something equally absurd. Superstitious fools," she sniffed. "Well, do as you think best. You know more about such things, I believe."

"Yes, my lady," I agreed.

"To start with I suppose you should do some exploring. Perhaps you should tour the house on your own—I don't want Thora's preconceived notions filling your head. Feel free to make yourself at home. We'll talk over dinner tomorrow night and you can tell me any ideas you might have after you're seen the house and grounds."

I sank down on the stool beside her resignedly, shaking off the weariness I felt after my long journey. "Perhaps you'd better tell me about this murder before we go any further," I said. "I remember hearing vague rumors of it last summer, but I didn't pay much attention." Actually, now that she had mentioned it, the details of the murder were quite clear in my brain, and I hoped that accounted for my feelings of misgiving. The style of journalism current then was nothing if not vivid, but I wanted the widow's version of that grisly afternoon.

The old lady nodded sagely. "Very wise, my dear. It's still painful to me." Here a dutiful expression of sorrow crossed her face, and I wondered how deep her emotions really went. "But I've been up against some cruel things in my life, and I've learned that the only way to face an unbearable fact is to face it squarely. Though I suppose there's not that much to tell in this case.

"I went out for my afternoon walk on a fogbound day last July. I always used to take long walks then before the rheumatism got so bad. Josiah would come with me more often than not, but that day he sent me on alone. There was something to take care of, he said, something for the man of the family to handle."

"And you went?" I prodded her, a little outraged at her humble acquiescence.

"Of course I went," she snapped. "You never knew my husband, my dear. He loved me very much, as I loved him, but he was possessed of the foulest temper in the Western Hemisphere." She sighed, almost with longing. "So like a blind fool I went for my walk, totally unaware of the terrible evil that was hovering over the island, waiting for my husband." She reached one thin hand to the table beside her and brought a frail crystal goblet of what I suspected was sherry to her lips. "When I arrived back Josiah was sitting alone on the lawn, his head drooping on his chest. I remember thinking, How odd, he must have dozed off. And on such a gloomy day. And I noticed that he was wearing his red waistcoat, which surprised me, for he usually kept that for winter wear. There was no one about, no one at all, and as I moved closer I saw that it wasn't his red waistcoat at all. It was blood, pouring from him." She shut her eyes in horror at the memory, and I let out my suspense-held breath.

After a moment or two of respectful silence her wrinkled eyelids opened. "He was dead, of course. Stabbed through the heart by a person of great strength, they said. The next few days were a nightmare. The island was overrun with people from the newspapers, asking impertinent questions. I nearly went mad."

I was about to open my mouth when the door flew open and Thora bustled in. "Now, now, what's all this?" she cried heartily, her eyes darting between the two of us with a sharpness that belied her cheery tones. "Why, you've been talking the better part of two hours, and poor Lorna here just arrived from a long trip. It's time both of you were in bed."

"Since when have you been giving orders?" Lady Margaret shot back with a somewhat diminished fire. "However, I dare say you are right. Put Miss MacDougall in the green bedroom and see that she's comfortable."

"The green bedroom?" Thora demanded, scandalized. "So that's how it's to be, is it?" she muttered under her breath. "Very well, my lady." She turned to me. "Well, dearie, wait for me in the kitchen. I'll be back after I get the mistress settled down for the night. Shouldn't take me long; I know you're tired too."

That was an understatement. I was almost blind from exhaustion; never in my life had I wanted anything as much as I wanted a bed that night. I curtseyed with old-fashioned politeness to Lady Margaret.

"Good night, my lady," I murmured, trying to stifle a yawn.

"Good night," she said, nodding benevolently. "Sleep well, my dear, and we'll talk more of this later."

I stumbled sleepily from the room, down the long dark hallways, shivering with the chill that emanated from the damp stone walls, my heavy traveling boots echoing hollowly. It took what seemed like hours to find the kitchen again, and now it was cool and quiet. Nancy and Katie had departed to their own interests, and silently I moved to the dying fire. The room was dark, with eerie shadows playing over the stone walls, and I sank down on the wooden settle, shivering nervously. My mind roved back over the last few weeks, the hurried packing, the tedious journey across three states. For the twentieth time I wondered whether I could bear it in this stone fortress, with miles and miles and a stretch of ocean between me and everything I had ever known—and a vicious murderer lurking about as well. I could feel exhausted tears welling up within me, and fought against them. One had escaped my vigilance, however, when Thora bustled back into the kitchen.

"There now," she said briskly, "she's settled for the night and now we'll do the same for you. I must say, she's taken a rare fancy to you, the mistress has. It'll be interesting to see what happens when the family comes home."

"When are they expected?" A flicker of interest fought through my fatigue. I couldn't imagine the other members of a family containing Lady Margaret, and I longed to see the children she had borne, the ones she so unhesitatingly described as possible murderers.

"Oh, they'll be here in a few days, I expect. Lady Margaret likes to have them down here as often as they'll come, and she usually gets her own way. She owns a controlling interest in the family company, you see."

"Yes, I do see." I followed her up the back stairs, my skirts brushing along the spotless floors with a soft whisper. Thora was an excellent housekeeper, and I thanked God I would not have to work with her. I appreciated an immaculate house, but not enough to be the one who made it so. My own tastes ran more to haphazard cleanliness rather than austere neatness. Perhaps there were advantages to my newfound if hazardous profession.

Thora must have been reading my mind, for she spoke as we started down a barren hallway. "This house is the very devil to keep clean," she muttered. "Well, that won't be any of your concern. Lady Margaret says you're to be on your own tomorrow—to get your bearings, so to speak. Breakfast's early—no later than nine."

"Nine!" I laughed in disbelief.

"Ah, I was forgetting you're from Vermont. You must rise with the cows." She shook her steel-gray head sentimentally and sighed. "Sometimes I think I would have been better off if I'd never left there." I shifted uncomfortably and the housekeeper gave herself a small shake. "Well, I'll have Nancy bring you a tray tomorrow and let you catch some extra sleep. I dare say you need it after your long journey." Her simple friendliness warmed me after the nervous excitement of the day, and I was grateful for her presence in this cold, strange house.

We went through an open doorway and a subtle difference was apparent in the furnishings of the hallway. Long oriental rugs, rich in color, shielded the cool floors; the oil lamps on the walls were of better quality than those in the halls we had passed through. We stopped before an open door and Thora gestured for me to precede her.

"I made up the bed and aired the room a bit after I settled Lady Margaret," she chattered as she followed me into the elegant bedroom. It was immense, with heavy oak furniture to match the dimensions of the room. A giant four-poster bed dominated the place, and a cool, wet breeze blew from the open windows. In a trance I moved to the window seat covered in forest green velvet, and stared out the leaded casement windows. The night was too dark to see the ocean, but the sound and smell were enticingly near.

"I'll close the windows now." Thora bustled forward, but I shook my head.

"No, thank you," I answered. "I always sleep with a window open. I can't abide stuffy rooms."

"You'll pardon my saying so, miss, but you've never lived on the ocean before. The sea air is dangerous to the lungs," she said firmly, reaching past me and closing the windows with a snap. "Your trunk is over by the wardrobe, and you'll find everything you need in its proper place."

I assumed she meant that the chamber pot would be under the bed and the hip bath and basin would be behind the elegant green dressing screen in the far corner. I nodded, secretly amused by her prudishness. "Where do the other doors lead to?"

"Other bedrooms, unused at the moment. This is far too big a house for this family nowadays: it belongs more to a time when there were constant house parties of twenty or thirty people every weekend. That's what it used to be like around here, before Josiah . . . died. Oh well, I suppose I should count my blessings," she sighed gustily. "Lord knows I couldn't manage taking care of a house party with help so hard to come by. Katie and Nancy are well meaning but a little bit on the lazy side, if you know what I mean."

I murmured something suitably sympathetic and she looked pleased. "Eh, it'll be a real pleasure to have someone to talk to now. Someone more my own station in life, if you know what I mean. You have a good sleep, now, my dear, and call me if you need anything."

"I will," I promised, having no such intention. "Thank you for everything, Thora."

"Well, now, it's my duty, more or less, to see you settled. You come and have a cup of coffee with me tomorrow and I'll set you straight on a few things around here. Good night."

"Good night," I echoed, and breathed a sigh of intense relief when the door finally closed behind her voluble personality. From what little I had seen of Thora Monroe I was aware of two things: one, that she liked an audience for her complaints and gossips, and two, that underneath her easygoing exterior she was very jealous of her exalted position in the Cameron household. I think she was suspicious of me, afraid I might steal her favored place of trust and near-gentility.

As far as I was concerned she had nothing to worry about. I found Lady Margaret fascinating and perhaps a bit frightening with her talk of murder. If I hadn't read the papers myself I wouldn't have believed her. But I had.

I would do what I had promised to do with a minimum of involvement and a maximum of care for my own safety. I undressed slowly and put on one of my serviceable nightgowns. Before climbing into the massive bed I went back and opened the windows. For a time I lay there in the dark, listening to the whispering of the sea and the stillness of the house, and then slept.

Chapter III

The sun poured in my windows and onto my eyelids, forcing me to clench them shut against such a rude intrusion. I wanted to sleep, sleep for hours longer. And then I heard the sea again, and remembered where I was. My eyes flew open and I leapt out of bed, wide awake.

I ran across the icy stone floor to the windows and looked out. A wide expanse of emerald green lawn met my eyes, stretching down to sheer cliffs, and then beyond was the shimmering blue jewel of the ocean spreading out limitlessly. I yearned for that ocean as a mother yearns for her child, and I wondered how long I would have to wait before I could swim in that silky sea. I knew full well that such an activity would shock my employers, and certainly Thora would have some harsh words to say, but I was nonetheless determined. I had always swum in the chill waters of our mountain lake, and I wasn't going to let prejudice stop me from doing the same in this vast and beautiful ocean. If I must I would sneak out when it got warmer and swim in the morning before the family and servants rose, but swim I would.

A knock sounded and the door opened before I had time to respond. Nancy's curly blond head poked in the room. "You're up already." She sounded surprised. "I've brought you your breakfast." She entered with a pert grace and set the heavy-laden tray on the small table beside the baronial chair in the center of the room.

"Thank you," I stammered, totally surprised. The tray was set with heavy silver, and such attentions to a servant seemed very odd to my naïve but suspicious mind.

"You're welcome, I'm sure." She dropped a curtsey, then seemed to think better of it, for she blushed, and added, "Lorna. Thora says to ask if there's anything else you'd like."

"This'll be fine, thank you," I murmured. "And thank Thora for me."

It was fortunate that I had no time schedule for the day. Thora had set the tray with blueberry muffins, tea, eggs, sausage, kidneys, toast, and oatmeal. I ate leisurely, devouring everything with the appetite that had long astounded friends and family alike. I only wished that the huge amount I usually ate would add a few pounds to round out my rather spare frame. I would have given anything for some of the fashionably elegant plumpness so popular then, but alas, that was not for me. I was doomed to my tall, boyish length; my only apparent sign of feminine beauty my thick, waist-length hair. And even that was an outrageous color, I thought, despite Katie's compliments.

I had a brief wash with the fresh warm water Nancy had brought with my breakfast, and then began the lengthy and laborious process of dressing myself. Bloomers, a chemise, petticoat upon petticoat, a whalebone corset I neither liked nor needed, and then my outer clothing. I rummaged through my trunk, disgusted with the serviceable navy-blue and gray dresses. Finally I pulled one out and dressed, then set to work on my hair.

The long red tresses were thick and unruly in my hands. I brushed and brushed, and the heavy curtain of hair took on some manageability. I braided it quickly and wound it around my head in a coronet. Winding the gold pocket watch that had belonged to my maternal grandfather, I slipped it into my pocket.

It took me but a few minutes to unpack my meager and sadly depleted wardrobe. I slammed the empty trunk shut, checked the watch to make sure the journey hadn't damaged it, and started out the door at the outrageously late hour of nine-thirty. I was about to shut the door behind me when a fresh sea breeze blew through the windows, reminding me that Thora would not take kindly to the notion that I had ignored her dire warnings about the noxious sea air. I went back, closed the windows with a sharp click, and was on my way again.

I didn't spend much time exploring the house. Nancy and Katie were busy cleaning in preparation for the weekend, and I had no desire to have them catch me snooping. The main part of the house, that is, the part reserved for the family, was large and elegantly furnished. Some of the walls were the heavy stone of the main house, some were paneled oak. The curtains were of damask and velvet in warm, rich colors, the furniture all very modern and built along the massive lines so favored in the latter half of the nineteenth century. I counted three drawing rooms of various proportions, from a warm pink sitting room designed for ladies to the leather and horsehair living room that exuded masculine taste. It was there that Lady Margaret had received me the night before. Two studies, again clearly divided for the sexes, three dining rooms, a library, and an immense ballroom rounded out the first floor of the family's rooms. Beyond them were the massive kitchen, a butler's pantry, Thora's rooms, a laundry, and what I assumed were various storage rooms for food and china. I was far too timid to risk Thora's disapproval by exploring them.

The second floor held six bedroom suites, complete with dressing rooms and sitting rooms along with the customary sleeping rooms, twelve small bedrooms, a large sewing room, a linen room, and a little-used schoolroom. The last looked deserted—I wondered when the grandchildren had last played there. I doubted they had ever seen the room. Toys and books were stacked neatly and covered with a thick layer of dust. It was a charming room, with a multitude of casement windows looking off in two directions—to the vast blue green of the sea and down the length of the island. From that vantage point one could see whoever came to call. A useful thing to remember, I told myself.

Beyond a wide door were the servants' quarters, sparsely furnished, scrupulously clean. It would have gone hard with my overproud nature to have been relegated to these lower-class quarters, and with belated thankfulness I recognized some of the advantages of my peculiar duties.

I could find no stairs to the third story. I had come across one locked door, and I assumed that it led upstairs. The lock puzzled me, and I promised myself I would take it up with Lady Margaret that evening.

And then I was free to explore the grounds. The house had told me nothing at all of its inhabitants, but then, my search had been cursory to say the least. Later, when the house was more or less deserted, I might have more luck.

I stopped in my room on my way outside and once more marveled at the elegance of it. It was clearly the finest of the single bedrooms, and I wondered why Lady Margaret had given it to me. Surely one of the more modest rooms would have done me as well. However, I was pleased with it, so why should I complain? I draped my heaviest shawl around me, for I could tell by the tossing, newly budded branches and the white-capped waves that a fairly strong wind had blown up. I hesitated as to whether I should wear a hat. They were *de rigueur* for young ladies at that time, and I hated them. Quite boldly, I decided against one. After all, I was forced to work for a living, I could no longer be counted a lady. And then, there was no one around to censure me except Thora, and I felt reasonably sure I could handle her.

I wandered the well-kept grounds in a slow, pleasurable dream. The salt tang was strong in the air, and it fed my fancies as it brought red into my cheeks. I ended up with a visit to the stables, planning to check up on my equine charges before I had to cope with my human ones, and found John busy with one particularly fine-looking creature.

"I'd watch out, miss. Samantha here's a mean un most times, and especially now with this sore on her neck," he warned me, and as if to demonstrate the truth of his words, the horse bucked slightly and rolled her frightened, angry eyes. I knew better than to interrupt at such a crucial time, so I wandered over to the other inhabitants of the stable: a tall roan, obviously even-tempered and friendly, a fat old chestnut, and a giant, superior-looking black stallion.

"I'll be helping out here, John," I called to him from the side of the friendly roan.

"What?" he demanded, his lined and puckered face enraged. "A woman? You'll get muck all over your long skirts."

"I don't intend to wear long skirts when I'm helping you," I answered him placidly.

He strode out of the stall, his obvious liking for me at war with his sense of propriety.

"Now, Miss Lorna, I don't know. The stables ain't no place for a woman. These aren't all as sweet-tempered as Ladybird over there. Why, Samantha . . ."

Before he had a chance to stop me I slipped past him and over to the angry horse. I whispered to her, low and soft, and she looked at me inquiringly, her glaring eye softening gradually. Then I moved in beside her, talking gently all the time, and she whinnied in response. Finally I fed her a piece of sugar I had thoughtfully saved from my tray and she was mine.

"Well, I never," Old John said. "You've a way with animals, along with the sight. I didn't know that, miss, or I wouldn't have argued."

I hated to have him believe that plain good sense with animals was somehow allied with the mysterious, supernatural "sight," but for once I took advantage of it, as long as it secured me a place in the stables without further argument.

"I don't like to talk about it," I said demurely, truthfully. "You do need help, John."

"Aye, it's true," he admitted doubtfully. "All right, I'll be glad of the help, that's for sure."

"Good." I seated myself on a rickety old bench with a total disregard for my clean clothes. I felt comfortable and at ease in the stables, and conveniently decided that here was as good a place as any to begin my sleuthing. "Could . . . could I talk to you, John?" I began in a carefully timid voice.

"Certainly, miss," he agreed, his voice taking on a solemnity to match my own as he went back to brushing the bay, Samantha.

"Could you tell me something of Josiah Cameron? I can feel his presence very strongly," I lied, "and I think if I knew a little about his life I would be better able to understand what it is he wants of me." This was all an outrageous fabrication, of course. I'd had no visitations from lost spirits other than a general feeling of apprehension, but I could see from the aghast but fascinated look on John's credulous face that I had picked exactly the right approach.

"Well, I never, miss!" he breathed, and redoubled his efforts on Samantha's coat. "Did you want to hear about his death, then?"

I shook my head. "No, that's not what seems to be the problem. I need to know about his life. What troubled him. You've been here a long time, you must have known him most of his life."

He nodded vigorously, casting nervous glances over his shoulder. "That I did, miss. My father served his father and my grandfather before him. Why, we grew up together, Josiah and I did. Anything you'd want to know just ask Old John."

"All right, I will." I settled back comfortably. "Where did the Cameron money come from?"

"Ah, that's easy enough, miss. You could find that out from mostly anyone in New England—it's a grand family the Camerons are, and that's for certain." He turned to me. "Josiah Cameron's great-grandfather began the business back in the middle of the last century. He was just come over from Scotland and he wound up here, having been told it was the closest thing to the old country as could be found. And at that time fortunes were just begging to be made.

"It's an unusual company, miss. Surely you've heard tell of it even as far away as you've come from. Why, the Cameron ships are still famous all over the world, for all that the shipping industry is leaving Maine behind. The Cameron shipyards now spend most of their time building blasted pleasure boats. Begging your pardon for my language, Miss Lorna."

I nodded serenely, and he continued, warming to his task. "Ever since the very beginning it's been the same way. Every generation has one brother building the ships and one brother sailing them. From the time the first Charles Cameron built the ships and the first Alexander Cameron sailed them, it's continued up until the present generation. Though of course now we have three sons instead of two to carry on the tradition. But then, Charles is from an earlier marriage, though we're not supposed to mention that in front of her highness." He jerked his head toward the house and I gathered that disrespectful term referred to her ladyship.

By then he didn't even need my gentle "Oh?" to spur him on; he was reminiscing full steam ahead, unlike those fancy pleasure boats the Camerons built. "Josiah's brother Charles married a woman of uncertain virtue by the name of Katharine Johnson, and things have never been easy here since. You talk about your hauntings, miss." He shook his grizzled head.

"What happened?" I recognized my cue and played my part.

"She drove Josiah's brother to an early grave. He was drowned back in '34 on the ship he'd been daft enough to name after his wife. *Witch Woman,* he called it and her, and there was no showing them the sense of their foolishness. He went out on the *Witch Woman* as soon as she was built, taking her on her maiden voyage to the Caribbean for rum and spices. The next thing they heard he was drowned off the coast of Florida.

"But the poor little widow didn't waste no time. There was her brother-in-law, now sole owner of the Cameron shipyards, all ready and waiting to comfort her." His voice was rich with an ancient anger. "In three months they were married, shocking half the state with such unseemliness."

"But where was Lady Margaret?" This was all coming as a surprise to me.

"Over in England. She hadn't even met Josiah then. And even though I disapprove of a lot that woman's done, she was a sight better wife and mother than that . . . that hussy was. Ah, but then I shouldn't speak ill of them that's gone. She died soon after their one son was born. That would be Charles, who runs the shipping business. They named him after his poor dead uncle," he added as an afterthought.

"She died in childbirth?" This sounded tragic rather than evil, and I wondered at Old John's malevolence toward the doomed Katharine.

"You might say that," he allowed. "Oh, she lingered on for a bit. A year, or two at the most. And then, when it was all over, Josiah left the business and went on a long vacation to recover from his broken heart." His tone was dry. "He returned a year later with twice as much money and that old termagant in there as his blushing bride."

"And the company's still doing well?" I questioned.

"Certainly it is. With Mr. Charles and Mr. Stephen to run it, better than their father ever did? And for all that Captain Alex is a wild one, you couldn't find a better captain, no, nor a sharper businessman when you come right down to it. He's wanting them to build these new iron ships, Miss Lorna, and the brothers and Josiah were fighting him tooth and nail. But they'll have to give in in the end, you'll see." He chuckled softly over the wisdom of the unknown Captain Alex. "And the fights he used to have with his father you wouldn't believe! The others, they used to bow and scrape and say, 'Yes, Father' all the time till it about drove poor Josiah wild. He used to tell me how he missed Alex when he'd be off on a trip. Though you'd never have known it from the way the sparks would fly when those two would get together. Why, I even remember on the day he died those two were going at it about something. They were shouting so loud you could hear them all the way in here. . . ." He let his voice trail off, as if he'd said something damning. And I was wondering if he had.

I rose and stretched my lanky frame in an unlady-like gesture. "Thank you for telling me about Josiah," I said sweetly. And thank you for telling me about his angry son, I added silently. "I think I'll walk down to the water before luncheon. This is my day off," I said confidingly, and watched the look of mortification fade from his seamed face. As far as he could tell I hadn't noticed the terrible implication of his thoughtless words.

"You do that, miss," he agreed. "But wrap your shawl around you —it's a mite brisk down there."

I made my way slowly across the lawn, lost in thought. Already it seemed as though I had pinpointed the murderer—and without having met any of the suspects. I was quite pleased with myself for my morning's discoveries.

Chapter IV

Dinner that night was a revelation in many ways. I dressed carefully in an outmoded but nonetheless flattering gray watered silk, coaxed my heavy locks into a slightly more elegant arrangement, and appeared at the door of the pink salon at the appointed hour with just a little trepidation. Thora had warned me that dinner with Lady Margaret was a full-scale affair, complete with seven or eight courses, at least three wines, and full dress sternly required.

"Ah, there you are, my dear." Lady Margaret greeted me with a graciousness that was only slightly condescending and therefore only slightly enraging. "Come in, come in. How charming you look in that little frock! Would you care for a glass of sherry? Or perhaps some ratafia?"

I would have preferred beer (which my shameless brothers had taught me to love) or a good mouthful of scotch whiskey, but I could tell that Lady Margaret believed firmly in ladies behaving like ladies, so I meekly agreed to the sherry and sat myself down on the rose-colored tapestry sofa.

She poured a meager glassful and handed it to me, then sank gracefully (despite her aged bones) into a plump armchair and eyed me with her sharp blue eyes. "Now, tell me, Lorna, my child, what you have discovered today."

Oh well, I never cared for small talk. "I think I know who murdered your husband," I said boldly, sipping the heavy-tasting sherry, my eyes demurely lowered.

"Who?" she demanded avidly, her faded eyes starting from beneath her creped lids.

"I couldn't say right now," I replied, a bit priggishly, I must admit. "I've talked with Old John, walked around the grounds a bit. It's mainly a hunch, I suppose," I confessed. "Something John said seemed to point in a certain direction, but I don't want to talk about it until I have proof."

"John!" The old lady sniffed. "I would take everything that old fool says with a grain of salt if I were you. He's ridiculously partial to one of my sons and could hardly be trusted to be unbiased. Why, ever since Alex could walk Old John has been his slave."

I kept my mouth shut, more convinced than ever that the mysterious Alex was our villain. If his most partisan supporter incriminated him, then there must be trouble lurking.

"Well, I've only been here one day, my lady," I remarked, twirling the amber liquid in what appeared to be a Waterford crystal wineglass. We had had a set that was very similar, which of course we had long ago sold. "After your children come the situation should be a little different, don't you think?"

She sniffed again. "I suppose so. But keep an eye out, girl. You aren't here for a summer vacation, you know." She looked as if she would have liked to rap my knuckles with her ebony cane, and I was glad she was holding her temper in check. I suspected that age was catching up with her. Her attitude toward me went through lightning changes. One moment I was "dear child" and "Lorna, my dear" and the next I was a recalcitrant "girl!" If the expression I'd seen on Old John's face hadn't verified Lady Margaret's wild accusations, I would have almost thought she had made the mystery surrounding her husband's death out of whole cloth. Well, I would wait to see her children and make up my own mind about the situation.

"It will be such a relief to have the children with me again," she sighed, her manner gentle again. "Especially dear Charles. Such a wonderful boy he is. He's always been special to me, even though he was born to Josiah's first wife. That woman!" she sniffed disdainfully. "He's so much like Josiah in looks; I'll always view him as my first-born, my little baby."

"Really?" I said encouragingly, sipping my sherry.

"It seems like only yesterday when I first came to this island with Josiah and little Charles. He was such a sweet child. You'll want to watch your step with him, Lorna, my dear. He's a very eligible bachelor, you know. He runs the building business, with his brother Stephen helping him, and a more thoughtful, sober, devoted son a mother could never hope to have. He's far more dedicated to me than my own blood children. He's been such a comfort to me through all these long years." She drained her glass of sherry, rose on slightly unsteady feet, and beckoned to me. "I have great things planned for Charles." She seemed to be warning me. "Don't be thinking that here's an easier way for you to earn your living, girl!" She drew herself up to her tiny height and there was a curious dignity about her. "We'll go in to dinner now."

We had always eaten well when I was growing up. Our long maple table was always loaded with massive amounts of food—more than enough to feed ten hungry children and whatever friends my father happened to bring home from Montpelier that day. But I had never tasted anything like this.

Thora was a genius in the kitchen. Course followed course of sumptuous food, most of it rejected by Lady Margaret's disdainful and bird-like appetite. I managed to partake nobly of everything, but even small helpings of baked haddock, clam quenelles, stuffed pheasant, lobster thermidor, four vegetables (and where they could have been gotten fresh at this time of year was more than I could imagine), potatoes *à la française,* pilaf, four desserts plus a wine with each course were almost more than my bottomless stomach could manage. I was feeling a bit stuffed as I waded through a third helping of rice pudding (a favorite of mine), and the expression on Lady Margaret's face was astonished disapproval, not unmixed with admiration.

"My God, child. I've never seen anyone eat so much in my entire life! Did they starve you in Vermont?"

I shook my head and swallowed. "No, ma'am. I like to eat," I added, rather needlessly, and she shook her head.

"Tell me, child," she said with a trace of sharpness in her voice. "That dress is charming, of course, but do you have anything a little more cheering in your wardrobe? Perhaps something green or pale blue? I can't stand any more dreary females surrounding me."

"Only my traveling dress," I answered shortly, unwilling to tell her that we had sold all my elegant dresses after father had his fall. "What I own will have to do. After all, I'm not here on a summer vacation." I threw that back at her quite shamelessly.

She ignored the impertinence. "Well, have Thora show you the sewing room. There should be ample materials to suit your needs. Make up three or four dresses of a somewhat frivolous nature. I trust you're an adequate needlewoman?"

"Adequate," I confirmed shortly.

"We have a sewing machine here so it shouldn't take you long. Help yourself to whatever you like—I have no use for sprigged muslins anymore."

"Thank you," I said, hating to accept her charity. "I will."

"Don't mention it. This will all benefit me in the long run, I hope," she said shrewdly.

"I hope so too, my lady," I murmured.

The next few days passed swiftly. I busied myself making three new dresses from the sumptuous array of materials I had found in the sewing room. For daytime I chose a far from sensible apple-green sprigged muslin. The material was light and filmy and more expensive than the rest of my wardrobe put together. I chose a fairly simple design—full in the skirt and snug in the bodice, with a high lace collar that displayed my long, slim neck to perfection. The flame of hair could hardly be disguised, and I decided that setting it off would be the only sensible way to handle it. I was a firm believer in flaunting things one couldn't avoid.

The second dress was more functional but nonetheless attractive. For this I chose some pale blue cotton and made it up into a simple day dress, more demure and retiring than the gay green one, yet still flattering to my slender curves.

Thanks to the wealthy Camerons' possession of that marvelous invention of Elias Howe's, the sewing machine, I completed these in a day and a half. My legs ached from the treadles, and yet I sewed on, fascinated by the machinery and the elegant stuff with which I worked.

Lady Margaret hadn't yet decided whether I would join the family at dinner (after that first evening I ate alone in my room), but I was daring enough to make myself another dinner dress from the exotic array of materials Thora had brought out for me. Back in the corner of the fabric closet, dusty and forgotten, was a bolt of satin. I pulled it out eagerly, enchanted with the strange blue green of the stuff—the color of the sea from casement windows.

"Is that still there?" Thora inquired over my shoulder. She had been fascinated with the wonders I was working, and came to oversee my labors whenever Nancy's and Katie's activities would free her. "I meant to throw that out years ago. It's all watermarked and dusty—give it to me, miss, and I'll have John throw it out."

"No!" I cried possessively, and Thora looked taken aback. I reconsidered my tactics. "Do you think it would be all right if I kept it? I could perhaps cut around the stained parts and make myself a new dinner dress."

"I'm sure that's up to you, Miss Lorna." (This term of respect had come naturally to her as she adjusted to my surprisingly exalted position in this household.) "I hope you can make something out of it—I, for one, hate to see anything go to waste." She sat her sternly upright form on the daybed by the window and prepared to have a comfortable coze. "And how are you liking it here, Miss Lorna?"

I sat down again at the sewing machine and appeared as busy as I could manage. "I love it," I answered truthfully. "It's so beautiful, here on the ocean. It's such a change from Vermont, you know." I sewed for a moment or two, then began in as casual a voice as possible, "Tell me, what are the children like? They're due sometime tomorrow and I'm agog with curiosity about them. Are they like Lady Margaret at all?"

"Well," she said portentously, "they are and they aren't. Charles is a dear, good boy but I have a feeling he thinks pretty highly of himself. I suppose, in his way, he's been a better son to the old lady than either of her real ones. Of course, she was never much of a mother to them, for that matter."

"Oh?"

"Too caught up in Charles and her own precious self, she was," Thora said succinctly. "But that's not to gainsay anything about Mr. Charles. A very handsome gentleman, he is. Many's the young lady who's lost her heart to him over the years. But then, Master Stephen and Captain Alex have had more than their fair share of doting young ladies, too. More than their share."

"Is Charles married?" I questioned casually, knotting a thread.

"No, he's not, and a bad thing it is, him being a bachelor at forty-two. His dear father was always after him to take a bride but would he listen? Not that Alex has, either. The only one of them who married was Stephen, and sometimes I think it was a dire mistake. Mrs. Stephen is too flighty by half." She snorted. "Ah well, Mr. Stephen was always only too willing to please his father. As was Mr. Charles. The only thorn in his side was Captain Alex, and underneath all the bickering and fighting Josiah dearly loved him for it." She rose abruptly and walked to the window, as if troubled by an ancient worry. "You'd best be prepared; his own mother hates him."

"Surely that's too harsh a term?" I inquired, a little shocked.

"Harsh it may be, but truth's always harsh," she said grimly. "For all Lady Margaret could care Alex might have drowned a thousand times."

"But why does she hate him? There must be a reason for such an unnatural feeling on her part."

"Oh, she has reason enough, I suppose. Alex was a little . . . disturbed when he was a boy. Terribly jealous of his older brothers, he was. Had to be sent away for a while."

The evidence against Alexander Cameron was building rapidly, and I abandoned all pretense of sewing. "What's he like?"

"Alex? Oh, he's as handsome as sin, and sometimes he seems almost as wicked. He's loved by the men who serve under him, hated by the young ladies Lady Margaret imports for his approval who never get anything but careless flirtations from him," she sniffed. "He's a loyal friend, a devoted son, for all that his mother dislikes him and his father fought with him. He knows more about the sea than any man I ever met, more about women, more about the forests." She looked at me openly. "He's a good man, Miss Lorna, and you want to watch out for him." She turned and headed for the door, scurrying a bit, as if she knew she'd said too much. And I realized that she too thought that Captain Alex had murdered his father, and would rather be strung up by her thumbs than admit it. I watched her go, pondering everything that she had said.

In the pink salon I had found a pile of fairly recent fashion magazines with some of the latest designs of Mr. Charles Worth of Paris. Boldly I chose a design that I knew instinctively was the most flattering to my slender frame.

The watermark on the satin had disappeared after a few rolls of the bolt, and I was left with seven or eight yards, quite enough to make myself that daring French evening gown with an incredibly full skirt and very little on top. Indeed, I felt justified, since there wasn't sufficient material to make much of a bodice. The heavy sea-green satin barely covered my small but well-shaped breasts and, shameless though it was, I couldn't help being pleased with the results. Even Worth of Paris would not have hung his head in shame.

As I was working on its final details Friday morning, I heard a carriage pull up into the front courtyard. I looked out my open window to peer at the people below, and one of the loveliest women I have ever seen appeared.

Even from a distance she was beautiful—her pale blond hair crowning her regal head, her dress (obviously a Worth original) was perfect in every detail. She looked around her with apparent disdain, and I saw her murmur something in a disparaging manner to the handsome man beside her as she sauntered through the massive front door, leaving her two small children to fend for themselves the best they could.

Anger rose in me at the sight of the two helpless babes, so like my youngest brother and sister, and I ran hastily to my room to toss the half-finished evening dress on my bed before rushing downstairs to greet my suspects and charges.

I met Thora at the bottom of the stairs. "Ah, miss, I'm glad you've come down—it saves my poor old bones a trip. They're wanting you in the pink drawing room right away. Master Stephen and his wife have come."

"Yes, I know. I saw them from the sewing-room window," I said hurriedly, unconsciously adopting her air of hushed importance. "Where are the children?"

"They're in the drawing room too, and proper fretful that one is, being cooped up with her own children for so long. She said to bring you immediately." Thora bristled with disapproval. I noted it absently.

"And here I am," I answered shortly, already disliking Allison Cameron intensely. "I'll go right now."

I knocked on the open door before entering, more as a polite gesture than the properly meek behavior of a servant. The cool, imperious blonde eyed me from her seat in the plushest, most comfortable chair in the room as her husband rose swiftly.

"You must be Lorna." He came forward and shook my hand with a heartiness at odds with the delicate pallor of his handsome face. He was not above medium height, in fact, he was an inch or two shorter than my Amazonian length, and slender to the point of poor health. His brown eyes were almost feverishly bright, and his hands, as they clasped mine in a friendly gesture, were cold. "My mother has been singing your praises for the last few minutes—we're so glad you've come to keep her company."

"That is my son, Stephen Cameron, who's greeting you so enthusiastically," Lady Margaret said dryly from her seat in the corner by the fire. Her grandchildren were at her feet, playing silently and happily, noting and dismissing my presence with the single-minded interest of small children. Grandmother's tiny china figurines were far more attractive than an overtall young woman with an unfortunate head of hair. "He's probably so delighted to see you because he thinks that since I now have a companion he can neglect me even more than he does already." Her voice overrode his protests. "And this is my daughter-in-law, Allison Byrd Cameron, and my grandchildren, Jenny and Young Stephen." Lady Margaret was in her element, the *grande dame* presenting her family, even if it was only to a lowly dependent. "This, everyone, is my companion and friend, Lorna MacDougall. She'll lend you a hand with the children, Allison, in hopes that you'll have a bit more time to spare for your poor aging mother-in-law."

The sulky expression on the lovely face instantly vanished as she rose and took her place beside her boyish husband. "I'm so glad to meet you, Miss MacDougall. I'm sure you'll be wonderful for dear Mama Cameron." Her sophistication had disappeared and she clasped her hands together with just the right amount of childish intensity. "It's just that I adore my children. I couldn't bear to leave them for even a moment, unless I was absolutely sure their guardian could be *perfectly* trusted." Her brown eyes suggested to me that I wouldn't do, yet I knew perfectly well she lied. She would have left her children with Attila the Hun if she thought she might miss some trivial party. I had seen her type before, I thought with stern New England disapproval.

"Come now, my dear." Her husband took her silk-clad arm jovially. "I'm sure Lorna will be excellent with the children. And you know how you need a rest." He turned his dazzling smile in my direction once more. "My wife's so delicate, Miss MacDougall. It's her nerves."

I nodded, thinking that he seemed a lot more sickly than she did. Beneath her powder-puff prettiness lay nerves of steel, I decided, and a sure instinct for getting her own way.

Lady Margaret obviously thought so too. "Well, Allison, if you wish to be in charge of your children, that is perfectly acceptable to me. I had thought we might make a few visits this time, since it's been almost a year since your father-in-law died, but if you prefer to remain here . . ."

"Oh no!" she cried, betraying herself momentarily. "Stephen would find it so tedious." She flashed a dazzling white smile in my direction. "I'm sure Lorna will be a second mother to them."

I hoped I would do better than that, I told myself grimly, returning her pleasant smile.

"You don't look well, Stephen," Lady Margaret continued abruptly. "Have your lungs been bothering you again?"

He flushed, and the delicate red stained his pale cheeks. "I'm fine, Mother. I've just been playing a bit too hard, I suppose. A few days' rest here on the island should do me wonders."

His devoted mother snorted her contempt. "I should have known it wouldn't be overwork that caught up with you. And more likely it was your wife's need of entertainment that's burnt you to the socket, not your own frivolity. Your man needs taking care of, Allison," she told her daughter-in-law sternly. "See that you do."

Allison pouted prettily. "I take excellent care of him, don't I, darling?" she questioned lazily. I watched her from my quiet corner and squirmed. I felt lanky and ill at ease in front of the petite beauty of Allison Cameron. My wrists seemed large and bony, protruding from the chaste blue cotton dress that had seemed so attractive before. Allison's complacent smile swept over me as she surveyed the room. She had obviously sized me up as possible competition and dismissed me quickly. But competition for whom, or what? I wondered, noting the look of glazed adoration in her husband's face.

"Is Alex coming down this weekend?" Allison turned from her husband's worship a bit too casually. Her pale brown eyes were far too intense for her seeming unconcern, and I wondered if Allison Cameron returned any part of her husband's devotion. She seemed far too interested in her brother-in-law.

"Alex?" Lady Margaret echoed, irritated. So this interest had not escaped her sharp eyes either. "Yes, he's agreed to visit his poor recluse mother for once. I expect him this evening. Along with Charles, of course."

"Oh, Charles." The beauty dismissed the elder brother with a wave of her slim white hand, while her husband seemed to perk up a bit.

"I'm glad Alex is coming," he said simply. "And you know perfectly well why he doesn't come more often, Mother. You don't make him feel very welcome."

"How dare you say such a thing?" Lady Margaret screeched. "I treat him as I treat you all. I have never been one to play favorites," she lied outrageously. "The only reason Captain Alexander Cameron doesn't come here more often is because he's selfish, that's what he is!" Her voice was rising with her temper, and Stephen's enthusiasm waned.

"Yes, Mother," he agreed nervously. "But perhaps you might go out of your way a bit this time to be nicer to the chap. He's your own son, after all."

"And who would know that better than I?" she demanded haughtily. "I'll treat him as my son when he starts acting like one. I suppose he still refuses to live with you in the Cameron town house?"

"Alex prefers to be on his own," Allison broke in with a trace of petulance in her light voice. "It's not as if there weren't enough room there for Charles, our family and a dozen more. But, no, he has to have his precious independence!"

Once more Lady Margaret's troubled glance swept over her, and I wondered if Allison's husband was as oblivious to her unusual interest in Alex as he seemed.

"I wish you'd both leave Alex alone," Stephen said tiredly. "And for once I wish we could have a peaceful weekend. I'm so weary of all this bickering."

"Who's bickering?" Lady Margaret demanded. "I was merely making a simple statement that my youngest son neglects me, and immediately everyone sees fit to criticize me."

"Not *youngest* son, Mother," Stephen said suddenly. "*Younger* son. You have only two sons."

Did I imagine the uneasy silence, the tension that filled the room? Perhaps I was taking my role as private detective too seriously.

"I wish," Lady Margaret said plaintively after a moment or two, "you could control your jealousy of your brother Charles. God knows he's been a better son than either you or Alex. . . ."

"Yes, Mother, so you've always told us," he said faintly. "From our earliest years. I'm getting rather sick of it all, if you must know." With that he strode from the room, but not without nodding to me politely with the years of well-bred training that had been drilled into him.

There was silence in the rose-colored drawing room for a minute. "He's not well, Allison," Lady Margaret said suddenly. "I don't like his color."

"Nonsense, Mama Cameron," Allison countered briskly. "All he needs is a few days' rest to put him right. You know how cranky he gets when he's overtired."

"Perhaps." Her mother-in-law viewed her skeptically. One of the children moved suddenly, and her attention spun around to me, still standing there feeling ever so slightly foolish. And it suddenly occurred to me that Lady Margaret had known I was there the entire time, provoking the scene for my edification. "Ah, Lorna, I forgot you were here. Take the children off somewhere, will you? When you tire of them you may hand them over to Nancy; she's good with them."

There was nothing I could do but accept my dismissal with good grace. I expected that Lady Margaret and Allison were about to have a most interesting conversation, and I would have given much if I could have stayed to listen. However, the children beside me had heard too much of adult squabbling as it was and were restless. "Certainly, my lady." I rose and the children followed my example, watching me out of apprehensive young eyes. I held out a hand to both of them and, taking their tiny hands in mine, we left their mother and grandmother with their secrets.

Taking a deep breath as we left the stuffy drawing room, I shook myself. All this demure docility on my part was taking its toll on me. I turned to my charges. "Where would you like to go?" I asked Jenny. She was a solemn, undersized young lady of five, dressed in stately clothes.

"Well," she said slowly in a precise little voice, "Stephen would like to go for a walk along the cliffs."

I turned to the sturdy little figure of her brother. He was about half her age and almost as tall as she was. His strong little limbs were still encased in baby fat, while Jenny's frame was as light and slender as a bird's. He nodded with a mischievous, lopsided grin, and I realized he was far less docile than he appeared. I would have my hands full with him.

"Very well," I agreed. "We'll walk to the cliffs. But you must never go near them unless you're accompanied by me or Nancy. Do you understand?"

"Certainly," Jenny answered, the word sounding strange in her young voice. "We know that already."

"All right, let's go."

The sun shone with unusual brilliance in the late May morning, and a stiff breeze with a tang of salt to it was sweeping across the island. I marveled once again at the seemingly endless good weather. There was a spell on this island, one that would soon be broken, I feared.

After a few moments Jenny began to lose her premature sense of dignity and soon she was chattering to me at breakneck speed about her friends, her proposed birthday party six months hence, her brother, her father, her pony, the house which her family shared with their Uncle Charles. Curiously enough, in all her rambles she never once mentioned her elegant mother. Uncle Charles was praised for his choice of presents, but it was Uncle Alex who seemed to merit her fullest approval. Even young Stephen stopped his joyous tumbles across the lawn long enough to repeat "Uncle Alex," with an engaging baby-toothed grin before he continued to stagger on fat, uncertain little legs well ahead of us.

Their chatter seemed to verify my belief that Allison Cameron's attentions were roaming. Apparently Uncle Alex, although he refused to live in the family manse, visited often enough for it to seem a trifle suspicious to my distrustful mind. On the other hand, my opinion of the mysterious Alex was rising at the children's praise. I felt I could trust their taste in adults far better than I could the opinions of the adults themselves. I began to look forward to Alexander Cameron's arrival with heady anticipation.

At the end of the faintly sloping lawn a small deck was built over the cliffs, surrounded with a sturdy railing. Long winding stairs led to the rocky beach below with its narrow oasis of sand, where I had spent most of my outdoor time thus far. Earlier I had planned to bring the ball gown down there to do the delicate embroidery I had designed, but perhaps the advent of the family would curtail my freedom for such enterprises now. I would help John with the horses, of course, and Nancy with the children. Already I had taken a liking to the little ones, and they to me. Stephen and Jenny slipped their hands into mine by their own volition as we stared out over the tossing blue-gray landscape. At the touch of their small hands I felt a deep pang of homesickness for my own brothers and sisters.

I had long ago decided that I was a woman who was a born mother, never quite complete without a child to care for. Yet this did not prevent me from having many other interests. In fact my feelings toward the male sex were often uneasy bordering on hostile. I cherished my independence and saw myself as a budding suffragette, and that had secretly delighted my father. But one part of my womanhood I could not deny—that I belonged with and to children, and that my life would not be complete without having my own. How I would accomplish this, with my vague plans of remaining a spinster and becoming a teacher, I did not know. I had not completely ruled out the daring thought of having a child out of wedlock, though heaven knows what teaching job, or any job for that matter, would be open to me if I were to do such a disgraceful thing. However, I was young enough at the age of twenty not to worry excessively about the future at that point. I could be content standing there in the exhilarating Maine sunlight with two small ones beside me, happy in a purely sensual way.

We were halfway across the lawn on our way back to the house when Nancy's plump young figure met us. "Oh, miss, I wondered where you could have gotten off to. The mistress says I'm to take the children and feed them and put them down for their nap."

"All right," I agreed, noting the mutinous look on Jenny's face and the sly one on Stephen's. "And I'm sure they'll behave themselves for you, won't you?" Jenny and Stephen looked surprised at being thus addressed, but, after a moment or two's consideration, they nodded. "And then after your nap perhaps we'll go exploring. Would you like that?" They brightened visibly and went off with Nancy with every sign of docility. I was conscious of a strange feeling, a wild desire to whisk them away from here, off to Vermont or somewhere else, to feed them and take care of them and love them. They looked and behaved as if they had had very little of the latter. I sighed, and made my way back to the house.

Chapter V

The remainder of the afternoon passed swiftly. The children awoke from their nap just as the sky began to cloud over and a chill breeze sprang up. A severe rainstorm was threatening, the first sign of less than idyllic weather since I arrived here, so I took them to the old schoolroom I had discovered on my earlier rambles. To my surprise they hadn't even known of its existence, and the delight of any new toys, however ancient and battered, kept them fascinated. I left them long enough to run down to the kitchen to beg dusting rags and a pail of hot soapy water and a broom from Thora. When I explained what I intended to do she seemed pleased.

"It's been years since that schoolroom was used, not since Mr. Alex grew up. It needs young people in it, and the young ones need it too. The mistress said to let it be, but I'm glad it's going to be used again. I'll send up one of the girls to help with the heavy work later on. Those windows will need washing for sure, after all these years."

"Yes, and the floors too," I agreed. "I'll make a dent in the layer of dust with these, though." I gestured to the cleaning tools she had provided.

"Aye, and I'll send Nancy up in a bit. She'll feed the children and put them to bed for you. Lady Margaret wants you to join the family for dinner. Mr. Charles arrived about half an hour ago and Mr. Alex, the Captain, that is, is expected momentarily." She looked pleased, and I wondered once more if the legendary Alexander Cameron had captured her middle-aged heart too. "Dinner's at seven-thirty, miss. The old lady says they won't dress tonight, seeing as how the children have traveled today. The Captain'll be soaked through if he don't get here before the rain hits."

But rain was gusting heavily when I returned to the dusty schoolroom. I entered silently, yet the children heard me, and they looked up at me furtively. I thought I could see fright in their young eyes. But surely that must be my imagination.

"It's only me," I called, and their tense little bodies relaxed. I wondered what kind of life they led with their parents and uncles, that children so young could be so apprehensive. "It's certainly raining hard, isn't it? Perhaps your Uncle Alex will have to swim to the island," I joked.

Jenny's pale round face lit up with joy. "Uncle Alex is coming tonight?"

"Yes, he is. At this rate, though, I think it will be long after you're in bed. But you'll see him tomorrow, for sure."

She nodded happily, and her thin little shoulders lost some of their premature tension. While she returned to Stephen's side, instructing him in the proper placing of the wooden blocks he was busy building and then smashing down again, I continued my cleaning in a thoughtful mood.

Nancy came and took the children from me an hour later. By then I had made a definite improvement in the over-all appearance of the room. It now seemed brighter, despite the gloomy downpour outside the dusty windows. I kissed the children good night and continued cleaning for a bit, then sat myself wearily at the small table, my mind full of the children and their peculiar existence.

Nonsense, I told myself. You haven't seen enough to know their lives are peculiar. Yet somehow I could not shake my sense of depression. An occasional clap of thunder only served to deepen my gloom, and I sat there in the darkening room, staring out across the rain-drenched island.

A knock sounded at the door. "Miss," Katie's voice whispered. The door opened a crack. "Miss," she called hoarsely.

"What is it?" I jumped up in alarm, disasters crowding unbidden into my mind.

"Oh, there you are, miss." Katie breathed a sigh of relief. "It's John. He needs help with the horses, Miss Lorna. Mr. Charles came in an hour ago, the Captain just arrived, and John's got more than he can manage."

"Certainly," I agreed swiftly, ignoring a little thrill of nervousness that coursed through me. "Tell him not to worry; I'll take care of things."

"He'll be right grateful," she assured me as she scampered down the hallway.

I hurried to my room, alight with a sense of mischief and adventure that would have gladdened my reckless father's heart. I stripped off my clothes: the restraining whalebone corset that I hardly needed, the six petticoats, even my chemise. Hidden under the winter petticoats in a lower drawer of my wardrobe was a set of my brother's clothes I had packed on impulse. Lady Margaret hadn't bargained for such outrageous behavior on my part, I knew, but surely I couldn't be expected to muck about in the stable with floor-trailing skirts. Once dressed, I pulled a knit cap over most of my hair and surveyed myself in the full-length mirror. The effect was far different from the one I had hoped to achieve with my satin evening gown. In the rough clothing I looked like a slender, half-grown boy. Carefully I stepped out into the hall and down the back stairs. Thora caught a glimpse of me as I slipped through the back door, and I heard a gasp of some strong emotion, horror or outrage most likely. The rain was whipping in torrents, and, grabbing a lantern from the back porch, I ran as fast as I could across the courtyard to the stables. By the time I reached their shelter I was soaked to the skin, and I'm afraid I had to thank the dark for concealing the difference between my real sex and the one I was affecting. The damp, clinging work shirt now made any subterfuge useless. Not that there would be anyone to see me, I thought. The stables were dark and deserted except for me, and the horses would scarcely mind. Besides, I had warned John I didn't intend to wear skirts when I worked out here, I thought defiantly.

I lit the lantern and held it high. Ladybird had obviously been ridden recently, but apparently John had found time to curry her before he returned to his inside duties. And that left the Captain's horse, which turned out to be a wet, trembling Samantha. Setting the lantern down, I moved toward her. She whinnied nervously and I murmured soft, comforting reassurances as I touched her cold, wet side.

"That evil man rode you through this nasty weather and left you, did he?" My voice was gentle. "Poor old Samantha, I'll take care of you." I continued a steady monologue as I fed her a piece of sugar and began to brush her down. Every time there was a distant clap of thunder she trembled, and the rain poured in at our feet from the courtyard door.

The usual sense of calm I had when I was working with horses was strangely absent this time. I had feelings of foreboding, and longed to finish so I could escape back into the house and the fire that would doubtless be waiting for me in my elegant room. But I dared not hurry; Samantha was nervous enough and needed careful handling.

It must have been his presence in my mind that made me look up at just that moment. My eyes were drawn to the door, just as a flash of lightning illuminated the yard, and there he stood, framed against the angry sky.

At another time I might have laughed at the perfect melodrama of his entry into my life. But somehow this was no laughing matter. In that brief instant of light I was aware of many impressions; of a tall, lean body soaked to the skin, of black hair and rakishly handsome face.

And then he moved into the stable as Samantha reared slightly, and I had to concentrate all my energies on the frightened horse. She must have picked up some of my uneasiness, and her nerves were worse than before. I soothed her quickly, whispering to her, too aware of the figure that entered the stable and moved close to the horse and me, the lamplight casting strange shadows in the night. When I felt I could leave the horse for a moment I turned to face him.

I am a tall woman, and yet I had to look up to see his shadowed face. "You're new here," he said briefly, running a strong tanned hand over the horse's hide.

I nodded, awash with conflicting emotion. I was getting off on a very bad footing with the redoubtable Captain, and I wondered how I would dare to meet him in an hour's time across his mother's formal dinner table. I kept my head lowered in the shadows.

"Well, you've a way with horses, lad," he said casually. "I'll take over now, though. You can go in and get some supper." He tossed a heavy coin in my direction and I caught it without thinking. I nodded nervously, and ran, past his disturbing presence, past the curious horses, out through the rain and into the kitchen. I slammed the door shut behind me and rested for a moment, trembling all over with suppressed laughter and nerves and the cold.

"Will you look at that?" Katie's voice was clearly amazed as she surveyed my bizarre attire. "Where did you get them clothes, miss?"

"That's enough, Katie," Thora admonished her. "Miss Lorna can wear whatever she chooses. Lady Margaret gave strict orders we weren't to question anything she did." She studied me wistfully as she spoke, controlling her own avid curiosity with a massive effort.

I took pity on her. "These are my brother's clothes," I explained casually enough. "I use them for working in the stables when John needs help—my skirts would get too dirty." Thora nodded, a little disappointed in my mundane explanation.

"Well, I'm sure that's your business, miss." She nodded and turned back to her stove. "Did you see the Captain out there? He got here just a few minutes ago."

I clutched the tossed coin in my hand so tightly it hurt, and nodded casually. "He thinks I'm a new stable boy. It might be better if he continued to think that," I offered tentatively, and Thora nodded.

"Certainly, miss. I'm sure you know best. Anyway, I've learned in

my years as help for the quality that they don't like to be told they
were mistaken about anything. Not that the Captain's like that, but
still and all . . ." She let it trail. "Dinner will be served in half an
hour, miss. If the Captain is ready, that is. The mistress says you are
to come to the green drawing room as soon as you are ready."

"I suppose I had better change first," I suggested, straight-faced.

"Yes, miss," Thora agreed soberly, and I dashed up the back
stairs, giggling helplessly.

I dressed quickly for dinner, chilled fingers fumbling with the
myriad of tiny buttons on my plain gray silk dress. I wanted to retire
into the background tonight. It would be far easier for me to find
out who murdered Josiah Cameron if Lady Margaret's family dismissed me as a rather nondescript, gawky young female.

My hair was still soaked from my mad dash from the house to the
stable and back again, and I wondered if the Captain would realize
his mistake when we met at dinner. I could hear the rain pounding on
the windows, and the bleakness of the weather dampened my spirits a
bit. Reluctantly I hurried downstairs, having taken too much time on
my toilette already. I stopped short before the door of the occupied
drawing room and took a deep breath, preparing myself for my second, more formal introduction to Alexander Cameron. I touched the
door with a slightly trembling hand, opened it, and entered.

Chapter VI

I was immediately conscious of a sense of disappointment. There was no tall, dark figure in the elegant room. Only Lady Margaret, deep in conversation with Allison, her pale eyes as disappointed as my own, and Stephen, chattering to whom I assumed was his half brother with an almost feverish animation.

"Ah, there you are, Lorna," Lady Margaret turned her basilisk eye upon me. "I thought you might be my scapegrace of a son. Come here and meet Charles." I advanced diffidently, with meekly lowered eyes secretly assessing suspect number four.

Charles Cameron was very handsome in a clean, well-built manner. He was not unlike his half brother, Stephen, although the latter looked like a shadow of Charles's robust good health. Both had the same short, curling brown hair and warm brown eyes that surveyed me with open friendliness and not the least trace of the superiority that Allison had made so apparent. They were both entirely different from what I could recall of my brief encounter with Alex Cameron's dark and dangerous good looks. I warmed to Charles immediately—there was no mystery here, I thought. Merely the fabled Cameron charm that Stephen also had in abundance. I smiled into his friendly face, suppressing the hope that the third brother might lack the charm of the first two. I was already thinking too much about him.

"I'm so glad you've come to us, Miss MacDougall," he murmured with obvious sincerity. "As I'm sure my brother has told you, my stepmother has long needed someone to keep her company through the weeks when we can't be with her. And such decorative company!" I'm sure I simpered becomingly in response to this flattery, and Lady Margaret viewed us with a fond but wary eye.

"What a cozy family reunion this is." A new voice came from the direction of the doorway, and we all turned with surprisingly uniform guilt, to meet the cool gaze of Alexander Cameron, Captain of the Cameron fleets, younger son of Lady Margaret, and my prime suspect in the death of his father.

He was an exceedingly handsome man, seen in the brighter light of the drawing room, though without that trace of slight effeminacy that often marred too handsome men. My eyes traveled up the long, lean length of him, his legs encased in unfashionably tight breeches, his dinner coat and white shirt carelessly elegant. And his face, so different from the easy good looks of his brothers, tanned from hours on the deck of a ship, framed with long, curling jet black hair. As black as a raven's wing, I thought fancifully, having heard that line somewhere in the verse I had read a year or two ago when I was young and romantic. His eyes met mine and caught them, and for a brief instant I felt almost lost in their cold, seemingly heartless depths. I had never seen eyes quite the same deep color blue—they seemed one more purposefully acquired effect designed to disturb me. I pulled my eyes away from him reluctantly, schooling my features into the properly respectful mask I had determined to show Lady Margaret's children.

"Alex, this is my companion, Lorna MacDougall. Lorna, this is my son, of whom you've heard me speak, of course. Captain Alexander Cameron." Was there a trace of belated pride as she introduced her son? Surely any woman would be proud of such a magnificent but frightening creature? I murmured something like "good evening," refusing to meet the somewhat speculative gaze. I could feel his eyes travel over me, from my damp red hair down the preposterous tallness of me, and I thought his eyes must be cold and calculating. Irritated, I met his gaze boldly, and the look of sudden amusement that flashed over the sternly handsome planes of his face unnerved me even more.

"Well, shall we eat, now that you've finally decided to join us?" Lady Margaret demanded querulously. "I'm sure the dinner must be completely ruined by now. Charles, your arm." Charles jumped to her assistance with alacrity, and, as they began their stately procession to the dining room, Allison ignored Stephen's proffered arm and grasped Alex with her nervous, clutching little fingers.

"I thought you were never coming," she whispered intensely, ignoring the look of pain that flashed over her husband's delicate face.

Alex raised an eyebrow coolly, looking down on her absurdly tiny form. "But of course I came, my dear sister-in-law. I promised my brother that I would." He detached himself from her hungry grasp and handed her to her husband, then turned and offered his arm to me, while Allison turned pale, then scarlet with rage. I had no alternative but to take his arm and try to enjoy the totally original experience of having my eyes level with a man's shoulder. Long before, I had even outgrown my strapping older brothers, and it was a novel opportunity to feel just the slightest bit dwarfed.

My opinion of Captain Alexander, however, was hardly improved by his callous treatment of his ill-mannered sister-in-law, and I could almost find it in my heart to pity her, had it not been for the sick and sorrowful expression on her husband's face. It was painfully clear that Alexander Cameron was a lot more of a man than poor Stephen, and I could scarcely blame Allison for succumbing to those sapphire-blue eyes. Alexander Cameron would be a formidable and dangerous man to love, I thought, and a great deal might be excused of Allison on that account. If Josiah had been anything like his youngest son, I didn't wonder he'd been murdered.

Alex seated me at Lady Margaret's left, and as I took my place my eyes met such savage hate in Allison's face that all trace of my usually formidable appetite vanished. Her eyes when they rested on Alex as he seated himself opposite her were beseeching, and I wondered if it was only adulterous love that was eating her up, hollowing her cheeks, and setting her pretty little eyes deep in pale mauve circles. Or was it something else? Something like fear? Or guilt?

I was unable to do justice to Thora's excellent meal, faced as I was with Allison and her delicate, bird-like appetite and the Captain's unnerving, silent eyes. I longed for the fastness of my own room, and reprimanded myself instantly. After all, I had promised Lady Margaret I would find out who had murdered her husband, and I was ignoring an excellent chance to pick up clues. I must try to regain some of my foolhardy courage if I was to play amateur detective, like one of those interesting characters of Mr. Edgar Allan Poe. But somehow, whenever my green eyes chanced to meet the cynical blue ones opposite me, all courage failed.

For the most part the talk was trivial, about friends and acquaintances I only knew from the newspapers, about stocks and holdings and their vast fortune. Under the influence of all this innocuous talk I had just begun to enjoy my meal when Alexander's drawling voice stopped me from my second helping of peach trifle.

"I see you've got a new stable hand," he said casually, swirling the wine around in his goblet before bringing it to his lips and draining it. "It's about time you got someone to help John. He's getting too old to manage the stables and the grounds himself. What's the new lad's name?"

There was a dead silence around the table. Katie smothered a giggle and rushed from the room, and only by sheer strength of will did I keep a telltale blush from mounting to my cheeks. But the Captain was looking nowhere near my direction, and I had to assume my secret was still safe, and his interest was purely innocent.

Lady Margaret appeared startled for a moment, then a sly expression passed over her wasted face. "You must mean Horace," she said, casting a mischievous glance in my demure direction. "He's good with the horses, and that's what counts. Not too bright, though."

"Do you think you should have hired him then, Mother?" Stephen questioned anxiously, toying with his dessert. He had scarcely eaten enough during the entire meal to keep a rabbit alive. "I mean, if he's dull-witted don't you think he might . . . well, imagine things? It's bad enough with the superstitious local people. Surely we don't need a simpleton roaming around here too."

"I didn't say he was a simpleton!" Lady Margaret snapped, and Stephen subsided unhappily. "He's merely a bit slow. As a matter of fact, that's the only reason why he's consented to work here. He doesn't understand enough to realize that someone on this island is a murderer."

"Shall we change the subject?" Alex requested with an expression of sudden acute boredom. "I heard enough about your senile fantasies last time I was constrained to visit here, and I don't wish to go over them again. Father was stabbed by a deranged tramp. The murderer's long gone now, and there's no use going over it again and again." He reached for the decanter that had been thoughtfully placed well within his reach, poured himself a generous glassful, and drained it. "Much as you'd like to think your children capable of murder, it's simply so much hogwash."

"Yes, I wish we could just forget about it," Allison's breathy voice piped in suddenly. "After all, it's over. It's no use crying over spilt milk, I always say."

Alex turned amazed eyes in her direction while the rest of us choked over the tactlessness of her remark. "My dear Allison," he drawled in his faintly husky voice, "sometimes your lack of taste positively astounds me."

"It's time for the women to retire and leave the men to their port and cigars. Though I think you might go a little easy on the port, Alexander," snapped Lady Margaret, stepping into the breach.

I escaped the room with a tentative sigh of relief. But I had barely sat down in the green drawing room when Allison began her attack.

"You needn't think all those shy little glances will get you anywhere, missy," she hissed at me from the adjoining sofa. Lady Margaret was already dozing by the fire, seemingly oblivious to this interchange.

"I don't know what you mean," I protested, outraged.

"You're hardly Alex's type, you know. He might not mind a bit of dalliance with you—perhaps he feels it his duty to deflower all the servant girls. *Droit du seigneur* and all that. But that's as far as it will go, I assure you. He's a cold, heartless beast, and it will take more than an insignificant little minx like you to move him. You ought to be ashamed of yourself."

The woman was clearly demented. Her eyes were ablaze with a curious intensity as she berated me for something that was happening only in her own tortured mind.

"Mrs. Cameron," I began, floundering helplessly. "Believe me, I have no interest in the Captain whatsoever! Why, he's a total stranger. Such thoughts are the last thing from my mind, I promise you." The idea of Alexander Cameron coming in and hearing this conversation was absolutely horrifying and I reached desperately for anything to convince her. In the face of her patent disbelief a brilliant (I thought) idea came to me. "Besides, I'm engaged to a young man back in Vermont. I'm here working for enough money so that we can be married. I would scarcely make eyes at a man the first time I saw him, would I?"

My righteous indignation seemed to mollify her. She subsided, murmuring apologies, and yet I wondered if she was truly appeased. There was a nervousness about her, totally unnatural, and I considered whether she might take drugs. The papers and women's magazines had been recently full of tales about the evils of addiction to cocaine and laudanum, which were just being recognized. Something must be responsible for her irrational behavior. I wanted to escape before her seeming source of discontent returned to our presence, yet I could think of no way to accomplish it. In all politeness I should bear Allison company, though what company I was to her jealous thoughts I couldn't imagine. And it would hardly do to wake Lady Margaret from her little snooze by the fire.

I sat back patiently, schooling my features into calm unconcern, inwardly fighting the tension that seemed to center around the doorway through which the men would eventually walk. If he had this unnerving effect on me, a total stranger, I suppose I shouldn't be surprised at the agony his . . . mistress was going through. Yet I couldn't be sure if she was his mistress. Perhaps that was her problem. Though from what I had seen of her she was more than willing and eager. And what man could resist her delicate, tiny blond charms? Surely not someone like Alexander Cameron.

The men returned eventually, and before Alex had even entered the room Allison had jumped up from her chair and rushed to the hall to grab his arm. "I must talk to you, Alex." Her voice was breathless and a little too loud, and Lady Margaret awoke with a start.

Stephen's unhappy face took on an even gloomier expression. "I think I'll retire now, Mother. Allison . . ." There was a pleading look in his brown eyes as he touched his wife's shoulder, but she shook off his restraining hand.

"If you wish, dear," she said hastily. "I'll be up in a short while. There's something I simply must discuss with Alex."

"Very well," he sighed, kissing his wife and mother with sober consideration. Before he left the room he flashed me a wan smile that almost broke my heart, and I could have slapped Allison for what she was doing to her poor weak husband, and for other reasons I didn't care to examine too closely.

"Where would you like to have our discussion, my dear?" Alex said briefly after his brother left. "Would you care for a stroll around the gardens?" The lightning flashed outside to complement his mockery, but Allison was too overwrought to notice.

"Please, Alex," she begged, almost touchingly, I thought. There seemed to be a trace of pity in him, for, rather than humiliate her further, he led her quietly from the room.

Charles raised his handsome eyebrows with gentle amusement, so much kinder than Alex's icy mockery, as he turned to his stepmother. "Well, I wonder what that was all about? I hadn't supposed anything of *that* nature was going on."

"I don't know what you're talking about, Charles," Lady Margaret snapped with unaccustomed irritation at her favorite. "Allison is always having megrims; we should be used to her fits and starts by now."

"That we should, Mama," he said affectionately, and she beamed at him. "Isn't it about time you retired, my dear? We don't want you overtiring yourself."

"Dear Charles. You always were so protective." Lady Margaret proffered her hand and he kissed it with the proper show of respect and devotion. I could see that Charles knew the old lady well enough to cater to her love of ceremony, and I warmed to him. I was fond of her already, and her wishes were harmless enough. It surely wouldn't have damaged her graceless younger son to have given her a bit more attention.

I rose willingly, glad of an excuse to leave the atmosphere of tightly controlled hysteria generated by Allison. "Lean on me, my lady," I offered, and she sagged against me gratefully.

We mounted the long winding stairs slowly, the old lady far more tired than she cared to admit. I felt my love for all vulnerable things well up, and my protective wings reached out to shield her along with her grandchildren. If I hadn't been so sentimental I would have realized she needed protection about as much as one of the thick-shelled lobsters we had eaten tonight.

"Come in with me, Lorna," she commanded as we came to her door. "We can talk awhile until Katie comes to put this poor old body to bed."

"Certainly, ma'am," I agreed, settling her into her plush chair in front of the banked fire. I rang the bellpull, then sat down at her feet.

"Well, what do you think of them? My children?" she demanded with a sudden upswing of energy.

"I don't know," I confessed frankly. "I think perhaps Stephen is ill."

"Stephen has always been ill." The old lady dismissed him coldly. "He has weak lungs—there's nothing the doctors can do about it. And to top it off he's too much in love with that selfish little bitch he married."

"I must confess that was about my opinion of your daughter-in-law," I said slowly. "She's obviously deeply troubled about something —if it's only her faltering marriage I can't yet tell."

"And Charles?"

I knew from her tone of voice I had better be ready to praise, and to praise indiscriminately, and I had no reason not to. "Charles seems very kind," I said somewhat mildly. "And quite handsome, of course."

"He is, isn't he? The best of all my children, and yet no child of mine at all." She sighed, not without a trace of self-pity. "I have planned great things for that boy. Great things." She leaned over and peered at me searchingly. "And what did you think of my son Alex?"

I thought back to his amused, slightly menacing figure, and I shook my head slightly. "He's a bit alarming," I confessed, strangely unwilling to bolster her obviously bad opinion of him. Despite the little good I had observed about him, I wanted to protect him from Lady Margaret's cruel suspicions. I told myself it was merely my innate sense of fairness. Even though with each action he seemed more and more to fit the role of murderer, I refused to condemn him until I had absolute proof. "I'm sure there's no real harm in him," I lied to his mother. I was sure of no such thing. There seemed to me a capability for very real, deep harm. Whether it was second sight or foolish feminine instinct on my part I did not know.

"And which of my sons will you fall in love with?" she asked with a shrewdness that startled me. "All the young ladies of my acquaintance, and some of the older and wiser ones as well, choose one of them. The sensible ones fall for Charles, with his sweetness and his ability; the motherly ones for Stephen, despite his marriage, because he seems so weak and fragile and tender. And then the romantic fools pick Alex. But there's a blackness in him, a blackness I neither know nor understand," she confessed, her lined and wrinkled face bewildered. "Be careful which one you choose, my dear."

"I have no intention of falling in love with any of them," I assured her with a brisk good sense I did not possess.

"Let us hope not," she said caustically. "You may leave me now, Lorna. Don't tire yourself out too much with the children tomorrow. Nancy is excellent with the little ones, and she adores them. As is only natural."

By the sly look on her face I knew I was supposed to question this, and dutifully I did so.

"She's their aunt, that's why!" she cackled mirthlessly. "Half the population in town's related to the Camerons in one way or another, and none of them on the right side of the blanket. Josiah accounted for Nancy and a good many others, and my sons seem to be doing their best to keep up the tradition. Don't trust them, any of them, Lorna." She cackled again. "I don't think your family would care to have you back on their hands with another little mouth to feed."

A small chill ran through me. "That would never happen, my lady."

"Never?"

"Never," I repeated firmly. "Before I leave I wonder if I might ask you a few questions."

"No."

"No?" I echoed idiotically.

"No, I will not answer your questions!" she snapped. "If I knew the answers I wouldn't need your help."

"But, Lady Margaret," I floundered helplessly, ". . . you'd make things so much easier if you'd . . ."

"Life isn't easy!" She leaned forward, watching me intently from her beady eyes. "Don't you realize, my girl, that I have a very good idea who murdered my husband? And that the idea of it is almost more than I can stand? No, you'll have to come to your own conclusions, without being influenced by me and my suspicions. If you come up with the same person then I'll have to accept it." She waved a slim hand of dismissal. "Good night, Lorna."

There was nothing I could do but accept defeat gracefully. "Good night, Lady Margaret."

I found myself in the cold stone hallway, lit by a single lamp. I wandered on silent feet down the hall, meaning to look in on the children before I slept. I had stopped outside the door for a moment, when my blood froze. Someone was in the room with the children.

My first impulse was to fling open the door and confront the intruder, but I immediately thought better of that notion. It would terrify the children, and I would look foolish indeed if it turned out to be a worried parent checking on the children. Though from what I'd seen of their parents, it seemed highly unlikely.

And then before I could move the door opened and Alexander Cameron stepped out into the shadowed hallway. He didn't seem to see me at first, so preoccupied was his expression. When he looked up and saw my motionless figure he seemed displeased.

"Miss MacDougall, isn't it?" he questioned coldly, knowing perfectly well who I was. "What can I do for you?"

"What were you doing in there?" I found myself demanding in a hushed whisper.

His look of displeasure changed to one I couldn't read. "Well, I'm pleased to see someone in this house has a feeling of concern. I was checking on my niece and nephew, and leaving a small present beside their pillows, as they have learned to expect from me."

When you come to sleep with their mother, I finished silently. I nodded, and made to move past him into their room, when he grabbed my arm with a steely strength.

"I told you I had checked on them. They're sleeping comfortably; there is absolutely no need for you to bother."

It would have been useless and undignified for me to struggle with him. I remained still and silent until he saw fit to let go of my arm. I was unused to being manhandled, and my rage rose.

"Do not," I said in an icy whisper, "touch me again."

He laughed, low and soft, and the sound enraged me. Before I could tell him exactly what I thought of his manners, he moved off down the hall.

I would have liked to slap his handsome face, but I told myself that I could not lower myself to his level. Besides, he would have probably hit me back. With all the dignity I could muster I retreated down the hallway, ignoring his polite call of "Pleasant dreams." He knew perfectly well I would have nightmares.

Chapter VII

I awoke the next morning with a pain in my head and a queer sense of excitement and depression warring within me. My sleep had been fitful, to say the least, full of dreams of Lady Margaret and her children, and the resultant sleeplessness made me feel groggy and out of sorts. I stared dismally at the black coffee Katie had brought me, oblivious of the warm sunshine that had followed last night's storm, and I wished it were Monday. I had just begun to be comfortable in my new home when the Camerons came and disrupted everything. And then I remembered the children and couldn't regret their presence. With real fortitude I pulled myself out of bed and took the first sip of the scalding liquid Thora optimistically referred to as coffee. Its only resemblance to the stuff I had grown accustomed to was its bitter quality and the capacity to wake you up in the morning.

At least it was a good day. I could take the children out for a hike, I thought, as I dressed myself in my pretty new green dress. There were a great many things we could do on such a fine day, I told myself firmly, lacing up my new kid shoes. There was no need for this melancholia.

I heard a knock at the door. "Miss Lorna?" Katie's husky voice called out. "Are you awake yet?"

"Come in," I answered. Her pale, attractive face appeared in the doorway.

"Where would you like the children to eat? Miss Allison says I'm to ask you—you're in charge of them, she says."

"In the schoolroom, Katie," I answered. "Are they dressed yet?"

"Nancy's with them now," she said, eying my outfit speculatively. "That's a pretty dress, miss." She looked thoughtful for a moment, then stared vacantly out the windows. "What do you think of the Captain?"

I turned sharply, wondering if she was foolish enough to think there was any possible connection between my choice of flattering apparel and the unfriendly Captain, but her face was bland and innocent.

"He seems to be a very interesting gentleman," I answered noncommittally.

"He is that," she agreed, sighing soulfully. "And so very handsome, don't you think?"

Her infatuation was apparent, and I wondered if its object was aware of it. It grieved me to see her falling prey to such a seemingly cynical fellow, but I forebore to warn her. After all, she certainly knew him better than I—perhaps he had hidden merits. Perhaps he didn't treat all women as harshly as he treated his sister-in-law.

"Handsome is as handsome does," I parroted repressively.

"Yes, ma'am." Katie was smiling with kind skepticism. "I'll tell Nancy to take the children to the schoolroom, then."

She left almost before I could thank her. Watching her saucy, disappearing figure, I was troubled. The Captain would be far better off on the vast ocean where he so obviously belonged, not here causing trouble.

The morning passed peaceably enough. Jenny and Stephen were entranced by the new toys their beloved Uncle Alex had left them, and I was too bemused to do much more than sit and watch them. Jenny and I had a reading lesson, and she was remarkably quick to grasp things. Stephen played happily in a corner, building towers with his new blocks and then gleefully smashing them down again.

Lunch was a suitably massive affair, with sausages, eggs, muffins, cake, and mugs of rich milk. The children and I ate until we could barely move, and we sat and stared at each other solemnly when we were finished.

"Would you like to go for a walk?" I suggested. "We have an hour before your nap time, and the sun seems likely to remain."

"Yes, please," Jenny said eagerly. "And we could go visit Uncle Alex. We haven't seen him yet and he likes to have us come and visit with him, you know. He says we never bother him."

"We'll see," I temporized, not eager to face their uncle's satirical expression. "In the meantime let's go and sit under a tree and I'll read to you."

"Hurrah!" Jenny shouted, and Stephen attempted a facsimile of Jenny's exclamation. We chose a book with a great many pictures and set out on our expedition, furnishing ourselves with sweaters and a blanket to spread out on the grass.

We found a newly budded maple tree halfway across the lawn and settled ourselves comfortably. Unlike most women, especially those with my flaming shade of hair, I thrived on sunlight. I loved the healthy golden color it gave my skin, which personally I found much more attractive than the fashionable pallor Allison enjoyed. With my height I could hardly hope to look delicate, and I preferred a look of lean resiliency. But since children are more susceptible to the sun's burning rays, we stayed far back in the shade while I read to them the adventures of Henry Rabbit and Arthur Mole. So intent were they that they didn't notice their mother and Uncle Alex deep in conversation as they wandered across the lawn. I kept my eyes firmly on the book as I noted their approach, stealing glances at them every now and then. Their conversation seemed unfortunate, and I wondered that the handsome Captain could be so immune to Allison's fragile charms. But perhaps it wasn't immunity to Allison but loyalty to his brother that stopped him from succumbing to her obvious entreaties.

"My darlings!" All of a sudden the beauty swooped down on her two unsuspecting offspring. She was dressed in another of her elegant toilettes, this one of pink dimity, and the recollection of her previous complete disinterest in her darlings made me want to slap her selfish, pretty little face.

The children remained passive in her crushing embrace. "Come sit with your mother, darlings," Allison cried with touchingly child-like ardor. "I've missed you so much!"

I could barely keep from snorting, and my eyes met Alex's cynical ones. He saw through her completely, I realized, and I wondered at Allison's naïveté in thinking she fooled him with this ostentatious display of mother-love.

"Shall I read to you, my dears? What was Miss MacDougall reading to you?" How could anyone resist such a charming picture, I wondered, with the lovely young mother and her two attractive young ones. I felt nothing but complete distaste for this belated sign of maternal feelings.

"No, thank you, Mama," Jenny answered her politely, distantly, and Stephen squirmed intractably. "We've finished for the time being. I think it's time for our nap, isn't it, Lorna?"

"Yes, it is," I responded to my cue, gathering up the various belongings we had brought with us.

"But darlings, don't you want to sit with your mama?" Allison cried, her pink and white face a perfect mask of trusting disappointment.

"No, thank you, Mama," Jenny answered, rising from her lap and placing one tiny hand in mine. Stephen pulled away and ran to my side.

"Say good afternoon to your mother," I reminded them, and they complied tonelessly.

"Good afternoon, Mrs. Cameron, Captain," I murmured politely. I was rewarded with the Captain's smile, sudden and charming, and I blinked in confusion, like someone coming from a dark place into the dazzling sunshine.

"Good afternoon, Miss MacDougall." Allison's voice was cold and angry. It appeared that she blamed me for her inability to charm her own children, unaware that they were precociously wise to her ways.

I could feel their eyes following us as we made our way back to the house across the wide expanse of lawn. I recognized the hostility in Allison's regard. I wished I knew what to make of Alexander Cameron. That brief, incredibly attractive smile shook me more than I would have liked to admit.

Nancy was bustling down the hall when we entered the house, and gratefully I gave up my charges. Much as I liked them, their constant presence was often too demanding. Watching them mount the long curving stairs, I contemplated the various possibilities open to me. To go back outdoors would be useless; the possibility of eavesdropping was remote.

I could retire to my bedroom and work on my sewing, of course. However, I had spent far too much time in my room already. I was at the point where I had to make some progress on the problem I had been hired to solve, however ignorant I had been of that fact. But I was unsure of which way to turn. Perhaps Lady Margaret would have suggestions.

"Nonsense!" she said sharply from her chair in the little green drawing room when I posed the question. "It's up to you—whatever you think is a likely avenue. If I could find out myself do you suppose I would have confided in you? No. I've told you before, it's your responsibility and I expect you to act upon your own."

"Yes, ma'am," I acquiesced, temporarily cowed.

"However, I may be of some use to you." She gave in suddenly, with a lightning-like change of mind that characterized the old and crafty. "All the children have, so to speak, disposed of themselves this afternoon. Allison will be resting her shattered nerves for an hour or two. Charles and Stephen have gone off-island on errands, and Alex will be busy in his workshop, I presume. In the meantime I

could spare you some time to answer a few questions. I was a bit ar-
bitrary last night—after all, you can't work completely in the dark."

I thanked her as effusively as I knew she desired, then queried,
"Alex's workshop?"

"Alex works in wood, you know," the old lady said with a trace of
warmth. "It has been our practice to have a figurehead on each of the
Cameron ships, even though such things are now outdated. For his
own ship Alex does the sculpting himself. And very nicely too, I must
admit."

"That surprises me," I confessed. I couldn't see the volatile Captain with the painstaking patience woodcarving required.

"Why?" She was very sharp, with that sudden change in loyalty I
found so disconcerting. "You don't like to think my son has any of
the softer, finer qualities, do you? I grant you, it's hard to find any
trace of artistic temperament nowadays. But in his youth he was
quite a fine painter also. And his water-colors!" She sighed. "But
nothing to compare with Stephen's poetry, or Charles's general excel-
lence in schoolwork. Alex was always the odd one, I'm afraid. We
had to send him away to school when he was quite young."

"And when was that, my lady?" I kept my voice neutral, waiting
for the information to pour out of the changeable old woman.

"Oh, I'd say when he was thirteen. He was bright for his age, there
was no denying that. But he never would apply himself, like dear
Charles. Now there was a son for a mother to have. Always courteous and thoughtful, always showing his elders their proper respect.
And Stephen worshiped him, absolutely worshiped him! Why, the
two of them were quite inseparable—we had to send them off to
school together. Alex we sent as far away as possible. There seemed
to be nothing he loved more than to cause trouble for Stephen and
Charles. He would make up the most disgusting stories." She shuddered delicately at the memory.

"Such as . . . ?"

"Oh, I really don't remember. Nasty things, things only a child
with a warped imagination would think of. I remember he came to
me one day and swore he'd seen Charles setting fire to some baby
kittens. I never heard of anything so infamous! And there was the
time he came to us with horrible burn marks up and down his arms
and pretended that Charles had held him down and burnt him!" She
shivered in remembrance. "It was then that I decided Alex couldn't
be left alone anymore. That he could actually do such a thing to himself in order to discredit his poor, half-orphaned brother in our eyes!"

"Terrible," I murmured ambiguously, my mind turning over these new developments feverishly. "But they seem perfectly friendly now."

"Oh, certainly, they do," the old woman agreed. "But only because Charles has been so tolerant of Alex's strange . . . hatred of him." She went on.

"Of course, no school could hold Alex. He ran away when he was barely sixteen—shipped aboard with one of Josiah's biggest competitors. I'd never seen Josiah so livid." She chuckled at the memory. "There was nothing he could do but give Alex his own ship the day he was twenty-one. And from then on there was no stopping him. He practically controls the entire fleet and all the captains, and they love him. He must show them a more endearing side than the one we see around here. Sometimes I wonder how I ever managed to give birth to such a difficult creature!" She sighed. "Sometimes I think it would have been better for everyone if he'd been lost on one of those early voyages."

This cold-blooded attitude horrified me more than I could dare to say. But I was determined to have the woman face what she was saying to me. "Why? Is Alex the one you think murdered your husband?"

She looked startled, and an instant denial sprang to her lips. Then she wilted. "Perhaps," she said slowly, painfully.

"That would be the easiest thing, wouldn't it?" I pressed. "To have him removed from your family. He's the perfect scapegoat." Anger was blazing in me, absolute fury at this evil old woman's neglect and cruelty. And yet I was helpless to do anything.

"You are impertinent, child," she snapped. "I want the truth, at whatever the cost. I'm too old to care much about anything anymore, but I must know this." Her voice sank to a whisper. "I must be sure I've been right about Alex all these years. I must be sure."

Unwilling pity slipped through my anger. "I'll find out the truth. I promise you that."

She nodded, and shut her eyes as she leaned back in the comfortable chair, seemingly at peace. I left the room quietly.

Chapter VIII

Aimlessly I wandered back out into the sunlight. Poor Alex, I thought compassionately as I seated myself on the terrace wall and looked out toward the sea. A mother who neglected him, a half brother held up as a paragon throughout his adolescence. Small wonder he had rebelled in a strange manner. The very sickness inherent in the lies he had told made my heart warm toward the poor lost child. I shut my eyes peaceably in the dazzling sunshine, full of humanitarian plans to bring kindness and a belated mother-love to the Captain.

I was in a pleasant haze, the beauty and calm of the day taking hold of me and soothing me into a tranquil state of semisleep, when a shadow blocked the sun. My eyes flew open in sudden apprehension.

"Did I frighten you, Miss MacDougall?" Alexander Cameron's voice was surprisingly low and beguiling as he seated his lean, taut body across from me.

"Why, no," I lied instinctively, nervously. I had been hoping the Captain would continue to ignore my presence: the full force of those intense blue eyes was highly unnerving.

"I've wanted to have a talk with you, Miss MacDougall, and now seems the perfect time," he said slowly, and I felt an irrational dread well up in me, rather like a student called to task by a stern schoolmaster.

"About your mother?" I suggested anxiously, twisting my long, slender hands in my lap.

"Partially." His voice was cool and detached. For a brief moment my attention drifted and I wondered what it would take to stir up some fire, some emotion in him other than the cold amusement with which he seemed to view the world. Surely there should have been some feeling in the man, despite his desperate childhood. His eyes betrayed him, their strange blue depths burning intensely in the bronzed, set planes of his handsome face. And then I remembered his smile the last time I saw him, so completely enchanting.

"I feel it's my duty to warn you," he continued, unaware of the un-dignified female thoughts that flew through my brain.

"Warn me?" I raised an eyebrow artfully. I had perfected that talent when I was seventeen, and now it stood me in good stead. There hadn't been much call for eyebrow-raising on a dairy farm in northern Vermont.

"Warn you," he repeated patiently, as if to a foolish child. "My mother can be a very enticing person, Miss MacDougall. For your own sake as well as hers I suggest you forget all about whatever strange and twisted schemes she has in mind." He spoke mildly enough, almost casually, and I forced my tone to match his, exercising my eyebrow for a second time.

"Whatever do you mean?"

"Don't play the fool like the rest of your sex," he said explosively. "My mother has quite obviously decided that you are the ideal person to sneak around the island and discover who murdered my father. Such a plan is doomed to failure and quite, quite dangerous. You seem graced with a bit more common sense than most; surely you can see what you're attempting to do is foolhardy." His voice was cold, so still. Idly I wondered what I could do to stir him up.

"If your mother's plan is so obvious I won't bother to deny it," I said recklessly. "What makes you think it's doomed to failure?"

He raised one beautifully formed eyebrow and I could have gnashed my teeth with envy. "My dear girl, this is not a parlor game! This is murder, cold-blooded murder. Tell me, my innocent one, do you think someone who is capable of spearing my respected papa with a kitchen knife would balk at the idea of tossing an inquisitive young female over our very convenient cliffs?"

I was fascinated at the lack of emotion in his voice as he spoke of his father. "I wouldn't know," I answered firmly, refusing to be cowed. "I suppose I'll find out soon enough."

He blinked in momentary surprise at my candor, and I congratulated myself on eliciting at least one emotion from his icy control. "You're a fool," he said after a moment. "You won't discover a thing; you'll merely stir up things best left undisturbed. I only hope you won't regret your decision."

"Is that a threat?"

"Let us merely say a friendly warning," he answered lightly. "If you change your mind let me know. I'll arrange two months' sever-ance pay and your passage back to New Hampshire or wherever it is you come from."

The offer should have been tempting, but I was unmoved. That in itself should have warned me of the trouble to come. "Vermont," I snapped, my green eyes blazing. "That's very generous of you, Mr. Cameron. Almost too generous. But I don't think I'll be needing your money." I swung my legs around to the ground and rose with what I felt was proper majesty. "Good afternoon."

"Good afternoon, Miss MacDougall." The cool amusement was uppermost again, but this time it seemed combined with an exasperated respect. Another surprising emotion, I thought with satisfaction as I floated as gracefully as my height allowed down the terrace.

By the time I reached the end of the first stretch of lawn I looked back, straight into the unreadable eyes of Alex Cameron. Shrugging mentally, I turned and continued onward, determined to set my thoughts in order by a long, vigorous walk on the windy beach.

My stroll along the ocean was uneventful for the most part. Two things remained uppermost in my mind, two things that I could not ignore. One, that Captain Alexander Cameron seemed almost desperate that his father's murder should remain a closed case. Yet the only thing he could fear was self-incrimination, and much as I disliked admitting it, everything was pointing at him as the culprit.

The second thought that ran through my mind was the unpleasant one that against my will I found the cold and cynical Captain more attractive than any man I had ever met in my twenty long years. So far I had sternly controlled this outrageous weakness, and would continue to do so, but in the meantime I could only wish that my vague and mysterious feelings of misgivings about the man would resolve themselves into concrete proof of his guilt or innocence. Though I placed little hope in it turning out to be the latter.

But I also knew full well, if Lady Margaret had not made it abundantly clear already, that the Cameron heirs were not for the likes of me. And the Captain himself was not only indifferent but verging on hostility toward me.

Scuffing up sand under my thin and impractical slippers, I sighed. And then I bent down, my eye caught by something flashing brightly in the wet sand.

It was a diamond earring, a very lovely diamond earring, sparkling brilliantly and obviously quite recently lost. As a matter of fact, it had been worn by Allison Cameron just last night—I remembered admiring it with just the tiniest spurt of envy as it caught the light of the massive chandelier. I was holding the jewel in my hand, staring at it speculatively, when I heard a sound behind me. I whirled around and without thinking stuffed it into my pocket.

"What have you got there?" Stephen's flushed, attractive face loomed a little below mine.

"A shell," I lied glibly, not quite knowing why. "I've been down here looking for treasures and I've come across quite a few good ones." I fished one of the sandy articles I had fortunately gathered earlier from my pocket and displayed it to him, and noted that his shoulders quickly relaxed some of their tension.

"Oh." He smiled, somewhat sadly, I thought. "Do you mind if I walk with you a bit, Miss MacDougall?"

I noticed his voice was courteous, cultured, unlike the harsh drawl of his younger brother. It was a pleasure to be with such a gentleman, I told myself, smiling at him sweetly. "Certainly, Mr. Cameron. Although I was just about to turn back—it's getting late."

"Then I'll accompany you back to the house if I might. I . . . I hoped we might have a chance to talk."

You too, I thought resignedly. I wondered if he was about to bribe me to leave the island like his brother had. If enough of Lady Margaret's children were to offer me money I could retire in style, I thought wistfully.

"Has my brother been bothering you, Miss MacDougall?" he asked suddenly, and I was so startled I stopped short in the sand.

"Charles?" I asked incredulously.

"Oh no!" Stephen was aghast. "I mean Alex. My wife told me that she saw you two out on the terrace this afternoon and that whatever you were discussing it didn't seem pleasant."

That spying little bitch, I thought with aggravation. "Your wife mistook the matter," I answered with a trace of coolness. "We were merely discussing your mother. There was nothing unpleasant at all, I assure you. The Captain was perfectly courteous."

"He can be pleasant," Stephen admitted, a troubled look on his handsome young face. "But perhaps I might offer a word of advice."

I looked up with hopeful encouragement. I was interested in Stephen Cameron's opinion of his possibly cuckolding younger brother.

There was a touch of bitterness in his light voice. "Those who enjoy Alex's good will often suffer for it. He's a very handsome man, my young brother, and there's a surprising amount of charm beneath that harsh exterior. He also has all the emotional maturity of a nine-year-old. You'd do well to beware of him."

The pain in his face was unavoidable, and my heart ached for him. I knew it was bitterness about his wife's infatuation, and yet I couldn't dismiss his harsh judgments as lightly as I so wanted to do.

"Well, I do thank you for your concern," I said after a long moment, wishing there was something I could do to comfort the poor man. "I'll keep your advice well in mind."

We had reached the bottom of the wooden steps that climbed up the cliff. "I hope you will," he said, pressing my hand. "And now, if you don't mind, I think I'll walk a bit more. I don't feel like returning to the house yet." Was there a trace of venom in his voice when he mentioned the house, or did I merely imagine it?

I nodded, adding, as he turned and started away from me, "Don't stay out too long, Mr. Cameron. The cold damp sea air is bad for the lungs, you know." It was presumptuous of me but I couldn't help it.

He smiled at me, and it almost broke my heart. "Don't worry, Miss MacDougall. The doctors said when I was little that if I made it to twenty-five I'd be all right. I'm thirty-three now and I intend to live for a long time." He cast an angry look in the direction of the house. "A damned long time," he muttered under his breath, and strode off down the beach.

I thought I'd had enough of the Cameron brothers, but when I reached the terrace I discovered one more waiting for me.

"Miss MacDougall!" Charles greeted me jovially, his healthy face ruddy and glowing. "I came out here hoping to meet up with you, and suddenly you appear like a nymph from the sea."

I was a trifle taken aback at this fulsomeness, and put my hand to my hair, assuming his flattery merely meant I was wind-blown. "Good afternoon, Mr. Cameron," I said with a little less enthusiasm. "What can I do for you?"

"Would you care for a turn around the garden, Miss MacDougall? My mother is busy with Allison right now and the children are still napping." He smiled at me with an innocent charm that seemed slightly false.

"Well, I don't know if I should," I hesitated, a bit coyly, savoring the image of meeting the Captain on Charles's arm.

"Please, Miss MacDougall," he said with surprising earnestness in his warm brown eyes. "It's not often I get the chance to go for a stroll in such lovely weather with such lovely company."

This obvious flattery made me a little uneasy, and I hoped the debonair Charles was not about to embark on a little flirtation with his mother's companion. I hardly felt like fighting off stolen kisses in the garden. At least not with Charles.

But I had misjudged him. He was the soul of kindness, really, pointing out the different varieties of early flowers to my inattentive eye. By the time we had toured the garden we were on slightly self-conscious first-name basis. I wondered if Charles, like Alex, had guessed my secret purpose and was trying to allay my suspicions.

We were heading back toward the terrace when Charles hesitantly broached the subject he had been hinting at all along.

"Lorna, I know this will seem presumptuous of me, but I feel it my duty to . . . er, I don't know quite how to put this."

With a sinking feeling I knew what he was about to say. I stood still and waited patiently.

Charles cleared his throat and continued with renewed determination. "I feel, my dear Lorna, that it is my duty to warn you about my brother."

Some imp of mischief made me say innocently, "Stephen?"

"No, no! I was referring to my brother Alex. He has a devil-may-care charm about him but you'd best be on guard where he's concerned. I would hate to see a sweet young thing like yourself taken in by him."

He obviously meant well, but my pride flared up at his friendly condescension. I was perfectly capable of protecting myself from Alexander Cameron's disputed charms, although it seemed likely that I stood in no danger of being exposed to them. The thought depressed me slightly.

"Thank you," I answered noncommittally. He was kind, and yet I could see how a rebellious child would love to get such a perfect creature in trouble. But a normal child would hardly go to the lengths that Alex apparently had. I shook my head.

"Perhaps we'd better start back to the house," Charles said finally after a long silence. "It's getting cloudy, and I imagine the children will be up and screaming for you. You've become quite their favorite, you know."

"Have I?" I questioned absently, wondering when Charles had spoken with them. So far he had managed to avoid them as if they were a rather ill-trained species of animal. Perhaps I had misjudged him. "Well, I'm glad they're fond of me," I said warmly. "They need someone to love unrestrainedly."

"Ah, but they have their mother," Charles suggested, and I threw him a swift glance to see if there was a trace of sarcasm in his demeanor. There was no expression beyond bland amiability, and I had to assume that he was sincere. It was hardly my place to enlighten him about his sister-in-law and her failings as a mother, so I merely nodded, changing the subject.

When I was alone with the children later that evening, watching them devour a hearty meal, I nibbled at a predinner snack and went back in my mind over the day's revelations. The sparkling diamond earring was safely tucked underneath my lace-trimmed chemises in my top drawer. I could think of no way to confront Allison and ask her point-blank what she'd been doing down by the ocean in fancy dress. She would either tell me to mind my own business, or lie, and either way I would be no wiser. No, I would simply have to slip it back into her room sometime and watch for her reaction.

As I thought back to the brothers Cameron, I had to admit that Alex was an enigma to me. He could scarcely be as cruel and cold-blooded as he was reputed to be—no one could. His piercing eyes and his flashes of humor betrayed him, yet he was too much on my mind, and I wished my far-from-reliable second sight would assist me. Now a proper gift, I thought wryly, would present me with the reconstructed murder in a nice little dream, with a bit of proof conveniently added, so all I would have to do would be to present the case to Lady Margaret and retire gracefully with the thanks of all and the teeth-gnashings of the villain. Unfortunately, life was not so neat and well ordered, and right now my gift seemed more of a hindrance than a help. These glimpses of another time and place served only to confuse me.

I sighed, nibbling at the mashed potatoes and gravy Thora had thoughtfully provided my immense appetite, and the children looked up, catching some of my obvious discontent. I smiled immediately, and their tense little bodies relaxed. The least I could do at this point would be to keep the children feeling relatively safe and peaceful. I could hardly let the mixed emotions toward their beloved Uncle Alex and their not so beloved mother show through.

Apparently I was to be given the night off. The Camerons were traveling to the mainland for dinner with close family friends, and I would be left to my own devices. They weren't expected to be back until quite late, and my services would not be required, thank you.

The house had never seemed so empty, so still. Katie brought me a heavy-laden tray, and it was all I could do to keep myself from sending it back. I wanted to join them in the warm, friendly kitchen, but I knew the idea was foolish. I had been given a special position in this household, a position I was expected to maintain with proper dignity. Besides, I knew Katie wouldn't thank me for a wasted trip, and my presence would put constraints on their easy dinnertime conversation, so I said nothing.

With a vague feeling of martyrdom I plowed my way through watercress soup, fish soufflé, beef and gravy, potatoes, spinach, and carrots. Three desserts were almost more than I could handle, but I decided it would be rude to return the tray half full. However, my mood and appetite were not of the best, and, setting the tray outside my door for Katie's eventual retrieval, I realized why.

I was feeling neglected, left out. For some foolish, childish reason I felt hurt that I hadn't been invited out to dinner with the family.

This business of being a servant comes hard, I told myself firmly. Think of something else to take your mind off such idiocy.

The only thing that suggested itself to my usually fertile imagination was a late-night search of the now inhabited bedrooms. I could return Allison's earring at the same time. I even went so far as to open the door, blinding myself firmly to the ghastly vision of Josiah's bloodstained body lurking just out of sight.

The hallway was long, dark, and deserted. I hesitated, and was lost. Slamming the door and locking it, I ran back across the room and leapt onto the downy softness of my bed. There's no need to give myself heart failure, I justified my cowardice. A nice comfortable book will do for the night. Tomorrow I could be the self-contained sleuth once more.

Chapter IX

I awoke early the next morning, long before the rest of the household had even begun to stir. It had been very late when the family had returned the night before, and I knew I could venture out without meeting anyone. The sun was rising with slow majesty over the calm, dark waters, spreading filigree fingers of light toward the shadowed house and across the wide expanse of wet green lawn. With far more than my usual morning energy, I threw the covers back and jumped out of bed. Back home I had often gone for early morning walks across the dew-spangled fields, and I knew that along the ocean beaches it would be even more enticing than by our land-locked lake. Hesitating barely a second, I dressed myself, brushed my tangled hair with only cursory attention, letting it hang loose down my back as I hadn't in the three years since I had become a young lady, and slipped out of my room, my bare feet noiseless in the old stone corridor.

Before I had reached the first floor my ever-present hunger pains began, and I detoured through the kitchen to raid Thora's supply of freshly baked bread. Arming myself with three thick slabs and a huge wedge of cheese wrapped in a heavy cloth napkin, I opened the solid oaken door and let myself out into the early morning sunshine.

My first stop was the stables. I fed the four horses a chunk of sugar each, greeting them warmly. They appeared pleased to see me, from Firefly, placid and cheerful, to bad-tempered Samantha.

"I've been neglecting you, my beauties," I told them, "but no more. You're the only ones I can trust around this place; you and the children." I sighed, and leaned my head against Samantha's smooth flank. She whinnied sympathetically, and I was comforted. Wandering out of the stables and across the lawns, I tried to fathom what this strange feeling of depression was that had hovered over me for the past few days. The only word for it would be lonely, I had to admit. How strange, I thought, after having spent most of my first twenty years trying to find a little time by myself, away from the demands of nine brothers and sisters.

And my thoughts traveled to the Cameron men. Alex and Charles and Stephen. Alex with his coldness that exhibited an unholy amusement about everything and everyone; Charles with his flattering attentions. And poor Stephen, with his foolish devotion to a shallow wife.

Up until now I had found men a boring necessity, useful for lifting heavy objects and providing food and shelter. The Camerons were a different breed, one I couldn't wholly understand as yet. They all made me very uncomfortable, from Alex, with his odd effect on my senses, to Stephen, who watched me with such hangdog sadness in his eyes, as if I might be the one to save him and return his wife to his side. As if I could.

And Charles was another thing, I thought, seating myself on the railing above the sea cliff and taking out my prebreakfast snack. I couldn't deny his portion of the legendary Cameron charm, and yet all that robust good health next to his sickly brother made me nervous. I munched reflectively on the thick, crusty bread and stared out across the blue-green water of early morning.

And then I was aware of a figure climbing slowly up the angled wooden stairway from the beach. My nearsighted eyes peered through the distance, and made out the curling black hair, the bare torso. I averted my eyes quickly, trying to control the blush that was spreading over my face. After all, I told myself sternly, you've seen men without their shirts before. Don't be a fool—now is your chance to find out something. Be friendly.

"You're an early riser." Alex spoke to me as he came to the final flight of steps. I could see with relief that he was wearing a pair of tight, calf-length breeches, and the sea water sparkled in his hair.

"So are you," I answered, pleased by my outward calm. I broke off a chunk of the Cheddar and ate it slowly, nonchalantly, my attention taken up with the distant skyline. When I looked around again he was beside me, his strange blue eyes resting lightly on me, fully aware of my bare feet and the hair hanging hoyden-like down my back, amused, I was certain, by my embarrassment. I smiled in what I hoped was a suitably casual manner, as if I were entirely used to having early morning conversations with half-nude men.

"Well, Miss MacDougall," he began pleasantly enough, "have you discovered any vital information yet? Or have you thought better of your decision to remain here?"

He could be very beguiling in the early morning sun, and my proximity to all that naked, sun-bronzed flesh made me suddenly wish I could do anything he asked me to. But it was all a cynical charm, I warned myself. He used it on all menials, on me and on his sailors. No wonder they long to please him. I refused to fall victim to it.

"No, Mr. Cameron, to both questions," I answered lightly, and took another bite of cheese. "And it's not that your brothers haven't tried to warn me away too."

He reached out and with one large hand grabbed the cheese away from me and bit into it with strong white teeth. I watched it disappear with feelings not unmixed with sorrow, and he smiled at me with sudden sweetness.

"What I like about you," he said seriously, "among other things, is your absolutely tremendous appetite. Don't you know that ladies are supposed to eat like birds?"

"What made you think I am a lady?" I was enjoying myself. "I'm not, you know. Ladies don't work for a living."

He considered this. "Perhaps you're right," he murmured slowly. "But then, I was never fond of ladies."

"So I've heard," I snapped with sudden bad temper.

He smiled again. "Tell me, exactly what did my brothers warn you about? Or should I say who?"

The telltale flush crept up to my face again as I remembered his brothers' careful warnings, and anger at this man for putting me in such an awkward situation made me speak before I could think, an unfortunate habit of mine.

"They warned me to stay away from you, Captain!" I said roundly. "They're afraid I might succumb to your overwhelming charm." The sarcasm in my voice made it clear that I found his charm tenuous, to say the least.

With that he threw back his head and laughed out loud, the sound ringing through the crisp salt air. "I never would have expected that," he said after a moment, looking down at me with laughter in his sapphire eyes. "Did they think of this themselves, or had you expressed some interest in my direction?"

I nearly slapped him for that one. "Not likely," I snapped, and he could see the rage in my eyes. It seemed to amuse him even more.

"Well, I can see I'm not having too salutary an effect on you this morning, Miss MacDougall, so I'll leave you to commune with nature on your own." Before I could respond to this he nodded with profound courtesy and left me abruptly. I sat in bemused and angry silence for a while, watching him make his way leisurely back to the house, whistling an old sea chanty as loudly as he could. Something had put him in an awfully good mood, and I couldn't help but wonder what. I waited, not thinking of much at all. Eventually I followed him to the house in search of a more substantial breakfast.

It was apparently going to be a quiet day. The entire family, children included, were going off on a sailing expedition. The rest of the help were given the day off, leaving me alone on the island.

I could see Lady Margaret's fine hand in all this. So far all I had delivered up were a few half-formed opinions, none of them particularly helpful. When it came right down to it there was no one on this island I considered incapable of murder. I could even picture Thora or amiable Charles delivering the final blow, though such visions seemed farfetched.

Deliberately I tried to steer my thoughts toward Alex. He was the obvious choice for a murderer; seemingly the only one around with the strength of will, the rough life and death of the sea in his background. I was sure that during his travels he had seen many differences settled with a knife or a gun, and had consequently learned to hold life cheap.

But I couldn't quite believe it. My logic told me yes, my instincts a resounding no. I could only hope that my instincts were right.

As I watched Thora and the two girls set off toward the landing dock, I felt vague misgivings. Even in daylight the house was much too big, too eerie for my total peace of mind. Even on such a day as this, with the sun blazing in a clear blue sky, sparkling off the still ocean, I couldn't rid myself of my uneasiness. It was almost as if someone was peering over my shoulder.

I wandered back through the deserted kitchen and into the main hall. The stairs curved majestically upward—I knew where my duty lay. A thorough search, room by room, was the obvious course. It mattered not that the long gloomy halls unnerved me. I had a job to do.

Four hours later I was in a state of frustrated exhaustion. I had gone through every drawer, pocket, every possible hiding place on the second floor, both the main section and servants' quarters, and what had I to show for it? Aching feet, a blinding headache, and a jumpy stomach from the nerve-racking effort of leaving everything as it had been. Plus a few interesting items:

In Allison's room there was an envelope stuffed full of crisp green bills hidden in her hatbox. I counted five hundred dollars, and I wondered why she should hide such a sum. I also discovered the full extent of her vanity in the lavish extravagance of her clothes. With great care I placed the sand-encrusted diamond earring in the hatbox beside the money. Just a little something to aid her sleepless nights, I thought with cheerful vindictiveness.

The earring's mate was nowhere to be seen. And I wondered once more whom she had been meeting down on the beach and why had it been so secretive?

Charles's room was as neat as a pin, which was as I suspected. There was nothing of interest there, merely a sheaf of papers connected with the Cameron enterprises. Papers I could make neither head nor tail out of. The rest of the rooms were as devoid of interest, except, of course, for the Captain's.

Adorning his walls was a collection, quite extensive and well cared for, of foreign knives of every conceivable shape, size, and use. From a Malaysian kris to a wicked-looking double-edged sword, he had a complete range of murderous cutlery. I stared at the wall in horror, wondering how I could have overlooked such a damning piece of evidence on my first tour of the house. I moved closer with a sort of sick fascination, and reached out to touch one smooth, sharp edge. I let out a little gasp of pain. Barely realizing it, I had let the unexpectedly sharp blade slice through my hand, and great nasty oozings of blood were dropping from the cut, splashing onto my clothes, onto the floor.

A wave of faintness washed over me. I ran from the room, slamming the door behind me. In my distress I nearly tumbled headlong down the stairs, but I caught myself in time. I dashed into the cavernous empty kitchen and thrust my bleeding hand under the pump.

The cool water soothed some of the throbbing pain, although it had little effect on the amount of blood that flowed in a seemingly endless stream from my wound. I leaned my head against the cool stone wall and the perilous dizziness abated. It was a hated weakness of mine, this giddiness at the sight of blood, and I could only be glad there was no one about to witness my shame.

"Are you all right?" A voice spoke from quite near at hand and I whirled around. Of course it was the last person in the world I wanted to see. Alex peered at me through the gloom.

"What . . ." I faltered, ". . . what are you doing here?"

"I came back early," he answered impatiently. "What have you done to yourself?"

"I've cut my hand," I answered testily. The blood was oozing out steadily again. I cast about and, seeing a chair nearby, sank into it gratefully.

"It's too dark in here," he muttered, striking a match and lighting one of the oil lamps. He set it down on the table beside me and took my injured hand in his large, capable one. "That's a nasty cut," he murmured, his touch surprisingly gentle. "How did you do it?"

"I . . . I . . ."

"Never mind." He grabbed one of Thora's best linen towels and wrapped it around my hand. "Hold that on while I look for some bandages. Thora must have some in her room."

"I believe she does." I swayed in the chair and he turned back to me.

"Here, now." Was his voice worried? "You'd better lie down." Before I could marshal my thoughts he scooped me up effortlessly, for all my height, and carried me into Thora's adjoining rooms, depositing me on her solid bed.

In a moment he was back beside me, tenderly unwrapping the dish towel. He rebandaged my hand expertly, and when he had finished I was able to look down at the offending member without feeling that blasted dizziness.

"It isn't quite that bad, you know." There was a trace of gentle amusement in his voice as we surveyed his handiwork in the twilight bedroom.

"I know it isn't," I answered. "It's just that . . ."

"That you have some feminine weaknesses after all," he finished for me, and his voice had a curious note in it.

I looked into his eyes then, in the dim light of Thora Monroe's stern New England bedroom, and his gaze held mine for a strange, breathless moment. Then he pulled away, almost as if he were burned.

"I thought my brothers warned you about me." And his voice was cold again. "You'd better rest for a while," he added. "I'm sure Thora wouldn't object to your staying here."

"No, I'm sure she wouldn't." My voice sounded hollow. Yes, I'd been warned. But I hadn't listened. It was all I could do to hold back the fretful, disappointed tears that threatened to spill over. And I couldn't even say why I wanted to weep.

I heard the door shut softly and a wave of depression washed over me. My hand throbbed, my head ached, tears slid down my face, and the bed beneath me was made of rock, as befitted Thora's strong sense of morality.

As my own sense of morality was happily elastic, the bed provided more discomfort than ease, so, sighing, I sat up and swung my feet to the floor. The dizziness was slight by this time, and, rising slowly, I was able to head for the door without stumbling, when my interest was caught by a photograph framed in heavy silver, occupying a place of honor on the dresser amid the surprisingly opulent silver-backed brushes. I moved closer to examine it.

It was a handsome, middle-aged man with the look of Cameron about him. The attractiveness, so similar to Alex's infrequent charm, was marred by an obstinate, bullying set to the mouth. It was inscribed with a firm hand, "To Thora, from her loving Josiah." In spite of my shock I decided he didn't look very loving to me as I slipped out of the room.

By the time I reached my bedroom door, I knew from the unmistakable sounds in the lower hallway that the family had returned once more. I could hear Lady Margaret's autocratic orders, the fretful sounds of tired children, Katie's (or was it Nancy's) soothing tones.

It would soon be time to dress for dinner, for the long ritual of delicious food and stifling tensions. Tonight I didn't feel equal to facing all the subtle undercurrents that pervaded the well-bred Cameron atmosphere. I didn't even care to find out whether Allison wore her newly restored diamond earring. Gluttony warred with a profound exhaustion, and the latter won. Besides, I thought, as I scribbled a note to Lady Margaret, Thora would be certain to send me up a hearty tray. My note read:

> Dear Lady Margaret,
> Please forgive my absence at dinner tonight. I have a blinding headache which seems unlikely to go away. Also, please make my excuses to your children.

I wondered if this would seem a bit cold and unsatisfying, so I hastily added a tantalizing postscript.

> I have had a very productive day.

That should silence her, I thought as I slipped the note under her door. She would find it when she came up to change, and I would have a night of peace. My only problem was to try and decide what tempting morsel of information I could trust the old woman with. The more time I spent with her, the more afraid I was that she would stifle all evidence leading to an unfavored suspect, allowing only clues condemning her chosen culprit.

What a fool I was then, what an innocent fool! I never even stopped to question my motives. I simply spent the evening by the open windows, my ears straining for any scraps of conversation that might have floated out on the soft salt breeze from the terraces below. My feelings, when I finally gave in and retired for the night, were not unmixed with disappointment, and it was a long time before I slept.

Chapter X

When I arrived downstairs the next morning, they were all gone. The children, Stephen and Allison, Charles and Alex. The house suddenly seemed very large and empty, and I found myself beset with a curious lassitude. I busied myself as best I could, trying to fight off the persistent depression.

Surprisingly enough, the next weeks passed swiftly. I would sit with Lady Margaret for long hours, reading repressive sermons on the folly of all things pleasurable. During the rest of the time I would ride or walk around the island, watching with wonder and delight as spring blossomed into summer lushness. I tested the water a few times with tentative bare feet, and shuddered at the thought of Alex immersing his entire body into the icy depths. And then at the thought of Alex's entire body I would blush and quickly think of something else.

The thought of Josiah's death haunted me. I had been purposefully vague with Lady Margaret as to the details of my findings up to that point. For some reason I was loath to mention the suspicious coincidence of Alex's knife collection, and that photograph of Josiah in Thora's room might cause more trouble than I cared to stir up.

Lady Margaret was satisfied with my glossed-over explanations. For the time being she seemed to have forgotten my original purpose in being here, and I spent my time as a sometime companion. The work was pleasing, leaving me plenty of time for riding and walking and dreaming. I was beginning to enjoy the first vacation I'd had since my father's accident, and I heartily wished old Josiah had died peacefully in his bed. But he hadn't died in his bed, he had been stabbed to death one warm afternoon by someone he had trusted, and despite the fact that the more I learned about him the more it seemed as if he deserved to be murdered, I couldn't simply forget about it and drift into the easy, elegant life offered me as Lady Margaret's companion.

I went on for two weeks like this, ignoring my reasons for being there, lolling in indolent sloth and excellent food. It came as a shock to me when I discovered it was almost July and Lady Margaret's odd assortment of children would be returning to the island by the end of the week. I had made no progress, I had been lazy and shiftless, and I was heartily ashamed of myself.

Determinedly I forced myself to face the unpleasant reason for my presence. I had yet to find out all I could from Old John, and an overcast afternoon toward the end of the week seemed a perfect time to further my knowledge. Lady Margaret had retired for a nap; Thora and the girls were involved in the seemingly endless cleaning that a house of this size requires. I changed into my pantaloons and shirt and strolled out to the stables.

A few minutes later I was seated comfortably on an old horse blanket outside the stables, studiously applying John's secret formula of leather balm to the harnesses, reins, and saddles under his careful direction.

"This place is a lot different than it used to be, miss," he remarked casually, his gnarled, cracked hands soothing the cream into the brown leather straps with odd tenderness. "Things were better when Josiah was alive, for all that the old man was a bit of a tyrant." He eyed me to see if this had aroused my curiosity. Naturally it had.

"Was he?" I questioned. "Thora has nothing but praise for him," I lied. Thora had seldom mentioned him.

The trick worked, as I knew it would. Old John snorted contemptuously. "Her! I thought it was common knowledge that she was the old man's mistress for nigh on thirty years. The sun rose and set with that man as far as she was concerned. There are others who weren't so partial," he added darkly.

"Such as?" I abandoned any pretense of disinterest.

"Such as his wife," he said flatly. "She threatened to kill him once if he didn't stop his womanizing. He wouldn't, she didn't, but she still bears a grudge against Thora." He eyed the piece of leather he was working on reflectively, spat, and continued, "Such as his children, which number more than you might expect."

"You mean Nancy?" I asked.

"More'n that. Thora and Nancy's mother weren't the only females Josiah trifled with over the years. And some of the others didn't fare so well. Look about ye, miss, and you'll see the Cameron stamp where you least expect it." He sighed gustily. "My own sister was one of the foolish ones."

"What happened?" I asked quietly, somehow knowing what he was about to say.

Old John's face had taken on a stony look. "She found herself in a family way one day, and of course it was Josiah to blame. And rather than bear the shame of it she threw herself off the cliffs over there." He jerked his head in their direction. "So there's a good many had cause to hate Josiah Cameron."

The Friday of the Camerons' return dawned dark and cold and stormy. A strong north wind was blowing up, and according to Old John, we would see miserable weather all weekend or he'd be an old fool.

"You are an old fool, John," Thora snapped at him, scrubbing the table with more energy than I had ever expended in a whole lifetime of scrubbing tables. "But this time you're right. I wish there was some way we could tell the children not to try and come out."

"They should know enough about the weather by now," John grumped back at her. "They'll come if the weather's decent, they'll stay away if it's not." He stomped out of the kitchen in a foul humor.

"Well, what are you standing about looking at?" Thora demanded of me in bad-tempered exasperation. "Go and see to Lady Margaret, or go for a walk or something. I'm too busy to bother with your everlasting questions right now!"

"Yes, ma'am." I prepared to depart.

"And take some cookies with you if you're going walking," she called after me. Thora had a fondness for me and my appetite.

The day remained the same—bleak and dark, but with no rain or fog to add interest to it. I sat with Lady Margaret and read Charles Dickens (whom I hated), mended sheets (which I hated even more), and waited.

It started with a bitter, howling wind. It seemed to blow right through the thick stone walls, and, despite my usual hardiness, I had to go upstairs for another shawl. Occasional flashes of lightning would brighten the early darkness of the sky, and a thick fog was rolling in over the island.

I placed Lady Margaret's fine cashmere shawl around her hunched old shoulders and lit another lamp against the unnatural gloom.

"I suppose my children aren't coming," the old lady said querulously. "I should have known, a little fog, a little cold, and they scurry into their fancy town house like so many mice, rather than face a little discomfort."

I could hardly point out that the fogbound chill outside would provide more than a little discomfort, so I remained tactfully silent.

After a moment I offered, "Isn't it better that they wait a day rather than risk danger or perhaps an infection?"

"Ah, you're thinking of Stephen," she said shrewdly. "And I thought it was Alex you had those green eyes of yours on. Well, it won't do you any good."

I had learned to control my blushes in front of the old lady's uncanny and outspoken insights. "Surely Stephen shouldn't be out in such weather?" I persisted.

"He's a weakling," the old woman snapped. "Josiah couldn't bear weakness in a man. There were times when I think he hated him. His own son."

"Did Stephen know that?"

"Of course he knew it! Josiah was never one to hide his feelings. Stephen may be a weakling but he's no fool. Only a fool could miss the contempt his father held for him. Contempt can drive a man to desperation, Lorna, my dear. And I've seen Stephen desperate more than once."

"Are you trying to tell me that Stephen might have killed his father?" I asked her point-blank. She didn't even flinch.

"It's a possibility, isn't it?" There was no emotion in her voice at all. "And I don't want you to overlook any possibility." Here was this strange mother offering up a new candidate for murder, and I wondered once more who she really thought had committed the crime.

I munched reflectively on the delicate seedcake Thora had provided with tea, and considered Stephen as a cold-blooded killer. The more I thought about it, the more possible it seemed. His father's dislike and probable taunting could have driven him over the edge of sanity into a mad rage. I had seen the traces of hysteria hovering behind his slightly feverish eyes, and knew that semihysterical people could be pushed too far. I was busy with this train of thought when the door flew open and Allison Cameron stood there, her children by her side, looking as if she'd crossed half of the Labrador wasteland to get here.

"What a miserable day!" she cried in her light, pretty voice, flinging off her lamb's wool cloak and tossing it on a chair. She glided over and clinked cheekbones with her mother-in-law. "And how are you, Mama Cameron?"

"I'm fine, Allison. You're late."

Allison pouted prettily. "Of course we're late; how could we be otherwise in this kind of weather? The fog is already so thick we could barely see our way from the landing." She sank into a chair near the fire and gave me a cold, smooth smile. "And how are you, Lorna? Have you been enjoying yourself here on the island?"

My hackles rose at her condescending tone, and my annoyance was not helped by the sight of her two children standing there wrapped in their warm coats, watching us with silent eyes.

Allison watched the direction of my gaze, and immediately resumed the role of perfect mother. "Lorna, would you be a dear and take the children up to their room? I'm sure the poor little things are tired to death. A light supper, I think, and then a story before bedtime."

But Lady Margaret had forestalled her by ringing the bell for one of the maids. "I prefer to have Lorna with me this evening. Nancy will do just as well. It's time the children got to know one of their aunts," she laughed with a bawdiness that belied her wizened frame, and sent the children off in spite of Allison's scandalized protests.

"Mama Cameron, I wish . . ." Allison began.

"Don't be such a ninny!" The old woman interrupted. "They're too young to understand what I said. Tell me instead how your trip was." Her voice was sociable once more. "No complications, missed trains or the like?"

"Well, as you can imagine, I had a terrible time trying to cope with the children all by myself. They were both in particularly *bouncy* moods. They were so excited about seeing their beloved Lorna again." She made a slight gesture of distaste. "Fortunately I had arranged to meet with Charles at the train station, and Alex was waiting at the dory so we all came across together. And speaking of that dory, Mama Cameron, couldn't we do something about it? It's so . . . inelegant! Why, I'm ashamed to ask my friends to come visit when they have to travel across in such a plebeian vessel."

Lady Margaret ignored this. "Why were you traveling alone?" she demanded. "Where is Stephen?"

There was a sudden uneasy silence. "Why, Mama Cameron, whatever do you mean? Stephen is here, of course. He left early so that he would miss the fog and the storm. You know what this cold, damp weather does to his lungs."

"He never arrived," she said apprehensively, and at that moment the door flew open and Charles stood there, panting and disheveled.

"Stephen's horse came in sometime this afternoon—riderless! That senile old fool John doesn't even know when he came in—he was off up-island checking on fences or something equally absurd. Stephen could be lying anywhere out there with a broken leg or worse, and in this weather!" He ran an agonized hand through his brown hair. "We've got to find him."

"Oh no!" Allison let out a little cry. I was surprised to see she had that much feeling.

"Alex, John, and I are about to go out searching," he said distractedly. "Why don't you get his room ready with plenty of quilts and the hottest fire the girls can make."

"Of course," Lady Margaret agreed.

"I think I'll find Horace and send him out too," I spoke suddenly.

"Do you think he'd be any help?" Lady Margaret looked at me sharply.

"You mean the half-wit?" Charles demanded. "By all means, send him. We will need all the help we can get."

Chapter XI

I was dressed in no more than five minutes, my long legs encased in my brother's corduroy pantaloons, my long hair tucked under a cloth cap. When I looked at my reflection in the mirror, I couldn't hope to keep my identity a secret, but with luck the dark night and the fog and a careful distance from the others would aid me. I would hate to think what would happen if Alexander Cameron discovered Horace was a female.

Thora was bent over the kitchen stove, which on this chill night was barely making a dent in the icy reaches of the kitchen. There were tears streaming down her stern face. She barely glanced at my outfit.

"You'd best take Old John's sweater," she said matter-of-factly, still stirring the pungent concoction which in this emergency had no ability to tempt me. "It wouldn't do for the Captain to find out who you are—we've enough trouble in this house tonight. There's a lantern out on the back porch for you. Head east—I don't believe anyone's gone in that direction yet. And look sharp—not that it'll do any good." She sighed gustily. "My poor babe."

"We'll find him," I said confidently. "The island isn't that big, you know. It shouldn't take us too long."

"You'll find him all right. Much good it will do you—with his lungs he wouldn't last five minutes out there." She turned to face me. "Well, what are you standing around gawking for—get going!"

I got. John's sweater was rough and heavy and redolent of horses, but it added necessary warmth and protection to my thin frame. The fog was so dense I could scarcely see my way out of the courtyard, were it not for occasional patches of clearing, and it was not without misgivings that I took off into the murky evening.

The others had gone on horseback, but I had no intention of doing so. I knew I stood a much better chance alone and on foot. I could become more attuned to the night air, to the sounds of the trees in the small forest beyond the house. I could hear the distant crash of the angry ocean on flinty rocks above the uproar of the wind. And I was counting on my intermittent gifts to be able to find Stephen before it was too late.

The ground was spongy and wet beneath my feet—there was a cold and evil dampness all around me, seeming to seep through my rough clothing, down into my very bones. It was only the thought of the weak and sickly Stephen, lying out in this miasma, and of his poor neglected children, who would probably fare far worse if they were left fatherless, that drove me onward. That, and the confident knowledge that I was going in the right direction, spurred me forward, even though I was somehow certain that death was lurking around me.

I came upon them so suddenly that I nearly screamed. Alex was bending over his brother's limp body. There was blood on his hands, and blood on Stephen's golden-brown head.

Alex's eyes glanced over me and dismissed me. He stood up. "Have you seen the others?" I shook my head, and then we heard the noise at the same time. Charles and John, arriving from their various parts of the island.

"Is he dead, Captain?" Old John asked meekly, slipping off his horse.

"Not yet." There was a bleak look on his face as he spoke. We stood there, silently, and I had the uncanny feeling that we were mourners at a grave.

Charles was the first to break the silence. "We've got to get him back to the house," he said urgently. "Here, boy, give me a hand."

It took me a moment to realize he meant me, and as I rushed to comply I was aware of a strangely intent expression on Alex's face. With some little difficulty we placed Stephen's limp body on Ladybird, the fat old chestnut, and John and Charles led him slowly away from the clearing. We watched them go, Alex and I, in silence. Finally he turned to me.

"We'd better start walking," he said briefly. "One death on the island is enough for now."

"But I thought you said he was still alive?" I questioned sharply, not even bothering to disguise my voice.

The Captain didn't seem to notice. Or perhaps he'd noticed enough already. "He'll be dead by tomorrow morning. Unless there's a miracle."

And even I knew how rare miracles were. We had prayed night and day for something to cure my father, to make his back whole again, but to no avail. Once broken, people were not as easily mended as toys. We walked the long way back through the liquid fog without another word.

I left him at the stables. I knew there was nothing I could do for

Stephen or any of the other Camerons for that matter. Nancy would be with the children, and that was all that counted. Right now there would be hot and sweating horses in need of a rubdown in this chill night air and some fresh hay and water.

I don't know what would have happened had anyone else gone to the horses. Would the others have kept quiet about what they would have found, or would they have spoken out? The large and painful metal burr that was embedded in Firefly's tender flesh, so that the poor thing shivered and snorted and backed away from me, as if I were the person who had done this to her. Instead of a sneaking, silent murderer. I wondered how long Stephen had ridden her before the burr had worked itself through the blanket and into her smooth skin. Had she thrown him where we had found him, or had he stumbled or walked through the ever-thickening fog until he had dropped from exhaustion? And then I remembered the blood on his head, the blood on his brother's hand. Was that blood from his fall, or had Alexander Cameron struck his brother down for some dark and dreadful reason? With a heavy yank I pulled the evil thing out of Firefly's back and placed it gingerly in my pocket. If such a thing had happened, I would find out. Someone on this island had tried very hard to kill once more, and quite likely would succeed again. But he wouldn't get away with it, I thought fiercely, rubbing away at the horse's hot and sweating flanks. It was no longer a question of money, of pleasing Lady Margaret. It was now a matter of necessity.

I went straight to my room, not stopping to comfort Thora's quietly sobbing form, not even checking on Lady Margaret. I shut the door, stripped off my clothes, and climbed beneath the chill sheets, too tired even to think.

I awoke sometime in the middle of the night. In the rush of last night no one had bothered to build me a fire, and the cold in the room was so solid and biting that all I could do was lie in bed and shiver. I told myself to go back to sleep—nights got a lot colder in Vermont. But the chill had reached down to my innards and I could only lie there and shake until I was able to summon enough will-power to get up and build a fire myself.

The moment I got out of bed I knew something was wrong. The evil was so strong in the house I could smell it. Without volition I went to the windows. My vision was drawn through the now clear night air to the only other lighted window in this monstrous edifice—Stephen's room, with its windows flung wide open in the icy night air.

I threw on my robe and ran out the door. Silently I sped through the halls, my bare feet scarcely touching the icy floors. I was young and strong, but the Cameron halls were long and winding, and I had just awakened from a deep sleep. Unable to help myself, I had to stop for breath almost at his door, gasping and choking as silently as I could.

It was as well I stopped, I suppose. Coming from his brother's room, a remote, hidden look on his face, was Alexander Cameron. He shut the door quietly behind him, and there seemed to me to be a damning furtiveness in his actions. Like a fool, I spoke to him.

"How is he?"

He wheeled around, and I thought I could read pain and guilt and anger like the mark of Cain in his forbidding countenance. "What the hell are you doing here?" he demanded coldly.

"I thought I saw the windows open in your brother's room," I answered with foolhardiness.

"You didn't."

"I decided I had better check."

"They're closed."

I tried to brush past him. "I still want to check," I said stubbornly.

"My brother is dead." It was anger on his face, a very real and frightening rage. Yet it didn't seem directed at me. Without another word he threw open the door, long enough for me to see the windows, tightly shut and bolted. But the telltale chill had not yet subsided.

"They were open," I insisted. "The room is ice cold, they . . ."

"Go back to bed, Miss MacDougall," he ordered me, his voice as icy as the room. "It's too late for any of that to matter. Forget what you've seen tonight."

"I will not forget," I said a little wildly. "I . . ." Before I could get another word out of my mouth he had scooped me up and was striding down the halls on silent feet. I was too stunned to protest, and when I tried to speak he crushed my head against his chest, so that I nearly smothered.

He kicked open the door of my room, strode in, and tossed me down on the bed. "You will remain here, Miss MacDougall, for the rest of the night. I don't need you stirring up more trouble and sorrow than we're bound to have naturally. Whether someone opened the windows or not is purely academic—it only hastened a slow, painful, and certain death. If someone here decided to ease it for him, then I won't hold them to blame." He moved away from the bed, then came back. "And if you open your lovely mouth, Miss Mac-Dougall, you may be sure that I will shut it for you in the most effective way I can think of. And that could easily include strangling you! So you'd better think twice about bothering anyone in this family with wild tales." And he slammed out of the room.

Chapter XII

Stephen was buried that Sunday. The hastily summoned doctor did not question the cause of death. Stephen's lungs had always been weak, and the long hours out on the cold, damp ground had done the final damage. For some reason I kept quiet about the burr I had found under his horse's saddle. At first it was a reluctance to cause further pain to Lady Margaret, not unmixed with a fear of Alex's temper. And then, following my interview with Lady Margaret the night before the funeral, it seemed a waste of time.

"Well," the old lady began once we were alone in her stiflingly hot bedroom, "that's that."

"I beg your pardon?"

"It seems quite clear to me," she said irritably, annoyed with my failure to grasp the convenient simplicity of things. "Stephen must have killed Josiah, and then, driven mad by grief and guilt, deliberately rode Firefly at a breakneck speed so that he was thrown." She toyed with her black satin skirt. "He never was an adept rider."

"But . . . but . . ." I began to protest helplessly, but she overrode me with a grand gesture.

"Now, now, don't worry, Lorna. You won't lose your job, my dear," she said with condescending kindness. "I've grown quite fond of you these past weeks. You can stay on and be my secretary. There are plenty of things around here to keep a young girl like you busy."

I decided to try and make her see reason. "I don't know how to tell you this," I said slowly, "but I think there are certain things you should know. The night Stephen died I woke up and saw his windows open in the cold night air."

The old lady was daunted only for a moment. "But don't you see, my child, it's simply further proof. He opened those windows himself, to make sure he would die!" She leaned back with a macabre look of satisfaction. "Don't you see?—it all fits so well."

"Too well," I said abruptly. "Stephen was too ill to get up and open those windows. Lady Margaret, don't you care that one of your sons is a murderer?"

"Of course I care," she snapped back, real anger in her now. "But what good will it do? Stephen is dead, Josiah is dead. I can't bring them back. I have to make my peace with the living. I believe, I firmly believe now that Stephen killed Josiah and then killed himself." There was a pitiful doubt in the old woman's faded blue eyes, and I took pity on her. She wanted so much to believe the horrid nightmare was now over. Rather than have to submit her to more doubts and fears, I would accept her verdict. For the time being.

But I refused to sit complacently by while a double murderer continued his or her pleasant life. I would find out who did these terrible things, and I would find proof too. And it would make no difference to me if Lady Margaret or even I desperately wanted a different culprit.

It rained that entire weekend, that long, tear-racked hideous weekend, from the morning after Stephen's death through his funeral. He was buried in the little family graveyard at the west end of the island, and I noted with surprise the large number of off-islanders there at the gravesite. More than once I saw the distinctive Cameron features on young men and women. Mostly they resembled Charles and Stephen, but the one that caused me the most pain was a young boy, scarcely six years old, standing beside Katie. Alex was with them, talking in a low voice, and the resemblance was unmistakable. The boy must be his son.

Sickened and angry, I turned away and looked across to the sea, now an angry blue-gray in the heavy rain. I refused to think about Alex and his licentious behavior, or about Katie and her obvious infatuation. Right at hand was a better warning than I could give her, and if she refused to heed it and continued to look up into Alex's deep blue eyes with helpless adoration, then there was nothing I could do about it. Except clench my fists so that even through the black cotton gloves my nails bit into my palms.

Old John was completely heartbroken. In the early evening I found him in a corner of the kitchen, his grizzled head bent in sorrow, his eyes glazed with despair. Thora was doing her best to comfort him, and I wondered once more about their strange relationship. Most of the time they never had a good word to say to or about each other. But in times of crisis it was to each other they turned, and I wished for a moment that I had someone to turn to as well.

"I'll feed the horses tonight, John," I offered quietly, not wishing to disturb him.

"That would be good of you, miss," he answered gratefully. "It seems like the heart's just gone out of me tonight, that it has."

As I was already in my pantaloons I went straight out through the misting rain. I had spent the entire afternoon in my room, leaving the family to deal with all the callers necessary to a death in the family. I knew I would be out of place down there, and I had kept out of the way, but now I was glad of a chance to get out.

Samantha was missing when I got to the stables, and I wondered who had gone riding on such an unpleasant evening. Perhaps Charles had seen some of the visitors to the boat. Or perhaps Alex . . .

I busied myself very swiftly with the oats and hay, determined to get out of there as fast as I could. The Captain had been in a wild, angry mood all weekend, without even a kind word for the extravagantly weeping widow, and the last thing in the world I wanted was a confrontation alone in this deserted stable. I was certain he knew just who the stable boy was, and it added to my speed.

I had just finished giving the horses fresh water when he rode in, hatless, coatless, his thin white shirt soaked through. With barely a glance at me through the lamplit barn, he dismounted and unsaddled his horse. His face looked reckless and a little brutal in the flickering light, and it took all the will-power and courage I possessed to walk casually to the door.

I had almost made it when he spoke. "Come here, Horace." There was a mocking lilt to his voice that should have warned me, but fool-like I went.

His arms went around me, and before I realized what was happening he had thrown me down on the pile of hay, his hard lean body covering mine, my wrists held in an iron grip. My hat had come off and I could feel my hair loose around my shoulders as I struggled with him, wildly, silently.

"You should have listened to the warnings, my dear Horace," he said in a low mocking voice, and then his mouth found mine.

I had nearly frozen to death, one terrible winter in Vermont, and this was very similar, the terrifying seduction of the cold enticing me to give up. I kept wanting to fall under the spell of his mouth on mine, to sink into the sweet and terrible lassitude his hands were causing me, yet I knew if I did so I would be lost. For a moment I answered his mouth, and I could feel his strong body pressing mine into the sweet-smelling timothy, could feel him relax just enough for me to take him by surprise. With a strength I didn't know I had I rolled over and jumped from his arms. Barely hesitating, I kicked him in the shin as hard as I could with my sturdy boots and ran from the stables as if the hounds of hell were after me.

If Thora or John noticed my agitation, they were kind enough not to comment on it. I ran straight to my room, slammed the door shut behind me with a resounding crash, and not only locked it, but shoved the heavy dresser against it. Then I threw myself down on my bed, gasping for breath with long shuddering sobs, trying to shut out the memory of his mouth, his hands, and cold mockery in his dark blue eyes.

Determined to avoid Alex at all costs, I waited until it was well past eleven the next morning to come downstairs. I felt completely unable to cope with the look I knew I would see on his face, and it was only when the hunger pangs became too much for me that I crept down the back stairs to the kitchen to find information and sustenance.

"Well, it's about time you were up!" Thora greeted me with a small return of her old spirits. "The whole family's left already, and you not there to say good-by."

I couldn't hide my sigh of relief. "Is there some breakfast left over?"

"Breakfast, is it? It's almost time for lunch!" she snorted. "And who was it you were trying to avoid?"

"Avoid? Me?" I laughed merrily. "Why, no one at all."

"Must be the Captain," John offered from his corner by the fire, nursing a cup of coffee in his gnarled hands. "He limped in here last night after you ran through, looking mad as a hornet. That must have been some argument you two had." He cackled with the first sign of life I'd seen in him since Stephen's death.

"It was," I answered calmly, serene in the knowledge that I wouldn't have to face Alexander Cameron for quite a while. And by then, if I worked very hard at it, I would have my treacherous temper and emotions firmly in hand.

The next weeks were long, cold and blustery, unenlivened by either sunshine or the presence of the Widow Cameron and her brothers-in-law. The weather was not unexpected—I recalled that June in Vermont had often been no more than a gusty, muddy extension of winter. If it was rather harder on us all after the halcyon days preceding Stephen's death we did not complain. The weather seemed a fitting complement for our mourning.

"Lorna, my dear," announced Lady Margaret one drizzling day. "I am heartily sick of all this everlasting gloom—if it goes on much longer I'll go mad. I've decided to have a party!"

"A party?" I echoed faintly, dropping my mending in my lap. "With Stephen so recently dead?"

"Come now, I wouldn't have thought a bright young girl like you would set much store by the usual conventions." There was a feverish glitter in her milky blue eyes, a glitter I had learned to watch for and beware of. If Lady Margaret became overexcited she had to rest in bed for days, which always necessitated my reading more Charles Dickens aloud than even his most devoted followers could stand. I did my best to calm her.

"Well, I don't," I replied in a soothing tone of voice. "But there are such things as . . . as good taste."

"Stuff and nonsense!" she replied roundly. "We'll start on a guest list this afternoon. I think a small party—perhaps only seventy-five or a hundred guests. Charles can engage an orchestra for us, and Allison will help—she needs something to occupy her time."

"Won't people be shocked?"

"Of course they will!" Lady Margaret twisted her heavy ruby ring around her arthritic finger. "But Camerons are above the rules that govern ordinary people—they'll be horrified but they'll all flock to attend." She leaned back and sighed. "I am so tired of this endless stream of mourning. I would like to have a trace of gaiety before I die."

In another moment crocodile tears of self-pity would roll down her furrowed cheeks, and I hastened to forestall them. "I suppose it would be fun," I said doubtfully, waiting for her to convince me.

She perked up. "Of course it will!" she declared. "And who knows, there might be some nice young man who'll take a shine to you. Perhaps some lawyer's clerk, or a young minister."

I made a face at the thought—all the young ministers I had met so far had been terribly bony and sincere. I was both annoyed and amused at Lady Margaret's opinion of the class I should marry into. Although I often told myself and her that I had no interest whatsoever in her remaining sons, she still had a gnawing anxiety that I would draw one of them into a mésalliance. Nothing could be further from my mind, I told myself virtuously.

The party plans went forward at an alarming rate—we soon found ourselves faced with a massive dinner and ball scarcely three weeks away. All who had been invited had accepted, just as Lady Margaret had foretold, and, despite the outraged letters from conventional Charles, Lady Margaret continued to arrange things in an overwhelmingly grandiose manner while I tried to shake off a premonition of total disaster.

"Well, Lorna," Lady Margaret announced to me at lunch one day, "here's a letter from Charles."

I was working my way daintily through my third helping of creamed chicken in delicate pastry shells, so I merely nodded encouragingly.

"He asks how I am, of course. The dear boy has always been so thoughtful, unlike his younger brother. He asks after you too." Here Lady Margaret peered at me over her reading glasses with an accusing stare. "You will be pleased to hear that the entire family is coming for the week before the ball. I will need help, and Charles has promised to come and take care of the last-minute details." She sighed and took a bite of her tiny portion of chicken. I wondered briefly how she could subsist on so little, and helped myself to another roll.

She continued to read. "He says Alexander has shown new interest in his boat! And it's about time, that's all I can say. It's been in the works for almost a year now. Time enough for it to be finished and launched. Alex had best get to work on the figurehead if it's to be ready in time." She smiled graciously. "The Camerons build very fine ships, you know. You must ask Charles to show you some of the portraits of the Cameron Line when he comes to visit. He has a portfolio of water-colors that were commissioned a few years ago. I'm sure you'll find them fascinating." She smiled to herself. "You see how much I trust you, my girl. It's not many totally ineligible young ladies I'd let spend time with my son."

"Thank you, ma'am," I murmured tonelessly. I'm afraid the thought of a tête-à-tête with Charles filled me with no excitement. Had it been the Captain I don't know how I would have responded. I couldn't wipe the memory of that night in the barn from my mind, anymore than I could scrub away the feel of his kiss from my mouth.

"Charles says that Alex might move back into the big house," the old lady continued, stealing a sly glance at me every now and then. "I must say I'm pleased at the thought—a match between him and Allison might be just the thing to settle him down. And Lord knows it should keep her satisfied, at least for a while. I hadn't wanted to notice before poor Stephen died, but she's been mooning over him for the past two years and more. He must have been foolish enough to encourage her at one time."

"Oh, surely not!" I protested thoughtlessly. "Not his own brother's wife?"

"I wouldn't credit my son Alex with too many scruples if I were you," she said crisply. "I've warned you before, my girl!" She sipped delicately at the translucent, lukewarm brew Thora called tea. "After lunch, Lorna, I want to go up in the attic and search for some old vases I have stored there. They would be just the thing for the color scheme I have in mind for the party. They're pink and gilt—terribly old-fashioned, of course, but I want the ballroom turned into a . . . a fairyland. I think there's too little fantasy nowadays. Life is far too serious. I won't have many frivolous occasions left to me and I intend to enjoy this one to the fullest."

Later, as we climbed up the twisting stairway into the musty old attic, I had no presentiment of danger, no hint that this place would come to mean something crucial in the tangled web of the Cameron family. I stood on the top step, staring around at the musty place.

"Open a window," Lady Margaret ordered peremptorily, choking slightly, and I rushed to do her bidding, grateful that her normal love of stuffy rooms had some limit. The hinge on the window was rusty, as most things are when they are left neglected in the salt air, and it was a few moments before I could open the stubborn latch. The sea breeze wafted into the room, and I sucked it into my lungs deeply, reveling as I always did in the unexpected freshness of it. I turned and saw Lady Margaret wandering among the boxes and trunks and discarded furniture, and I joined her. She pointed to a dusty trunk.

"I think they might be in there." She dusted off an old chair with her lace handkerchief and seated herself daintily. "If you would be so good as to open it for my inspection."

"Certainly." I dropped cross-legged on the dusty floor and began fussing with the fastenings. They gave with little effort and I opened the trunk. Lady Margaret's frequently uncertain memory had not played her false this time, for beneath several faded damask table-cloths were three excessively ornate, cupid-laden pink vases.

"Splendid!" Lady Margaret exclaimed. "You may close the trunk now, my dear. We don't want mice to get in."

I did as she ordered and rose, brushing the dust from my skirt. "Why don't you have Thora and the girls clean up here?" I suggested, perhaps tactlessly. "I'd be glad to help them." The old lady was preparing to depart and I hadn't had time to look around properly. I was intensely curious about this locked place.

"No!" she snapped. Then in a calmer voice she continued, "There are a great many private things up here. Things not meant for Thora's prying eyes." She turned and walked slowly, wearily toward the stairs, leaning heavily on her ebony cane, when my attention was caught by a small object in the corner. I must have uttered some cry, for she turned back sharply.

"What's this?" I asked, pointing to a small wooden crib piled in the corner with a lot of disused furniture.

"Obviously, my child, it is a crib," she answered tartly. She moved over to it and prodded it with her cane. "Both my sons used it."

"Alex did?" I found myself asking, finding it impossible and yet curiously endearing to think of her cynical son as a helpless baby.

"Certainly," she said sharply. "He wasn't always the giant he is now. I want to leave here, Lorna."

"But . . . what's that?" I had noticed something even more startling. An immense cradle lay in the corner under one of the dusty windows, a cradle surely large enough for a full-grown adult. I turned to her questioningly and she sighed.

"What does it look like?"

"It . . . it looks like a cradle for a giant," I answered. "Or an adult. But what sort of adult would need a cradle?"

The old lady nodded. "Exactly, my dear. You think about it. This cradle was used by a member of our family—one we don't talk about who is now mercifully dead. I'm sure you'll have the goodness not to mention it again."

"But . . ." I floundered helplessly, as she made her stately way across the room, her long skirts trailing in the dust. Something clicked in my mind, like a piece of a puzzle falling into place, and yet, I couldn't quite grasp it.

"I would like some assistance, Lorna," the old woman's autocratic voice came from across the room. "Bring the vases and come immediately."

"Yes, my lady," I murmured, still loitering.

"Lorna, we will leave this place at once!" Her voice rose to a shriek, and I hastened after her with only a backward glance at the tantalizing trunks and boxes and the eerie cradle.

I had quite a bit to think about in the following days. What secrets did those trunks and boxes hold? And what member of the family could have required a bed like that? A cripple, perhaps? Or someone with the body of an adult and the mind and reflexes of a child? That was the more frightening, somehow, and yet it could hardly have been the poor victim's fault. It seemed to me that in some way the answer to the murders that had plagued this island lay in that attic, and yet, try as I might to concentrate on it and let my mind relax, no illuminating vision came to me. The past seemed dull and lifeless, and when I tried to force it into my mind, the face of Alexander Cameron as he leaned over me in the stable came instead to disturb me.

Chapter XIII

The sun was shining brightly once again, after what had seemed like a year of cold, gray days. I sat on the plush train seat in my fancy green traveling costume, clutching Lady Margaret's precious parcel in my kid-gloved hands, and lazily contemplated running off with its contents to Boston or New York or even California, eventually dismissing the idea as impractical, not to mention immoral. In the small, innocuous-looking cloth bag I had carefully secured inside my reticule was a fortune in jewels. The famous Cameron emeralds, which I had coveted the moment I laid eyes on them, the fabulous rubies that had been passed down for generations in Lady Margaret's own family, and a large and very beautiful assortment of diamonds far superior in quality to the flashy things Allison sported. I was taking the jewels to be cleaned at Lady Margaret's personal jeweler on the mainland. I would drop them off this afternoon when I arrived, spend a few hours shopping for myself, and then find my way to the Cameron town house. The jewels would be ready first thing in the morning, and I could catch the first return train back.

I viewed the prospect of my little adventure with mixed emotions. I was very curious to view the Cameron town house, and to see how Lady Margaret's remaining offspring were surviving the murder of Stephen. Or the accidental death, as they preferred to view it. But I was more than a little wary of meeting Captain Alexander Cameron again, especially after that stunning kick I had landed on his shin. But as far as I knew he had yet to move back into the bosom of his family, and I could merely hope that I would be able to avoid him for the short time I would have to spend on the mainland.

In anticipation of my brief freedom I had a tentative plan in mind. The great Italian soprano Festa La Gurci was scheduled to sing the part of Violetta in *La Traviata* at the Civic Opera House that night, and I was determined to hear her. I had always had a weakness for Verdi, and for La Gurci as well. One of the loveliest moments of my life had come when she appeared in Montpelier one summer. No doubt the tickets would be sold out well in advance, but I could still hope there might be one lone seat somewhere in the large auditorium. I most particularly wanted to hear *La Traviata*—I had wept buckets over *La Dame aux camélias* when my mother judged me sufficiently mature to read it. For some obscure reason I was in need of a good, refreshing cry about something that didn't touch me personally, and I longed for the purgative effect of a good, heart-rending opera, especially with La Gurci's lovely voice soaring around me.

Needless to say, I was out of luck. I delivered the jewels with a sigh of relief to the wizened old jeweler, made my way as quickly as I could to the opera house, and discovered that tickets had been gone for three weeks. Concealing my disappointment, I smiled at the supercilious ticket seller and gave him my name and direction should anyone happen to turn in an unwanted seat for that evening.

The town was large compared to most I had seen, and I spent as long as I could wandering through the shops, stopping to have a late lunch and then an early tea at one of the charming teashops, matching ribbons for my ball gown, and searching for some inexpensive piece of jewelry to set off the sea-green shade of my dress. I'm afraid I was scarcely satisfied after handling Lady Margaret's beautiful gems, but I picked a thin silver necklace at last that I decided would simply have to do. When I could put it off no longer I hailed a hansom cab and gave him the Camerons' address.

It was a beautiful house in the midsummer twilight, and quite different from what I had expected. I had thought it would be a massive pile of New England granite, towering and forbidding, as close to the island mansion as it could be. Instead I faced a neat and tidy white clapboard of noble proportions, its large size welcoming rather than daunting. I took heart and climbed the winding wooden steps with more enthusiasm.

A maid answered the door and surveyed me with an expression bordering, just bordering, on insolence. She looked enough like her half sister Nancy so that her parentage was obvious, and I wondered if Josiah had fathered most of the servant classes around here. Before I had a chance to announce myself, Allison Cameron floated into my vision from the darkened hallway, dressed extravagantly in one of the most elegant creations I had ever seen. It was a deep black, as befitted her state of mourning, and clung to her shoulders by the will of God and her undeniably magnificent breasts. Diamonds sparkled at her neck and throat, and in her tiny ears were the diamond earrings I had found on the beach.

She stared at me blankly. "Well," she said after a moment. "Let her in, Grace." Grace did so, and I found myself standing in the gloomy hallway more in keeping with the usual Cameron style of décor.

"We were expecting you earlier, Lorna," she said in her light, charming, condescending voice. "The children are already asleep, and I'm about to go out. The opera, you know."

Bravely, I controlled a spasm of envy. "I'm sorry, I didn't realize I was expected at any particular time."

She waved one slim white hand negligently. I could see widowhood agreed with her. "I had thought you might help Cook with some small chores while you were here. However, I'm sure we can over-look it this time." There was a slightly ominous chill to her child-like voice. "You can put her in the small room behind the kitchen, Grace. I'm sure that will suit Lorna very well." The malice glittered in her brown eyes.

There was nothing I could do but turn to follow the sullen maid. Before I reached the door at the end of the hallway Allison's light voice floated after me.

"Oh, and Lorna."

"Yes, Mrs. Cameron?" I hated myself for saying it but I could see no alternative.

"I know you meant no harm, my dear, but next time do you think you could use the back door? We like to keep the front door for guests, you understand."

I am undoubtedly a saint, an absolute saint. Without hesitation I smiled back brightly with a sweetness to match her own. "Of course, Mrs. Cameron. I understand you only too well." And I swept from the hall with swift dignity, leaving her openmouthed and frustrated in her effort to humiliate me further.

The room they put me in was little more than a hole. The olive green walls were cracked and peeling, the cot had a thin cotton blan-ket and darned sheets, the mirror over the broken dresser needed resilvering, and dust lay in every corner. I did not think much of Allison's lack of supervision in the house cleaning. I reflected that when my mother could afford servants the smallest section of their quarters had been as spotless as the family's part of the house. Or perhaps they had been keeping this room as squalid as possible as a suitable welcome for me. If so I had never fully realized the extent of Allison's dislike for me.

"Everyone's already eaten," Grace informed me coldly, her black eyes surveying me with impersonal disdain. "As soon as you're ready Cook will find something for your supper."

"What time is it?" I asked faintly.

"Half-past seven. All the best families eat their supper no later than six-thirty in the summer. Don't you know anything?"

"I suppose not."

My voice must have sounded suitably humble, for Grace unbent slightly. "Well, then, I imagine you're new in service. It takes a while to get the hang of it. Though you won't go far if you continue to get on the bad side of people like Mrs. Cameron."

"Do you have any idea how I angered her?" I asked softly.

"No, nor do I care to find out." She leaned against the shabby dresser and sighed, losing some of her first-housemaid dignity. "I must say, I don't like it here half as much as I used to, when old Mr. Cameron and Mr. Stephen were alive. It's too gloomy by half!"

"Then why don't you go somewhere else?" I asked curiously.

"I have as much right to be here as anyone," she snapped, flashing me a sly glance. "They're not going to get rid of me so easy." She stood up, obviously having lost interest in me as a confidante. "See that you're ready soon. Cook has a terrible temper, and she don't like having to prepare two meals."

Cook *was* in a terrible temper, I thought morosely, moving the cold and soggy beans around on my plate. The kitchen, though a trifle cleaner than the room allotted to me, was redolent of cooked cabbage and grease, and my appetite had successfully vanished. I watched Cook's disapproving bulk move around the kitchen with deliberation, every motion expressing her resentment of the affront that she should have to wait for another servant before she could clean up and retire to her room. I took a leisurely mouthful of cold boiled beef and smiled at her sweetly from my seat in the corner. It was a little past eight, and I knew that in about twenty minutes' time the curtain would go up on *La Traviata,* with tin-eared (I was certain) Allison in rapt attendance. I could have spit with anger and frustration.

From a distance I could hear the front door open and close, could hear steady footsteps down the long hall to the kitchen door. Instinctively I shrank farther back into my corner seat.

"Hello, Florence," Alexander greeted Cook with a degree of fondness. She bloomed before my eyes, and I wondered if he had the same effect on all women. "Have Charles and Allison left already? I was held up at the yard."

He was very handsome tonight, I told myself dispassionately. His formal clothes were beautifully cut, fitting his long, lean body to perfection. He'd had his hair cut slightly, but the black curls were still beyond his collar, and the tan hadn't faded from his face. He seemed more at ease than I had ever seen him. And then I remembered our last meeting and shrank back even farther into the corner.

I should never have stirred. The movement caught the corner of his eye and he whirled around. We stared at each other in silence for a moment, I with a look of defiance, he with an expression of amazed . . . it almost seemed like delight.

"What the devil are you doing here?" he inquired mildly enough, moving toward me. "There's nothing wrong with my mother, is there?"

The idea didn't seem to distress him overmuch. "No, she's fine." I pushed the tasteless meal away from me. "I came here on an errand for her."

"An errand?"

"To have her jewelry cleaned," I answered briefly, wondering why I felt hesitant about disclosing my mission.

"I see." He pulled out the chair opposite me and sat down in it, much to the horrified fascination of Cook and Grace. "And what are you doing eating here in the kitchen like an orphaned waif? Why didn't you leave with Allison for the opera?"

I bit my lip. "I wasn't invited."

"Don't you care for opera?" he questioned abruptly.

"I love it," I answered simply.

He surveyed me out of those dark blue eyes, an unreadable expression on his face. "Well, then, what are you waiting for? The curtain goes up in fifteen minutes. Go and change."

A small thrill of excitement swept through me, one that I knew wasn't occasioned by the thought of the opera alone. "I haven't anything to change into," I objected.

"Borrow something of Allison's."

I let out a little gurgle of laughter. "We're hardly the same size or shape, Captain."

His eyes moved over my body in a manner I found subtly daring. "True," he said after a moment. "Well, then, you'll have to come as you are."

"But I can't!" I objected. "What would people think?"

"Come now, Miss MacDougall, you never struck me as someone who would care overmuch for people's opinions. If you like we'll sit in the orchestra instead of the family's box." He stood up and swept the dishes off the table in front of me. "And afterwards I'll take you to the finest restaurant in all of Maine. Now how could you resist that?" His smile had all the charm I knew he was capable of, and it made me even more nervous. I couldn't keep from remembering the last time I had seen that mouth, and the response it had elicited from me. "Come now, Miss MacDougall, don't you trust me?"

It was a challenge, one that I couldn't ignore. "I doubt if you're capable of behaving like a gentleman," I said coldly, and heard Grace give a delighted little gasp.

He laughed, and I found the sound strangely exciting. "I swear to you, my dear Miss MacDougall, I will behave toward you as if I were my brother Charles. Not one indecent suggestion shall cross my lips, not one improper advance to you will I make. And I swear it before Grace and Cook as my witnesses. Does that satisfy you?"

I hesitated no longer. I knew full well it was playing with fire, but it had a fascination I couldn't resist. I could suitably protect myself by keeping a strict formality between us. And I did so want to see the opera. "All right." I rose. "If you don't think there'll be trouble obtaining seats."

"My dear, my very dear Miss MacDougall." He raised one eyebrow mockingly. "I am a Cameron. In this town that is only a little short of royalty. Any seat in the house will be ours."

I made a fool of myself that night, I suppose, as I have many other nights. We drove to the theater in record time, our cabdriver nearly knocking over two passers-by on his way to earn the undoubtedly large bill Alex had flashed under his nose. The same man who had so smugly informed me that tickets were unavailable nearly prostrated himself on the red plush carpet of the opera house in his haste to provide the illustrious Captain Cameron and his companion whatever seats they desired. Alex flashed me a brief look as if to say, "I told you so," before we hurried down the aisle in the darkened theater.

I wept all the way through it. It started with a mild tear or two when Alfredo was forced to leave Violetta, and by the time she died in his arms I was sniffling in earnest. I sat there in joyful misery, trying to control my tears, when a bronzed hand reached out with a fine linen handkerchief. Gratefully I accepted it and proceeded to stuff it in my mouth to stop the sobs that threatened to overwhelm me.

Fortunately, the rest of the audience was as enamored of La Gurci as I had been, and after a series of seventeen curtain calls I was once more calm. The house lights came up, and Alex stared down at me with gentle surprise.

"Have you recovered?" he questioned wryly.

"Of course." My tear-filled eyes met his, then looked away hastily. Straight into the outraged expression on Allison Cameron's face as she leaned over her box.

"You're in for it now," Alex murmured. "We had better beat a hasty retreat."

For a moment I didn't move, my eyes glued to Allison's in fascinated horror. Never had I seen a look of such pure, unadulterated hatred. It made me physically sick.

Alex took me by the arm and hurried me out of the theater, an unreadable expression on his face. "That was unfortunate."

"Why?"

He stopped for a moment on the crowded sidewalk, looking down at me with grim amusement. "If you don't know, Miss MacDougall, far be it from me to enlighten you. You're safer in your ignorance."

I didn't like the sound of that word, safer. But I knew better than to press the matter. Reluctantly I took the arm he offered and continued down the street.

The restaurant was every bit as good as he had said, and I stuffed myself on everything from lobster Newburg to incredibly delicate French pastries. I let the Captain order for us, and it was not without suspicion that I observed the satisfying (if gluttonous) amounts of delicious food delivered to our table. Alexander smiled blandly at me over the candlelit feast, exerting every ounce of charm he possessed to lessen my coolly polite suspicion. Truth to tell, I was still both horribly embarrassed by my unrestrained tears at the opera and chilled to the bone by the hatred on Allison's pretty little face. The sooner I got back to the safety of the island, the better.

I wish I could say I was immune to the Captain's charm, but I wasn't. Our brief struggle in the stables must have affected me even more profoundly than I had thought. For a first kiss it had been shattering, to say the least, and I could only try to shut it out of my mind. I gazed back at the fascinating Captain with a seemingly impersonal interest as he told me enticing tales of his travels through the West Indies.

"I suppose we'd better start back to the house," he said eventually, lighting a cigar with a practiced air. I looked around me with a start, and noticed we were alone in the restaurant.

"How late is it?"

"After three," he said, grinning, and I jumped up in horror, spilling the last bit of coffee.

"It can't be!"

"It is. I'm afraid I should have paid more attention to the time— you were doomed to have enough trouble with Allison anyway. If she realizes, as she's bound to, what time I brought you home . . ." He let the sentence trail, and I felt a small shiver of apprehension.

"But why should she mind?" I questioned foolishly, imagining perfectly well the mad jealousy that could take control of that seemingly simple-minded lady and turn her into a raging virago.

"I couldn't say." Alex shrugged his shoulders. "Allison is prone to rather sick fantasies, I'm afraid. You're not planning to stay on the mainland long, are you?"

"I'm going back tomorrow."

"Good." The easy, enchanting mood that had so beguiled me had vanished, leaving me with the cold-tempered Captain Alexander Cameron I remembered only too well. But with a ten-minute ride in an unchaperoned, closed carriage still ahead of me, I could only be glad his affability had gone. Because some foolish, vulnerable part of me wanted him to try once more what he had tried in the stables, and this time I wouldn't have kicked him. It was far better not to have to worry about such things, I assured myself forlornly.

The ride back to the Camerons' white-painted house was accomplished in dead silence. I sat beside the Captain's still figure, trying hard not to even breathe, while he stared ahead, puffing on his cigar, and I couldn't stop myself from wondering miserably if it was guilt that was haunting him so.

When we finally arrived at the house, Alex got out with me and sent the hansom on its way. "I'll walk home," he said abruptly, starting up the steps to the front door.

With a sinking heart I saw the lights burning brightly in one of the front rooms, and knew that someone was waiting up for me. I couldn't shake the awful vision of Allison, her fair hair streaming down her back like a mad Ophelia, a knife in one slim hand, greeting me at the door.

"I . . . I was told to use the back door," I said hesitantly when Alex threw me a coolly questioning look.

"Don't be absurd," he said sharply, taking my limp arm in his rough grip and half pulling me up the wooden steps to the house.

It was with profound thankfulness that I saw Charles open the front door to us. I had allowed Alex's mood of apprehension to influence me too strongly, so that even the look of disapproval on Charles's face failed to abate my feelings of relief.

"Isn't this a little late for Miss MacDougall to be out?" Charles taxed Alex as if he were an erring schoolboy. I flinched, waiting for Alex to lash back at him with that cold cruel temper I had caught glimpses of.

Apparently I was no longer of any concern to him. "You're right, of course. You always are, aren't you, Charles?" With a mocking salute he was gone, out into the warm summer night without a backward glance at me.

We stood in the hall for a moment, Charles and I, and the uncomfortable silence grew. After a moment he spoke. "I'll have to apologize for my young brother's manners, Lorna. Though I believe I did warn you about him."

"So you did." My voice was unenthusiastic. "Good night, Mr. Cameron."

"Lorna . . . er, Miss MacDougall, could I speak with you?" His voice was scrupulously polite. "In the study?"

"Now?" This was not terribly courteous of me, but I believed I knew what he was about to say, and I wasn't in the mood to be reprimanded for ideas above my station right then.

"If it's not too much trouble. You're leaving tomorrow and I don't know when we'll get a chance to talk undisturbed again."

"Very well." I followed his sturdy, broad-shouldered form into the well-lit room and stood defiantly by the window.

"Please sit down, Miss MacDougall," Charles said smoothly, with the same false charm Alex had employed earlier, I noted bitterly.

"I prefer to stand," I said stiffly. "Perhaps I should save you some trouble, Mr. Cameron. You are about to say that you don't consider it proper for your brother to be seen at a social gathering with a . . . with a servant. I didn't want to go with him . . ." My voice was getting a little wild. "I tried to tell him it wasn't a wise idea . . ."

"But my brother can be very persuasive when he wants to be," Charles said soothingly, coming over to me and placing his hands on my shoulders. "Please, Miss MacDougall . . . Lorna! You're misunderstanding me. Sit down."

Miserably, I sat.

"Lorna, there's nothing whatsoever wrong with your going to the opera with my brother—if it weren't for my brother. As a matter of fact, when I heard Allison had left you behind I was about to come back and fetch you myself when I saw you sitting there with Alex." He cleared his throat. "This is difficult to say, Lorna. I thought I'd made it clear enough before, but I had forgotten my brother's charm. He's not for you, Lorna. He's had at least three women in keeping in the last few years, and all of them no better than they should be. There was a widow in Boston, an actress from New York, and a divorced woman right here in town. Up to now he's stayed clear of innocents like yourself, but I'm afraid your charming high spirits have overcome his small sense of decency. He's becoming more and more like our father." Again there was that bitterness in his voice, and

I abandoned my rather sulky mood and stared up at him with considerable interest.

"But what about that boy at Stephen's funeral? He surely must have been a product of some wild oats?" I questioned.

Charles's brow furrowed in thought for a moment, then cleared. "Oh, you mean Robbie. Looks just like Alex, doesn't he? No, I'm afraid it's our late father who was responsible for that. I think, I hope to God, that Robbie's the last one of a long line. You can't imagine how distressing it is to find brothers and sisters wherever you turn."

"Perhaps that's why Alex tends to keep away from the village maidens," I suggested somewhat lightheartedly, and immediately retreated at the sight of Charles's shock over my bit of levity.

"This is hardly a humorous situation, Lorna. I'm afraid there can be no doubt that Alex has dishonorable intentions toward you, and I . . . I'd take a horsewhip to him if he ever brought you pain."

I looked at his intense, handsome face in mild surprise. This was a new start, and entirely unexpected. Before I had a chance to respond he rushed on, flushing slightly, as if he'd said more than he was planning to.

"Forgive me, Lorna, I wasn't meaning to trouble you with anything new tonight. Please, consider what I've said, and you'll realize that whatever your attraction is to Alex, it's something best forgotten. He's . . . he's evil, Lorna. And I couldn't bear it if you were hurt."

I stared at him blankly. There was evil on the island—I'd felt its presence more than once, but never had I felt it emanating directly from Alex. Could my ridiculous infatuation have blinded me, who was usually so astute in these matters? I hated to think it, but I knew I had to consider it a possibility. I rose, calm once more.

"I thank you for your advice and concern," I said softly. "I'm very grateful, but really, there's nothing to worry about. The Captain and I had a very pleasant time tonight, but that's as far as it went. I'm in no danger of losing my heart to him."

Charles grasped my hand in his warm, soft one. "Can I believe that?"

"Certainly, since I tell you so. Good night, Charles."

He hesitated, almost as if he wanted to say something more. But the moment passed. "Good night, Lorna. Pleasant dreams. And don't let my mother work you too hard. She can be a tyrant." He laughed ruefully.

But she's not your mother, I thought silently, puzzled. I smiled. "I won't. Can we expect you out there soon?"

"Soon," he promised. "Soon."

Chapter XIV

The trip back to Cameron's Landing the next day was uneventful. I had barely slept at all when I left Charles—the combination of the lumpy mattress and my disturbed thoughts kept me tossing and turning till the first rays of dawn crept sullenly through the grime-speckled window in my cubbyhole. I dressed silently, sneaked out to the kitchen, and raided Cook's surprisingly munificent store of bread and cheese and dried fruits, and crept out the door before the lady of the house had a chance to rise from her scented sheets and tax me with last night. Though I shouldn't have worried; as evinced on the island, Allison could scarcely drag herself out of bed before eleven.

Lady Margaret seemed pleased with the results of my errands on the mainland. She paraded about in her jewels, filled me in on the latest acceptances to her ridiculous party, and was in a better mood than I'd ever seen her in. The island seemed to have survived my absence for a day and a half with little change, or so I thought until I went into Stephen's room that afternoon while Lady Margaret took her prescribed nap. The place had been stripped.

"She ordered it done while you were gone," Nancy said from behind me, scaring me out of a year's growth. A year's growth I could have done without nicely. "All his clothes, all his papers, everything was burned." A spasm of unhappiness crossed her round little face and I remembered belatedly that he had been her brother too. I wondered if Stephen had ever been kind to his little bastard half sister, who earned her keep waiting on her more fortunate kinfolk. And I wondered if those sweet mild eyes often held the look of half sorrow/half rage that they held now. A frightening amount of grievance could be built up by someone in her situation. I, for one, would have found it intolerable. And there were many of them in that selfsame situation, thanks to Josiah Cameron's alley-cat tendencies. The very thought of the randy old man filled me with distaste.

"Why did she do that?" I questioned mildly.

"Who knows why she does anything?" Nancy asked bitterly.

"She's wiped him out of her life as she does with anything she don't like." She turned and left me abruptly.

Jenny and Stephen were coming that weekend. I had only been able to snatch a few minutes with them while I was on the mainland, and they had seemed well enough, if rather subdued. They'd be much better off roaming around the island in the once more pleasant weather than shut away in that stuffy house while their mother chased after Alex. Though when I remembered that icy look of hatred she had cast me, I wished it were a bit longer before I had to face her. I felt she needed more than a few days for her anger to cool.

"Here they are, Mama Cameron." She arrived Friday morning with the children in tow. "It's so good of you to take them while I visit a few friends. This sea air is so good for them." Her shallow brown eyes moved to me and she simpered becomingly, the dislike obvious in her expression. "I swear, Lorna, I don't know what magic you used on my children, but they talk of nothing and no one else but you the whole time they're with me. It was so nice of you to find the time to snatch a few minutes with them before you crept out. I would have thought you would have taken advantage of your visit to catch up on some sleep, especially after such a late night, but no, you were up and out like a thief in the night before I could even ask you how you enjoyed your evening." She laughed lightly, and I wanted to slap her.

"What's all this?" Lady Margaret demanded. "You didn't mention anything about an evening out, Lorna. You know I can't abide secretiveness! Tell me about this, Allison, since my companion doesn't seem to think it's any of my business."

Allison smirked, well pleased with herself. "I don't know that it is any of our business, Mama Cameron. After all, what goes on between her and Alexander should be their own private affair."

She was making it worse, of course. "What?" shrieked the old lady. "Tell me at once, you sneaking little wretch."

It was too much to hope she was addressing Allison. I stood there, pale and calm and absolutely furious. "I'm sure your daughter-in-law would gain so much pleasure telling you that she should be the one."

Lady Margaret looked from the smug pretty face to my furious one, and chuckled suddenly. "Very well, Allison. Tell me."

"It's nothing, Mama Cameron. Alex merely took her to the opera the night she spent in town, then somewhere else—I can only guess where—till three o'clock in the morning. One must assume she's found an easier way of earning her living," she said spitefully. "And you know Alex, he's so susceptible to any halfway attractive woman. She obviously played upon his sympathy in getting him to take her to the opera, which of course would be quite above her touch normally, and then worked her wiles on him from there on."

Allison stopped abruptly, as Lady Margaret's howls of laughter were drowning out her vicious remarks. "Hogwash!" Lady Margaret said finally, mopping her streaming eyes. "But I do thank you, Allison. That's the first good laugh I've had since your husband died." She chuckled again, then started coughing and hacking into her black-edged handkerchief (she was assiduous in small funereal conventions if not in the major ones). "I suppose, Lorna, that Alex found you in whatever garret Allison put you and out of sheer boredom took you to the opera and out to dinner afterwards? Is that right?"

Gratefully, I nodded.

"I find it inexcusable that you did not tell me, but there's no harm done. As for you, Allison Byrd Cameron, with your absurd accusations, calling my son susceptible to any half-attractive woman is amusing. All his women have been first-rate beauties. He wouldn't look twice at you, my dear, and he certainly wouldn't waste his time with Lorna. You make her sound like some wicked scarlet woman instead of the awkward virgin that she is. He took her out to spite you, Allison, and out of sheer boredom." The old lady waved me away, not even noticing the expression on my face at being referred to as an "awkward virgin." "You may leave, Lorna. We'll have words about this later, I assure you."

Allison smiled sweetly at me, in no way despondent that her mischief-making had failed. "I hope that you don't mind taking care of the children, Lorna. That *is* what you're hired to do, isn't it?"

"Well, what do you think about this, Lorna?" Lady Margaret snapped at me, clearly not in the best of humor. "I want you to have plenty of time for your regular duties. We have a lot to accomplish before the ball and my dear family doesn't seem disposed to do more than enjoy the fruits of my labors. Perhaps I shall call the entire thing off." Her withered, lined face took on a petulant droop.

"If you wish, ma'am," I answered calmly enough, though still seething inwardly. "Shall I write to Senator Goodridge for you?"

"Never you mind," she said shrilly. "I'll take care of that if and when I find it necessary to do so. In the meantime you may take these children out to visit Thora while their mother and I have a little talk about filial devotion and troublemaking." She eyed the now quaking Allison with a stern eye, and I could almost find it in my heart to be sorry for the creature. Almost.

Surprisingly enough, the next week passed very happily indeed. Lady Margaret was disposed to be exceedingly pleasant, and the children behaved like minor devils, which pleased me. Their pained politeness when they had first come to me disturbed me no end, and I was happy to see them act more and more like normal, mischievous children.

One week before the ball Lady Margaret's wayward children returned. Allison came first early Friday morning, with a pile of luggage more suited to a European grand tour than a couple of weeks by the sea. She embraced her children with just the right amount of motherly devotion.

"My darlings! How I missed you!" she cried glibly, her delicate, expensive hat with its real ostrich feathers dyed black trembling with emotion. Her children suffered her embrace grimly, jumping away the moment they were released from her perfumed arms. They moved back to my side, eying their mother with the patent distrust only seen in the eyes of children who have been betrayed.

Allison's raptures were checked for a moment. Then she turned to me, the brown eyes in the enchanting little face frankly confiding, rather like a frog eying a nice fat mosquito, I thought. "I do hope they haven't been giving you too much trouble, Lorna. I feel terrible about leaving you with my little angels *and* Mama Cameron. You're so practical, though, I'm sure you had no trouble coping. While poor little me, I'm so high-strung, you know." She shook her blond curls and sighed, and I experienced a moment of wishing she were high-strung, preferably from a nice high rafter. The smugness of her vapid little face made it apparent that she had had some degree of success with Alex. Well, I wished her joy of him.

"I had no trouble, thank you, Mrs. Cameron." I kept my annoyance in check and my voice level, signaling to the children that they could leave. They did so immediately, their devoted mother taking no notice.

"You must call me Allison," she said engagingly, slipping one of her black silk arms through mine and leading me through the hall. "I'm sorry we had that little misunderstanding last week. Alex has assured me there was nothing to it, which of course I should have known right away." She smiled at me with only a trace of malice. "I want us to be great friends. After all, we're of an age, you and I," she said, loftily dismissing the ten years' seniority that showed nowhere but under her delicate, willful little chin and in the hardness of her brown eyes. "Tell me, Lorna, how is Mama Cameron? Has she been well lately? I thought, well . . . I thought I might have detected signs of growing . . . forgetfulness on her part last time I was here. As if she weren't all there in her mind any longer. You've been closer to her, surely you've noticed." She was a little too close, and the smell of her perfume, the sickly sweet scent of roses, was cloying in the air.

"No, I hadn't noticed any such thing," I said flatly. "She *is* eager to see you, though, and she doesn't like to be kept waiting, as I'm sure you know. She's in the green drawing room."

"Really?" Allison withdrew her arm from mine with a sour expression on her face. "Well, I suppose I should see her then. I expect she wants my assistance with this wretched party. I must say, I would have thought you would have attended to all that. After all, that's what you're being paid for." Her high little voice was peevish.

Really, the woman was a little unstrung, with her lightning changes of mood. I could find it in my heart to be a little sorry for her, since she seemed to have forgiven me for my pirating of Alex that night. Perhaps she had no need to be jealous. The thought bothered me.

I said softly, placatingly, "Almost everything is done, Allison. She wanted your opinion on some of the finer points of decoration for the ballroom. She said you had a gift for such things."

Like a spoiled child her expression cleared at my blatant flattery. "It's true I do have a way with flower arrangements and such." She preened slightly. "I'll go to her right now. Perhaps I might offer to help with the flowers for the party. Though I must be careful not to overtax my strength," the recent widow warned.

"I'm sure that Lady Margaret will be grateful for whatever you feel able to do," I murmured, sure that Lady Margaret would bite her head off if she started any of those die-away airs in her presence. "If you'll excuse me."

"Certainly, certainly." She waved me away absently. I was almost out the door when her soft voice called me back. "Oh, Lorna."

"Yes, Allison." I paused, my back still toward her.

"My brothers-in-law are due sometime this weekend. Charles will be here tonight, I know. And I'm sure you'll be able to enlighten us as to when the Captain is expected to arrive." Her voice was venomous again, and my surprise overshadowed the nervous jumping in my stomach.

I turned to her, my eyes wide in unfeigned amazement. "Why, we haven't heard a thing from the Captain. I don't think Lady Margaret expected him until next week sometime."

"I wasn't talking about Lady Margaret," she snapped, and swept from the room, her silken skirts rustling along the stone floors.

Apparently she wasn't over her obsession. Though what she felt threatened her pale beauty in my lengthy dowdiness I failed to see.

As I wandered back to the kitchen I thought to myself that she needed help of some sort very badly. What kind of help was more than I could imagine; maybe a clergyman, or their family doctor. Although the Camerons were not typically God-fearing Scots, perhaps in the old days they had attended church more regularly in the neighboring town of Windham. Whether Allison would willingly talk with anyone I sincerely doubted.

Chapter XV

All that day and evening my nerves were on edge. Charles arrived around five o'clock, urbane and charming as ever, casting warm glances in my direction whenever he thought no one was looking. It made me even more nervous. He had no information whatsoever on Alex's plans, but I found myself dressing for dinner that night with extra care anyway.

Dinner went along easily enough, despite my constant starts. The food was delicious, and there was no changeable Alex to rudely comment on my surreptitiously immense appetite. Allison seemed to dine solely on meat and vegetables, eying the potatoes and dessert longingly. I suspected she might have a weight problem, and the thought pleased my malicious soul. Although a few more pounds on her fashionably trim frame would have made her look healthier, I decided.

"We're blowing up for a storm," Charles declared as we adjourned to the drawing room. "I suppose Alex won't make it tonight." As if to verify his statement lightning flashed outside, and Allison jumped, letting out a tiny, refined shriek.

I willed myself to relax. "Would you like some help when you retire, Lady Margaret?" I asked after a polite interval. Charles and Allison were deep in what appeared to be a friendly conversation, and I hoped to slip from the room without further attention from either of them. Charles's eagerness for a tête-à-tête had abated somewhat with my obvious reluctance, and I wanted to escape before he tried again.

"No, my dear, that's all right," she dismissed me sleepily. "I'll have Katie help me when I'm ready. You go on up to bed if you wish."

I escaped without notice and shut the door behind me. I had left on somewhat false pretenses—I had no intention of going to bed. I loved wild storms, and I was going for a walk down to the ocean to watch this one in all its fury. At least, I told myself, slipping a shawl around me, I would be safe from the specter of Alex's imminent arrival. I tiptoed into the library and opened the french doors. The wind was raging, bending the birches till it seemed as if they might snap in two. A bright half-moon shone fitfully from behind the angry, shifting clouds, and without further ado I slipped out, shutting the door firmly behind me.

The ocean's furious crashings and poundings came to me across the lawn, and I felt a surge of excitement inside me. I bent low into the wind, holding tightly to my shawl as the wind tried to rip it from me. I made my way slowly across the neat expanse of lawn, down the suddenly flimsy wooden stairs to the beach, my heart pounding, my pulse racing. Some wild, pagan part of me was scudding through the sky with those angry clouds, a part of me was in the water swirling and thrashing at my feet. I lifted my face to the ocean spray like an offering. And then two strong arms reached out and caught me and I realized I wasn't alone in that wild night.

As I turned and looked up into Alexander Cameron's impassive face with the black hair blowing wildly about it, I recognized against my will the reason for my excitation. The moment the storm blew up I knew he would be here, as he came the first night in the pouring rain, and without thinking I had gone out into the night to find him. And now that I stood with his strong hands on my arms, holding me there, helpless in the storm-tossed seascape, I was suddenly frightened. Our meetings always seemed fraught with tension, changing from heated arguments to a light banter to attempted rape. I wished I knew what was going on behind that mask he so often wore. I stared up at him, saying nothing, watching and waiting for something that vanished from his equally stormy face before I had a chance to identify it.

He let go of me abruptly, and I put my hands up to rub the pained spots where his hands had gripped me so tightly. That I caressed my arms where his flesh had touched mine was barely discernible in the dark of the night.

"What are you doing down here in weather like this?" he demanded.

"I . . . I like storms."

A smile cracked his stern face, almost against his will. "Do you now? When you've been on a ship through a real nor'easter you might think differently. Even this tiny island is none too safe."

"Is this going to be one?" I asked, courting danger by wanting to prolong this moment of feeling alone in the world with him, alone in the storm.

"I don't think so. Perhaps we'll have one just in time to ruin

Mother's blasted party. I doubt it, though—it's not the season for them." There was a mild bitterness in his face as he stared out at the crashing waves. "Are they expecting me up there?"

"No," I answered. "They think it's too stormy for you to come tonight."

"But you knew different," he stated, his queer blue eyes shining down on me, and I could say nothing, neither confirm nor deny it. He knew anyway, and there was no need for me to waste words with him. "We'd better go in," he said after a moment, sounding suddenly very tired. "We don't want them jumping to any more conclusions, do we?"

"N . . . no," I stammered, grateful for the dark of the windy night. Lightning shot through the sky and straight into the tossing seas and a crack of thunder followed immediately, seeming to shake the sand beneath our feet. Rain began splashing down in large drops.

"We'd better run," he said, and, grabbing my hand in his calloused one, so different from Charles's soft grasp, he pulled me up the stairs and across the lawn as the rain poured down on our heads.

When we reached the terrace Alex shouted at me through the tumult, "Did you leave a door unlocked when you came out?" Helplessly I shook my head and he swore lightly. "Well, there's no help for it, then," he said, and, still keeping a tight grip on my hand, pulled me over to the drawing-room door and banged loudly.

A second later the door was flung open and lights and voices poured out into the night. Alex dragged me into the house, ignoring my attempts to free myself, and we stood dripping in the middle of the drawing room, my hand still in his iron grip, with Lady Margaret and Allison and Charles all staring at us with amazement and disapproval.

"Lorna went out to watch the storm and ran into me," Alex said casually, finally releasing my hand. "Hello, Mother." He bent to kiss Lady Margaret's withered cheek, ignoring her look of censure. "Good evening, Charles, Allison. I'm sorry I'm so late, but I was held up in town on business."

"Must you drip on my Aubusson rug?" his mother demanded icily. I jumped, flushed with mortification.

"I'm so sorry, Lady Margaret," I stammered. "I just wanted to . . ."

"That's perfectly all right, child." She turned to me with a surprisingly gentle graciousness. "I'm sure it wasn't *your* fault. You go on up and get into bed and I'll have Katie bring you up a hot toddy. We don't want you catching cold."

"Thank you, ma'am." Scurrying from the room, I nearly ran into Katie, who was waiting by the door with an avid expression on her face.

"The Captain is here, ain't he?" she demanded eagerly, her eyes alight with an almost sensual excitement, and I felt a flash of discomfort. Did I look like that at the thought of the Captain's presence? I dearly hoped not.

"Yes, he's here," I said shortly. "I'm going to bed now, Katie. If Lady Margaret sends you up with a hot drink for me don't bother. I'll sleep like the dead tonight." I shivered at my unconscious choice of words. I wondered how well Josiah and Stephen slept.

"Yes, ma'am." She was barely listening, her eyes intent upon the door. I ran up the stairs and down the long hallways to my room then, and slammed the door shut behind me. I leaned against the solid oak, panting more from emotion than exertion. The storm was raging outside my casement windows, and my mind felt a kindred spirit with it. The weather was warm enough for the family to do away with fires, and the only light was the candle Katie had left burning when she had turned down my bed.

I locked the door and stumbled toward the bed, dropping my sopping clothes to the floor as I went, fumbling with my blasted stays. I shall never sleep, I told myself wearily as I dropped onto the bed clad only in my chemise. I crawled under the heavy covers, too tired to change into a nightgown, and wished I had that hot toddy Lady Margaret had mentioned. I would never sleep, I knew it, I would never. . . .

Chapter XVI

The next morning dawned bright and clear. I was awakened quite early by the unmistakable sounds of heavy housework. Throwing back the covers, I flew to the windows and flung them open into the bright summer sunshine.

"Good morning," a voice called up to me. It was Charles laughing up at me from the dew-spotted grass, looking boyish and happy.

Blushing slightly, I nodded in return and withdrew, ignoring the unbidden thought of what Alex's reaction would be to the sight of my deshabille. Not at all what I would wish for, I reminded myself grumpily, dressing with more haste than the hour necessitated. I wanted to be up and waiting when Alex made his appearance this morning. For once I wanted to be in calm control of the situation.

I sailed into the breakfast room, then stopped cold. He was already there, waiting, it seemed. He looked up briefly from his plate of eggs, kidneys, and such, and greeted me with a total absence of enthusiasm.

How could I have thought I would ever have this man, or any situation which involved him, under my control? Never one to give in without a fight, I murmured a polite "Good morning" as I strode toward the heavy-laden sideboard.

I considered for a moment, hovering between the toast or the muffins, the kidneys or the kippered herring, the omelet or the poached eggs. I decided impartially on everything, and carried my loaded plate to the table with all the dignity I could muster.

At breakfast time we had no predetermined seating arrangements, and I hesitated for only a moment before seating myself beside the stern Captain with a boldness that would have amused my father.

Alex looked up then in blank surprise, and I smiled back with unimpaired cheerfulness. "Lovely morning, isn't it?" I began conversationally as I slathered butter on my muffin. "I couldn't stay in bed a minute longer."

"So I observed," he said dampeningly, turning to gaze out the window toward the calm blue sea.

"I always feel it's best to get up when you feel like getting up because what's the use in staying in bed when you no longer want to don't you agree and it is such a very lovely morning that I thought I just might go for a walk I think early morning is the best time for a walk don't you and besides I like my walks to be solitary unless someone is with me I know that doesn't make sense but you know what I mean." I ended a little breathless and almost in tears. I was suddenly so nervous, feeling quite alone there with him in the great house, that I chattered like one of those deathly debutantes he had tried so hard to avoid. And I had wanted to appear mysterious and alluring, rather like Allison's bizarre image of me, as cool and aloof and invulnerable as he was. Instead I had ended up sounding like a gushing adolescent.

So upset was I that I subsided into total silence, staring at the mass of food in front of me with no appetite whatsoever.

After a minute or two he turned back from the window, on his no longer stern face an expression of reluctant amusement. "Aren't you going to eat that ridiculous breakfast?" he asked suddenly. "You won't get another bite till noon or even later."

Curiosity banished my unnatural depression. "Why not?"

He toyed with his cup of coffee. "You're taking the children on a long picnic so Thora can begin turning the house inside out for my mother's foolishness."

"Where will I take them?" I questioned, a bit bewildered.

"Surely you've had time during your investigations to explore the island, Madame Detective," he said with only a little coldness. "You should have discovered our favorite picnic places. As it is, the burden is not on you. I have consented to serve as chauffeur and general nursery maid."

I choked on the coffee I had begun to swallow, and it was a few moments before I could breathe properly once more. "Oh," I said brightly, and proceeded to demolish the meal with newfound appetite. A full day with Alex, with no other adult around to spoil it, was my idea of a rather dangerous heaven. But I was, against my will, becoming too much of a fool to care.

The children greeted the news of our planned excursion with shouts of unrestrained delight. It was all I could do to keep them reasonably well behaved until the hour of departure. Thora was rushing up and down the back stairs, red-faced with exertion, demanding of me whether we wanted chicken sandwiches or duck sandwiches, lobsters or clams or both. My decision was always on the side of quantity, and by the time eleven o'clock rolled around our appetites were so aroused by the constant discussion of food that I was sure the three of us could have devoured a horse.

We made a stately procession through the hallway, the children spotless in their matching sailor outfits, myself looking prim and neat in my governessy clothes. John and Alex were waiting in the front courtyard, with Firefly hitched up to a wagon laden with enough supplies for a cross-country trek instead of an afternoon's outing.

"What a lovely pair of young ladies I have the honor to escort." Alex bowed very low and Jenny giggled complacently. I nodded with due graciousness and lifted the children into the back of the wagon. Preparing to mount into the front, I found myself stiffening uncontrollably as Alex's strong, tanned hands went around my slender waist and lifted me up into the seat. I could feel myself blushing idiotically and I cursed my complexion. He jumped in beside me and took up the reins, and in a moment we were off.

The flurry of getting started and making the children seat themselves on the little bench Old John had thoughtfully provided covered up my temporary discomfiture. By the time I had turned my attention back to the front of the wagon, my color had been restored, and I was able to respond with equanimity to Alex's offering that the weather was quite lovely.

I breathed deeply of the salty air. The weather was indeed lovely—the sky a perfect, deep blue with only a wisp of cloud here and there. The smell of the sea was strong and fresh in my nostrils, and the soft summer air combined with some intangible sense of joy to exhilarate me. The sound of the children's voices, mingled with the not far distant whisper of the sea, and the presence of the man beside me stirred me in ways I couldn't begin to fathom. I let myself lean back against the leather-padded back rest and merely soak up the odd sensations, without trying to decipher them.

We came eventually to a small cove with a sureness that told me it must have been a favorite haunt of Alex and his brothers in their earlier days, and the children scrambled from the wagon with dispatch. I fairly leapt out, unwilling to have those disturbing hands touch me again. Alex looked at me sharply and smiled, and that smile was even more disturbing than his hands would have been. He seemed to have sloughed off his moodiness with the repressive atmosphere of the house, and there was a lighthearted air about him.

"I don't believe in waiting for men to help me," I said aloud, trying to justify my behavior. "I'm perfectly capable of climbing in and out of a wagon by myself."

"I'm sure you are," he said soothingly, his azure eyes alight with amusement. "I have no intention of raping you, my dear Lorna," he added in a lowered voice, and I knew I blushed a deep crimson. I turned and scampered after the children like a frightened rabbit.

We played an exhausting game of ring-around-the-rosy, then London-Bridge-Is-Falling-Down, then tag. When the awkwardness of my conversation with Alex had abated somewhat, I allowed myself to collapse gracelessly in the sand, cursing him roundly for his ability to disconcert me. My long, slim hands were trembling slightly, and I buried them in the sand, suddenly intent upon a sand castle. The children left their small mounds of wet sand to help me, and studiously we ignored Uncle Alex as he unpacked the lunch and set out an elegant picnic. To my surprise he sang a song under his breath as he worked, and I was hard put not to stare. I could only wish the man weren't so unpredictable—that he would either stay withdrawn or charming, but not alternate maddeningly between the two.

So caught up was I in my edifice that I barely noticed him until his tall shadow fell across the sand. "That's the house," he said quietly, and I was surprised at his choice of words. Not "my house" or "my mother's house." Just "the house." The children had wandered off toward the food. With sudden, no longer suppressed violence he reached out and knocked my delicate structure flat, then turned on his heel and strode off down the beach. I watched him with mixed emotions, controlling my sudden inexplicable longing to follow him, to comfort him somehow. And yet his strange fury had frightened me, after his previous lightness of mood. Sighing, I rose from the sand and kicked the rest of the castle flat, so that no trace remained, and joined the children in devouring a hearty meal. I worked for a bit, teaching them their letters, drawing short words in the sand. We finished on the name ALEX, and then they slept like the innocent things they were, and I watched the sea.

He was a long time in returning. I could see him from a great distance, walking slowly back along the sand. I kept my eyes on him all the while, and he met my mild gaze with stiff politeness.

"I apologize for my previous boorishness," he said in a stilted voice when he was a few feet away. "It was inexcusable, of course, and I can only hope you will be generous enough to overlook it."

"It's perfectly all right," I murmured, watching him as he stared out at the sea. He turned suddenly and his eyes met mine, and in confusion I lowered my gaze to the sand, and his name etched out in capital letters for the children's reading lesson. Without thinking I quickly obliterated it, but not before he could see it, and he laughed, relaxing in my embarrassment.

"Are you hungry?" I offered timidly.

"There's food left?" he said in mock amazement, throwing himself down on the blanket beside me and reaching for a sandwich. "I would have thought you'd devoured it all. I must have upset you more than I thought."

"I don't eat that much!" I denied hotly.

"My dear, you eat like a horse." He finished his sandwich in three bites and reached for another. "I hope my outburst didn't disturb your appetite?" His dark blue eyes were curiously tender, and I looked away uneasily.

"No," I lied, mumbling. "Look at the color of the sea." I quickly changed the subject. "I've never seen it so blue."

"Haven't you?" He sounded amused. "Down in the Caribbean the color is even more lovely than this. It's a warm, shimmering blue and the water feels like bath water to the touch."

"It must be very beautiful," I murmured, trying vainly to keep the envy and longing out of my voice.

"Someday I'll take you sailing." His voice was like silk, sliding over my skin. "I'll show you all the strange and beautiful places in this world."

I turned back to him with a thin veneer of skepticism covering my childish dreaming. "I don't really think so," I said softly, staring down at the tiny grains of sand beneath my fingers.

His hand reached under my chin and forced my head up to face him. I tried to lower my eyes with a flash of child-like mutiny.

"Look at me," he said peremptorily. My eyes met his for a breathless moment, and that moment stretched and grew. "Lorna." His voice was soft and urgent, and unconsciously I responded to that urgency. "Lorna," he said, and his eyes were like smoke, "I want you to leave here."

The words were so very far from what I had expected that I pulled away from him abruptly.

"Don't look at me like that," he said sharply. "You're in danger here, with that pretty little nose poking into places it doesn't belong."

"I can take care of myself," I said staunchly, staring off into the horizon. "I don't need your advice."

"I think you do," he said, and one strong hand was placed on my unresisting arm. I could feel myself weakening, drawing closer and closer, until our bodies were almost touching, when we heard Jenny stir.

The ride back to the house was far too short for me. I was uneasy about the place, about the idiotic ball that was advancing on us rapidly. I wanted to stay in the dangerous, enticing world comprised of Alex, the ocean, and the sweetly dozing children. I couldn't have cared less if I ever saw the other Camerons again.

Instead I marched back into the house, head up, shoulders back, a martial gleam in my eye. I was damned if I would let them all know my vulnerability—they all suspected too much as it was. I went back to my room and changed into my green cotton dress with the full, swirling skirts, and took my long red hair from its coronet of braids, brushing it fiercely. The sun had added color to my face today, and it made my cat's eyes shine more brightly in the burnished gold of my skin. I looked ready to take on an army, or at least the noble Camerons.

There was a curious constraint in the air when I entered the drawing room. Charles and Allison were once again deep in conversation, and I wondered belatedly what they had to discuss with such earnestness. Lady Margaret was glowering at everyone in general, and Alex was staring out the windows toward the sea, a drink the color of amber in his hand, belligerence in his stance. I felt a brief contraction in my stomach, no more than a small twinge, just enough of a reminder that I wasn't as invulnerable as I pretended. The way his black hair curled around his neck, the weather-beaten and now angry face, his long, strong body all reminded me of something I would rather forget.

It was not one of the Camerons' better nights. The damask tablecloth gleamed in the candlelight, the crystal wineglasses sparkled, the food was ambrosial, and a sullen anger hung in the air, rather like a storm building up to a point where it would crash down about our heads. Allison sat toying with her food, a sulky and frightened look on her child-like face. Lady Margaret ate in outraged silence, her disapproval of all her children bristling. Even Charles, jovial, handsome, good-natured Charles, had fallen under the spell of the evening. There was hatred and evil about, I could feel it growing and swelling, and it made me ill. I pushed my plate away, unable to make more of a dent in the mountain of food I had served myself.

As for Alex, he sat across from me, saying nothing, eating nothing, drinking steadily. To my covert amazement he finished a bottle of Lady Margaret's excellent red wine singlehandedly and started on another. And this on top of the obviously potent drink of whiskey he had been indulging in when I had first come down.

"I don't suppose," Alex said suddenly, and I jumped, "that you would consider calling off this extremely ill-advised party of yours?"

Lady Margaret stared at him haughtily. "And who are you to tell me when my plans are ill-advised?" she demanded. "It's seldom enough I see anyone, confined as I am to this island. I haven't got much time left—this will probably be the last party I feel up to giving, and I would think you would for once have the consideration to humor me and try to make things easier, instead of obstructing my plans in any way you can think of."

Having heard this lament many times in the last two months, I knew perfectly well that a little discretion could cheer the old lady up and put her back in a reasonably good mood. I also knew perfectly well that Alex in his present humor would do his best to make it worse.

"You'll live forever, Mother," he drawled, refilling his wineglass for the umpteenth time. "Haven't you heard, only the good die young?" He drained the glass, and poured himself still another. I wondered that he could swallow so much of the stuff and not show it. "You're asking for trouble with this party, Mother, and only someone as desperately self-centered as you are would continue with it in the face of obvious disaster."

Lady Margaret rose from her chair, her tiny figure trembling with rage. She threw her linen napkin down on the table, knocking over her wineglass. In a horrified fascination I watched the red wine spread and soak into the cloth, unable to suppress a shudder. In the candlelight it looked like blood.

"God knows what I ever did to deserve a son like you! You've been nothing but a hateful, spiteful, jealous changeling since you were born. I wish you'd drowned long ago on one of your voyages instead of coming back to . . . to . . ."

Alex smiled at her lazily. "To what, Mother?" he goaded.

"To kill your brother and father," she cried furiously, and a terrible silence fell over the room. Even Lady Margaret knew for once she'd gone too far.

As for me, it was all I could do to keep from jumping from my seat and running to him, to try and protect him from that evil witch that had given birth to him. I should have known he'd have no need of my help.

"Well, it's enlightening to know what you really think of me, Mother," he drawled after a shocked moment or two. "In that case, perhaps I'll phrase my warning a bit more bluntly—if you insist on having this ridiculous party you'll live to regret it. And I'm very much afraid that someone else won't." With a graceful, careless move he was gone from the room.

"Really, Mother," Charles said sternly after the door had shut behind his half brother, "that was a shocking thing to say. You know perfectly well that Alex had nothing to do with Father's and Stephen's deaths."

"Do I?" Lady Margaret turned to him with a coldness she had heretofore reserved for others. "Am I sure of anything?"

It was a subdued group of Camerons that adjourned to the drawing room. Lady Margaret sat apart from everyone in a state of sullen rage, occasioned partly by her feelings of guilt. I couldn't even coax her from her bad temper by the offer of a little Mr. Dickens. Actually, I had no desire to lessen her transgressions. I hoped she'd rot in hell for her cruel words to her only remaining child. That he'd asked for it made no difference to me. I stared at her tired old face and felt no pity.

When I could stand the tension in the room no longer I curtly excused myself and left them all. One of my feet was on the massive winding stairs when from the dark recesses of the hallway Alex appeared.

I was sorely tempted to continue up those stairs rather than hold a private conversation with him. My curiosity got the better of me, and I turned to meet his dark gaze with as much nonchalance as I could muster.

"Have you reconsidered my suggestion?" he asked abruptly. Alexander Cameron was always a man to be completely in control, and it was only because I had watched him so long and so often that I realized suddenly that he was very drunk indeed.

"Suggestion?" I echoed.

"That you leave here," he clarified shortly.

I wondered absently why tonight of all nights he had decided to get drunk. Saying nothing for a moment, I tried to formulate an answer. As I stood there my eyes fell to his mouth, now thin-lipped and stern with his sudden anger, and I found myself remembering the taste of that mouth on mine.

"And stop looking like that, damn it!" He might have shouted it, but his voice was low and fierce.

"Looking like what?"

"All soft and helpless and clinging." He spat out the words like insults.

"I . . . I don't understand," I whispered helplessly.

"Don't you?" he demanded. He stared at me in brooding silence for a moment. "All right, perhaps you don't." He seemed suddenly very tired, and I wanted to take that proud head and cradle it against my breast. "This is the last time I'll warn you, Miss MacDougall." His voice mocked my name. "From now on you'll have to fend for yourself if you insist on staying here. I wash my hands of you."

"I was never your responsibility!" I felt close to tears, and angrily I fought them back.

"Weren't you?" he asked softly. Without another word he whirled around and left me in that darkened hallway, feeling alone and curiously bereft.

Chapter XVII

That marked the beginning of an exceedingly long and nerve-racking week. Every moment I was expecting to see Alex's tall form appear beside me, only to find it was Charles. The Captain was obviously avoiding me, and I told myself I was glad. But I jumped at my own shadow, and even self-absorbed Allison commented on my tenseness.

To further complicate matters the week was one long, unending stream of tradesmen, caterers, decorators, and by Friday evening we were burdened with eight houseguests. Most of these were innocuously affable business friends and elderly gentlemen and their wives. The one exception was the first thing that broke through Allison's cold dislike of me and united us in wrath: Lady Margaret's favored entry into the Alexander Cameron matrimonial sweepstakes.

When Pamela Sutton first alighted from the elegant carriage the Camerons kept for distinguished guests, my breath was taken away. I had thought Allison very pretty in a spoiled, pink and white manner, but this girl was an absolutely captivating beauty. From the top of her elegantly hatted black hair to the toes of her tiny well-shod feet she was perfect, almost like a porcelain figurine. She stared at me haughtily as she swept into the hall, and greeted Allison with chilly courtesy. I would have been more amused than bothered had it not been for the sudden reappearance of Alex from the mysterious world of his workshop.

"Alexander." Her voice was light, cool, and charming. And ever so slightly imperious.

"Pamela." He came forward, with barely a trace of reluctance, and took her tiny hand in his large, work-worn one. "I had no idea you were expected."

She laughed a small, musical laugh and tapped his arm playfully. "And are you pleased? It's been absolute centuries since we've seen each other."

He raised an eyebrow. "Has it? I hadn't realized it had been so long." He was teasing her, and my anger distressed me more than the disgustingly flirtatious scene I was witnessing.

"Take me in to your dear mother, Alexander," she had the temerity to order him. "I must be a dutiful guest."

"Mother invited you, did she?" Alex looked faintly amused. "I see." He made no move to accompany the lady, and she gave a slight shake, almost a stamp of her foot.

"Alexander." Her voice was definitely on edge.

He looked down at her from his great height, a curious expression on his face. For a moment his eyes met mine, and all my rage and misery were apparent. There was a brief softening in his face, before he turned back to his mother's choice.

"Certainly, my dear. I trust you won't mind the dust on me. I've been busy."

"In your workshop, I suppose," she said with a knowledge that pained me. "You always were wasting your time in some way or another." Her indulgent voice made my skin crawl.

"Yes, I was." The look he bent down toward her was almost a parody of flattering concern. They disappeared down the hallway, and I looked across at Allison's still form, at the almost maniacal hatred in her brown eyes.

Without a word she turned on her heel and left, and I stood there with a curiously painful, betrayed feeling.

For the next few days I had more than enough aggravation to keep me occupied. Alex's attentions fulfilled his mother's fondest wishes. His behavior to the lovely Miss Sutton was assiduous and revolting, and the Cameron charm was in full force. Miss Pamela accepted it all as her due, playing up to him very prettily, and Allison and I seethed, I inwardly, she with a great show of frustrated rage. I had one consolation—even if his intentions were as serious as his mother could wish, she wouldn't have him for long. He was hardly the type to be faithful to a cold-blooded china miss like that one.

The night before the party was a taste of things to come, in more ways than one. Thora came up with a twelve-course dinner, admirably served by the temporary butler and footmen and maids, and the house was filled with bright lights, chattering guests, and flashing jewels. Lord only knew what the next night would bring, I thought grimly, plodding through the massive meal with less than my usual appreciation. I had been snubbed by a senator's wife, an ex-governor's wife, Miss Sutton, Allison, two bankers and their spouses, and I had had enough. Whenever my eyes sought out Alex in that crowd of overbred magpies, he had his dark head bent down close to Miss Sutton's delicate one, totally immersed in her no doubt fascinating small talk. Lady Margaret beamed through it all, her dreams come true, and I wanted to wring her skinny old neck.

After dinner was much, much worse. I felt wretchedly ill at ease in my frumpy gray silk, the only evening dress I owned besides my new green one, which occupied a place of honor in my closet. I felt trapped, surrounded by those glittering, laughing, condescending people and their mindless conversation. When my parents had guests the conversation had been either erudite or useful. The newest writers, the most prolific strain of corn were of equal importance at our table. But not the malicious backbiting gossip that enveloped me so that I wanted to put my hands over my ears and scream at them to stop.

Minutes flew by like hours as I sat alone in the corner of the massive green drawing room, ignored by the Camerons' bejeweled guests, left with nothing to do but concentrate on the nauseating spectacle of Pamela Sutton flirting archly with a tolerant Alex. Even Charles had deserted me—his mother had commanded his presence by her side and a dutiful son did not disobey.

When it finally seemed that I had endured this torture long enough, I rose and began to thread my way through the crowd. I was forced to pass right next to Pamela and Alex, and belatedly I tried to duck my head.

"Oh, Miss MacDougall." Pamela's slightly shrill tones seemed to pierce through the noise, the talking and laughing. There was a sudden hush, and I stood there feeling horribly conspicuous, tall and gawky and plain.

"Miss MacDougall, I'm feeling a bit chilled. Would you be good enough to fetch my blue shawl from my room? It's lying across the chair in the sitting room." Her full pink lips curved in a satisfied smile as she put me firmly in my place for all to see—a servant, forced to do her bidding. I toyed briefly with the idea of refusing her outright. All eyes were on me, it seemed; I could feel Lady Margaret's coldly assessing ones, watching for my reaction. I couldn't bring myself to look at Alex while he allowed his lady-friend to humiliate me.

"Certainly, madam." I made my voice a perfect blend of subservience and insolence as I curtseyed mockingly. I had the brief satisfaction of seeing an angry mottled red flood her delicate cheeks. I swept from the room grandly.

The halls were cool and dark, and I ignored the little shiver of apprehension that assailed me by stomping angrily up the stairs to

Pamela's room. I shouldn't care about such slights, I was merely an upper-class servant, when facts were faced.

Pamela's shawl was where she had tossed it, draped across one of the little slipper chairs. I looked around casually, scarcely interested in Pamela Sutton's almost vulgar display of wealth. Jewels were strewn across the dressing table, clothes littered the floor. I sniffed disdainfully and left the room, moving toward the stairs with such preoccupation that at first I didn't notice that the hallway was curiously dimmer. And then the apprehension that I had been fighting off suddenly became full-fledged fear, and I moved down the deserted hall a little faster.

As my nervous feet reached the top of the stairs I felt only a strange, tingling feeling at the back of my neck, a faint warning. I heard the noise a second before it touched me, and I had time to duck. Something came down heavily on my shoulder instead of my head, and I was pitched forward into the vast inky darkness, down those deadly steps.

In desperation I clawed out at the rushing stairway, and somehow I was able to bring my wildly tumbling body to a halt less than half-way down. I lay there, panting, my body a mass of aches and pains, my mind nearly blank with the slowly receding terror.

I lay there motionless, waiting for him to come and finish me off, but all was silent. Slowly, very slowly, I pulled my body into a sitting position. Nothing seemed broken—the throbbing pain was universal but not unbearable. Leaning heavily upon the wooden banister, I pulled myself to my feet. The hall was silent and still—whoever had tried to murder me was long gone. He hadn't waited to see whether he had succeeded or failed.

I bent down with some difficulty and retrieved the silk shawl. The worst of the pain had lessened by then, lessened enough so that my mind was a seething mass of suspicions I couldn't begin to sort out. I reached the bottom of the stairs and moved carefully across the floor to the open doors, the laughing, carefree people who shielded a murderer.

This time there was no sudden silence, no hush. The laughter and talk continued to flow about me as I made my way across the room to Pamela's minute elegance. I dumped the shawl unceremoniously onto her outstretched arms and left. There had been no look of surprise on her companion's face, but then, whoever was behind all this would have to be a consummate actor. I made my way slowly, with painful caution, to my room, fighting off the too easy tears of pain and fright. The halls were silent, almost too silent, and to my tortured imagination came the sound of breathing. I moved a little faster, and as I neared my room sudden laughter welled up from the dark reaches of the empty corridors. The sound was the final, terrifying last straw, and I ran with aching limbs down the hall and into the seclusion and safety of my own room, slamming the heavy door behind me and bolting it, breathing with angry, frightened sobs.

"Calm yourself, Lorna," I said out loud, breathing more slowly after a moment or two. There was no sound of chase from the hallway—whoever had tried to kill me must have given up on his quarry for the night. I moved slowly over and opened the windows, letting the soft summer air blow in on me. The sea was calm that night, and the moon almost full, and somehow the happenings of the night seemed even worse in the face of the island's beauty. Tomorrow would be a lovely day for the party, I thought morosely, and I looked over at the dress hanging in the open closet. Katie had pressed it for me, and I knew its simple, elegant lines would make me appear underdressed next to the gaudy creatures below. I had no jewelry besides the dull silver necklace to set it off, and I knew that to the others I would look hopelessly drab. The perfect governess. I sat there at the window and brooded over the cruelty of a fate that had sent me here to be attacked, enticed, humiliated, and . . .

It must have been nigh onto an hour when there came an imperious knocking at my door. Someone's impatient hand rattled the locked doorknob.

"Why was your door locked?" Lady Margaret demanded haughtily when I eventually let her in.

"It must have been an accident," I lied instinctively.

"Perhaps," she murmured, unconvinced. She shut the door behind her. "I'm glad you're still awake. What with all this hubbub I doubt we'll have a chance to talk before the guests leave, and I'm counting on you tomorrow night."

"Yes, ma'am," I said politely, helping her to one of the elegantly padded chairs by the cold fireplace. She had a leather box under one arm that she grasped tightly. I seated myself opposite her and waited. At that point I had no intention of telling her about the attempt on my life. That could wait until her cherished party was done with, when I had something more concrete to offer her.

"Is that the dress you're planning to wear?" She gestured to the sea-green satin with her cane, and I nodded. "Good girl. You have far better taste than those ninnies downstairs. You'll look lovelier in that gown than they will with all their frills and furbelows. I must confess that Katie let me have a glimpse of it while she was taking it to be pressed, and I decided to lend these to you." She held out the leather case and I took it hesitantly. "Well, don't be bashful, girl. You've done me many services, and I decided it was time to show my appreciation. I won't ever have it said that Margaret Cameron doesn't play fairly." She sniffed. "Well, go ahead. Open it!"

I did so, and nearly let the box drop on the floor with astonishment and awe. Inside, nestled in a bed of blue velvet, lay what were surely the beautiful emeralds I had taken to be cleaned. "Lady Margaret, you can't!" I gasped.

"I didn't say I was giving them to you, girl. They're a loan, and they'll look a sight better on you than they ever did on me, that I must say." She leaned back, an expression of satisfaction on her crafty old face. "They were Josiah's wedding present to me. He meant well, and they are beautiful, but they were made for a much younger woman than I was."

This startled me out of my jewel-laden reverie and I looked up quickly. "You were old when you got married?" This was tactless, to say the least, but my surprise overcame my courtesy.

"Use your head, girl," she snapped. "I'll be seventy-five this year and I married less than forty years ago, after Charles's mother . . . passed on. When Josiah Cameron proposed to me it was my last chance." She looked proud and defiant at the old pain, and a great many things that had confused me before fell into place. A woman well set in her ways must have had a hard time coping with motherhood in her forties, especially with a difficult child. Perhaps it was no wonder that she had been so unresponsive with her younger son.

"I had no idea," I murmured in response. "I just didn't ever bother to count, I suppose."

"I suppose you didn't," said Lady Margaret, though her attitude was not unkindly. "It doesn't matter—it has no bearing on anything." She leaned forward. "Lorna, I'm counting on you not to interfere with Alex and Miss Sutton. It's been brought to my attention that both my sons find you very attractive. I'll accept your word that you won't come between Pamela and Alex."

So the emeralds were a bribe. I wanted to throw them back in her face. "Of course," I agreed coldly. "Though with Miss Sutton hanging on his every word I'm not sure the Captain will even notice."

She let out a wheezing chuckle. "You don't like that any more than Allison does, do you? Serves you right. I'm very pleased with the way things are working out. If Alex proves to be amenable I would find a match with her most suitable. Most suitable indeed. I'm sorry, my dear," she said with sudden tenderness. "He's not for you, you know."

"I know that perfectly well," I said stiffly. "And why you think that I would want him is beyond me. He's a coldhearted womanizer, a . . ." I stopped, mortified, when I realized she was nodding in avid agreement.

"Haven't I told you he was no good? He never has been. I'm glad to see you haven't fallen under his spell like that little ninny Allison. You wear my emeralds tomorrow night and you'll shine with the best of them. I want you to enjoy yourself too, you know. You've been . . . a good girl," she finished lamely, unused to paying compliments. "It's been good for me to have you here."

"Thank you, my lady." I appreciated her effort. "And I'll take very good care of the emeralds."

"See that you do," she answered crossly, rising with great difficulty from the chair. She threw off my helping hand. "I can make it on my own—I'm not quite helpless yet. Good night, my dear."

"Good night," I answered, watching her weary old figure move from my room with stately grace. I looked down at the jewels in my lap, and thought about what greed and the love of pretty things such as these would do to a person. To a person such as Allison, perhaps. Sighing, I moved over to the window seat and curled up, watching the sea dreamily. I wished I were far out in the blue, on a beautiful winged boat, far from the shore and all these strange tyrannies. Away from handsome sea captains who smiled with their eyes and lied with their mouths.

I must have drifted off, for the next thing I heard was voices far below me on the moonlit terrace. My first thought was that I was eavesdropping on a private flirtation, and I moved to shut the windows when a word came to me. The word was murder.

I scarcely dared to move, so intent was I upon hearing the rest of the conversation. But, alas, I was too far away to hear more than a few snatches.

". . . you promised . . . money . . . I could still say something, you know." This was a woman's voice, high and clear in the night air, curiously like Allison's. A man's voice answered her, low and rumbling, and I couldn't make out a word. I leaned farther out, trying to catch a glimpse of the conspirators, when something dropped off the ledge and went scuttling down the side of the house with an alarming clatter.

"What was that?" the woman's voice cried out in fright, and

quickly she was silenced. When I dared I looked out again, but there was no sign of anyone out there. I undressed and climbed into bed, troubled beyond measure. I knew perfectly well that voice was Allison's, and I was horribly, terribly afraid that the man had been Alex.

Chapter XVIII

I didn't fall back asleep until the first rays of dawn were streaking across the water, and consequently I slept deeply and quite late. The first thing I saw upon awakening was Stephen sitting peacefully on the floor, playing with the priceless emerald earrings while Jenny paraded in the high, wide neckband. I let out a shriek and jumped from bed, scared them half out of their wits, and it took a great deal of careful, tactful discussion to calm them again. They were still so much like frightened fawns, really, that it broke my heart. I couldn't regret yelling, however. They needed more normal treatment, with perhaps a few well-deserved spanks thrown in for good measure.

"Katie brought us in here a long, long time ago," Jenny informed me solemnly as I dressed. "She said she had important business to attend to, and that you'd wake up soon enough. But you didn't, you slept and slept." Her voice was accusing.

"Well, you should have woken me up," I answered reasonably, pulling on my stockings and fastening them.

"Mama told us she'd have us beaten if we ever woke *her* up," she answered with dreadful calm.

Hiding my dismay, I said crisply, "Well, you know me well enough by now to know I'd do no such thing." I pulled on my whalebone corset with a sigh of resignation and began the tiresome task of lacing it loosely around my slender torso, once more cursing a society that forced its women into such an instrument of medieval torture.

"Lorna," Jenny said in a shocked voice, "aren't you going to have Katie come and help you lace up?"

"Nope."

"Mama spends half an hour getting laced every morning. She needs two people to help her," her daughter confided artlessly, and I chuckled.

"Well, I'm so skinny tight lacing wouldn't make much difference," I laughed, taking my hair out of its long braids and brushing it thoroughly.

"Uncle Alex doesn't think you're skinny," Jenny said.

I dropped the brush. "What?" I turned to face her and she backed away nervously.

"Nothing," she murmured, looking guilty.

"I'm not angry, Jenny," I reassured her with more calm. "I just want to know what you said."

Her brow cleared. "I said Uncle Alex doesn't think you're too skinny. He told Mama so when she called you a skinny, nosy bitch."

"Oh, really?"

"Yes, and he told my mother to leave you alone or he'd hit her in the teeth. I wish he would," she reflected.

So do I, I thought, as I remonstrated with her about such undaughterly utterances. "What else did he say?"

"I don't remember. Except that he said he wished he could see you with your hair down again. Which is silly—he couldn't have seen you with your hair down your back. Only little girls wear their hair that way." Illogicality on the part of her uncle troubled her.

"Well, he saw me early one morning," I explained, hard put to control the warmth that was flooding through me. "Maybe you could help me wash my hair today while Stephen takes his nap. Would you like that?" She nodded vehemently, and I leaned back, well pleased with the day's offerings. The only cloud on my horizon was the memory of that near-fatal push last night. The aches in my body were less than I had feared, and the purple bruises were thankfully on my legs and would remain undetected.

I thought back to the night before, to the feel of a sharp push at my shoulder. But my memory was vague and clouded—I couldn't be absolutely certain that someone had actually shoved me. Perhaps I had tripped. I looked out across the wide blue expanse of the ocean. It was a lovely day, I was a young girl going to my first ball, and I had a lovely dress to wear and magnificent jewels to go with it. I couldn't be gloomy.

But there was more to come. When I arrived downstairs with the children trailing behind me, I was confronted with what amounted to sheer pandemonium. Strange girls and staid-looking men were rushing to and fro, arms laden with tablecloths, napkins, vases full of flowers, bowls of fruit, champagne glasses, cleaning accouterments, and the like. Thora stood in the midst of this like an admiral directing a naval battle, sending her ships this way and that, always on the lookout for a possible collision. Her noble brow was aglow with the heat and exertion and her glance toward me was scarcely affable.

"Breakfast's out and waiting for you, Miss Lorna," she called.

"You'd best hurry if you want to eat—I'll have to have these girls clean out that room in the next half hour." Her disapproval of my slothful habits was evident.

"I'm sorry I slept so long," I murmured, grasping the children's hands to keep them from interfering with the incredible flow of traffic around us. "Where is everyone?"

"They've gone out sailing," she answered, obviously a little distracted by my presence. "Mr. Charles took them all out on the family's new sloop that was brought up from town special for the occasion. Everyone's gone except for Alex and that Miss Sutton. Lady Margaret sent them out on a picnic and good-riddance to them," she exclaimed with fine bad temper. "Now you get out of here and leave me to do my work if you don't want the house to disgrace us all tonight!"

"Yes, ma'am," I murmured numbly, leading the children into the deserted breakfast room. All my fine fancies about the Captain had vanished in the cold cruel light of the morning. That he should have taken that . . . that simpering, slimy creature out alone in the woods! I felt helpless with an irrational rage. That he would dare to do such a thing! I stared morosely at the food in front of me. It was cold and tasteless—the eggs were jellied, the muffins seemed stale, the coffee lukewarm and rancid. It suited my mood.

"Aren't you hungry, Lorna?" Jenny questioned, munching happily enough on cold toast.

I gave myself a mental shake. It serves me right, I thought, for letting myself sink into this ridiculous pit of emotion over such a man. He'd warned me; everyone had warned me.

"I'm fine, Jenny," I answered with a little more cheer. I took another bite out of the blueberry muffin and found it surprisingly tasty. I devoured four more, drank a few more gulps of the still-bad coffee, and was set for action.

"I think, children, that we had better plan to spend the entire day out of doors. We'll just get in Thora's way if we remain in here. So, in honor of the ball, we'll have no lessons today."

"Hurrah!" Jenny shouted with surprising vigor, and Stephen echoed it with some degree of exactness. "Can we do anything we want?"

"Almost," I temporized. "I thought we might make our own picnic and take it down to the beach. That way we could watch the boats and maybe even go wading."

"Mama won't let us go wading," Jenny said hesitatingly.

"Well, I will," I answered boldly, jumping from my seat. Action was better than useless brooding. It was none of my concern how Alexander Cameron spent his time and with whom.

Accordingly, I gathered up the children and escaped from the turmoil that had once been a moderately peaceful, well-run home and retreated to the seaside.

The day had grown stiflingly hot, with scarcely a puff of wind to mar the stillness. I could imagine Charles's boating party becalmed somewhere in the distance, and I chuckled to myself with un-Christian glee. If only Pamela Sutton had seen fit to join them, my evil amusement would have been complete.

These pretty, useless people who had descended upon Cameron's Landing with their silks and jewels filled me with a strong emotion I called contempt but knew perfectly well was jealousy. Had I the money I would have been as irresistible as Pamela, as lovely as Allison, I told myself disconsolately, kicking the skirt of my navy-blue serge. Already the back of my blouse was plastered to me with sweat, and I wished more than anything I were back in short skirts again.

We settled down in the lee of a small cove, spreading an old blanket over the sand and quickly divesting ourselves of shoes and stockings. The water was cool and inviting, lapping at our feet, and I could have wept with longing for its blue depths. Yet even I had enough sense of propriety to know that I could hardly divest myself of my clothes and splash out stark naked. Later, I promised myself, later. I compromised by taking advantage of our relative seclusion and brazenly stripping myself of my stifling long-sleeved shirt. Sitting there in my unbuttoned camisole top, the soft breezes caressing my bare arms, I felt more at peace than I had in quite a while.

I prolonged our picnic well into the late afternoon, knowing that by then the bustle would have settled down up at the big house. After all, our delicately nurtured guests simply could not see the way a house was run, could they? The children and I gathered up our picnic things and wandered back across the lawn. Unfortunately we reached the back door just in time to see Alex and Miss Sutton return homeward, Miss Sutton's lovely head erect beneath her pink ruffled parasol, not a hair out of place, not a wrinkle in her outfit from her delicate pink kid shoes to the pink kid gloves on her soft white hands that had never known a day's work. I reached a hand up to my head absently and felt the pins coming out; my entire body felt damp and sticky and gritty with sand. Her cool eyes met mine for a second, then she looked away, as if I were a not too attractive piece of the landscape.

"You shouldn't say that word, Lorna," Jenny said in shocked tones. "Uncle Alex says that ladies should never use words like that, only gentlemen. And only on extreme provocation."

"I have had extreme provocation," I answered, ruffling her already tousled head. "And if I don't pull myself together," I continued to myself in an undervoice, "Cameron's Landing is going to have another murder to contend with. Supercilious bitch." The bad word brought pleasure to my tongue, and I repeated it softly, savoring the sound of it. We entered the kitchen and I immediately wished we hadn't.

There wasn't a spare inch in the place, either on the floor or the counters. The specially hired help stood around in various attitudes of boredom, their primary work over, awaiting the evening's duties. Plates and dishes piled with delicacies were loaded on every spare bit of table space, and my mouth watered at the sight.

I saw Thora bearing down on us, and I spoke quickly before she could order us out. "We're just leaving, Thora. Could you send some dinner up to the schoolroom for the little ones? And perhaps Nancy to help with putting them to bed?"

"That I could, miss," she said, nodding, her face red and sopping with the heat of the day. "Mr. Charles has been asking for you."

"Oh, has he?" I murmured vaguely. "I didn't know they were back."

"Yes, miss, everyone's back. Shall I tell him you'll see him in the green drawing room in half an hour?" Was that possibly a matchmaking gleam in her eye? I was appreciative of the thought, but the last thing I wanted today was Charles's eager attentions.

"I'm afraid not," I answered, smiling to cover the sharpness of my refusal. "I have to take a bath and rest before the party. I won't have a minute to spare until nine o'clock. Tell him I'll see him then."

"Land o' mercy!" She threw her hands up in the air. "Do you know how many baths the girls have got to fill and empty tonight?"

"I am going to have a bath tonight if I have to heat and carry the water myself!" I said abruptly. Then more quietly, "Please send Nancy up the minute you can spare her."

Thora quailed a bit before my unexpected bad temper. "Well, we'll see what can be arranged, Miss Lorna. Perhaps if you could take your bath right now before the other ladies are ready?"

She had had a much harder day than I had, and I was ashamed of myself. "Certainly, Thora. Thank you very much. I'm sorry if I yelled."

She smiled, grateful for my apology. "That's perfectly all right,

Miss Lorna. It's been a hot day. And it'll be a hot night too, you mark my words."

"I'm afraid you're right," I agreed, shepherding the children up the narrow back stairs. We had barely arrived in the schoolroom when Nancy came scurrying in.

"Thora said you . . ." She stopped midsentence and stared at me in amazement. "Oh, miss. You look . . . different."

"What do you mean?" I demanded, moving to the small mirror hanging on the wall. "Oh, my God."

I was a beautiful, unfashionable golden brown, my skin aglow from my thoughtless hours in the hot sun that day. I had been careless all summer, and today's burning rays had finished their work. Compared to Miss Sutton's delicately protected complexion, or Allison's pink and white prettiness, I looked like a member of another race. I would be shunned, if not refused admittance outright tonight, I thought with the hysteria that too much sun and tension could bring on. I could have wept.

"Actually, miss, you look real pretty," Nancy offered. "Just different, that's all."

But I don't want to look different, I wailed inwardly. I want to look pink and white and pretty like the other ladies Alexander Cameron's wayward fancy seems to light on. I cursed my stupidity roundly, silently.

"You look beautiful," Jenny said stoutly. "Much prettier than any other lady around here."

"You do, indeed, miss," Nancy agreed heartily. "And your bath should be almost ready by this time—maybe some of it will wash off," she added tactlessly.

I wandered back to my room aimlessly, my mind preoccupied with the forthcoming ball. The hip bath was pulled out and steaming water filled it. I stared at my reflection in the clear depths for a moment— the shining eyes, the burnished skin. I shook myself sharply. "Foolish creature!" I mocked myself, pulling off my clothes and taking out my heavy red hair. I had looks enough, even if they weren't just in the common style. The emeralds would match my dress and my eyes, and I was going to enjoy myself fully, come hell or high water.

By the time I had succeeded in washing and rinsing my heavy mane and my body, the once-scalding water was cool. Stepping out of the bath, I threw a towel around me and moved to the open windows to stare out at the sea while I began the tedious task of combing out my tangled hair. The salt air blew warm and gentle on my wet skin, and I gazed out dreamily at the deep blue of the ocean, all sense of time lost to me. For an hour or two I wasn't going to worry about a thing; I would sit in the windows and wait for my hair to dry and not let anything trouble me. I would have enough to cope with before the night was through. For now I could rest.

It was getting dark when I heard a knock on the door. I rose from the window seat slowly, lazily, and wrapped myself in my dressing gown. As I opened the door I had to duck to keep from meeting Katie's fist in my face as she raised it to knock once more.

"Here's some supper for you, miss." She thrust a tray into my hands hurriedly. "Everything's topsy-turvy downstairs, what with it being only an hour till the dancing begins. Have you seen the lanterns yet?"

"No," I replied absently, intent upon the food.

"They're a beautiful sight along the front driveway. They haven't lit the ones out on the lawns yet—they're waiting for the musicians to set up." She stared at me curiously for a moment.

I stiffened. "Is something wrong?"

She shook her head, startled. "No, miss. You just look different, that's all. Prettier, if you don't mind my saying so."

She was obviously sincere, and rather surprised at my long-hidden attractiveness. My spirits rose. "I got a little too much sun today, I'm afraid."

"Is that what it is?" She looked frankly amazed. "Well, miss, I may have to try it on my day off. It does give you a sort of . . . glow."

"Why, thank you, Katie. You've cheered me up."

"Now, why would you need cheering up on such a night?" she demanded. "Your dress is the prettiest one here tonight; much prettier than Miss Sutton's. Don't you pay her no mind—the Captain isn't serious."

"What are you talking about?" I demanded with a fine show of surprise. "What would the Captain's business have to do with me?"

She smiled slyly. "What his business has to do with all the women in this house. I'm on your side, though. That Miss Sutton is a prime bitch, and Miss Allison ain't much better."

I started to protest further, when Thora's bellow floated up from belowstairs. "She's calling me, miss. I'd better go. You ring if you need some help with your hair or anything. I'll make sure I can spare you the time." And off she ran with a flurry of starched petticoats, leaving me floundering helplessly with unspoken denials.

"It's not true," I told myself, setting the tray on my little desk and eating heartily of the cold chicken salad and rolls. "Absolutely not a word of truth in it," I muttered between mouthfuls. I was beginning to feel slightly nervous as I devoured the small dinner, and I decided to begin the laborious process of dressing for the ball tonight. It would take me long enough—most ladies in the house would have at least one maid to assist them in their toilette. I couldn't even take advantage of Katie's kind offer—Thora would have a fit if one of her best workers were taken from her for even a minute.

I started with lace-trimmed pantaloons that my wealthy Aunt Megan from Glasgow had sent me. They successfully covered the welts and bruises I still had to remind me of my tumble down the stairs last night, and only the trace of stiffness would be unavoidable. Then a blue lace garter belt with tiny pink rosettes on it, to hold up the first pair of silk stockings I had been able to afford in a long time. Then four petticoats: two muslin, two silk, each with a froth of lace that I had spent three long winters tatting patiently. I looked disparagingly at my corset with its firm bones. I had to face facts, though, I would probably dance. Strange male hands would rest on my sweltering back, and heaven only knows what thoughts would occur to them if they didn't encounter the customary armor of the day.

Sighing, I put it on, lacing it tightly with annoyance. I had slight trouble catching my breath at first, but I stubbornly refused to loosen it. I would wear it and suffer.

And then the dress itself, with its yards and yards and yards of skirting. When I finished fastening the tiny hooks, I turned to face myself in the mirror, and my courage nearly failed me. I had forgotten how very indiscreet that bodice was. My small, firm breasts were scarcely covered by the sea-green satin, and the effect, though undeniably fetching, was indecent. All that expanse of golden-toned flesh, so very different from the Dresden ladies who would be the guests tonight. My eyes shone with excitement in the exotic face I could hardly recognize as my own. I brushed my long hair, then, at the last moment, gave in to cowardice. Instead of leaving it hanging down my back I wrapped the long auburn waves around my head and stuck a few haphazard pins into the creation. The effect was artful and a little wild, rather like a sea nymph, or that poor lost mermaid I had wept over in Hans Christian Andersen's fairy tale. I retrieved Lady Margaret's emeralds from under the mattress where I had hidden them, and placed them on the table. The necklace went around my neck: a wide choker of emeralds that set off my swan-like proportions to perfection. Small emerald and diamond earrings were next, just peeping through the drooping auburn curls, and the bracelet I clasped around one slender wrist, thanking God once more that

for someone as tall as I at least I could boast of delicate bone structure. A brooch remained in the box, and at the last moment I fas-
tened it in my hair with the aid of a few more hairpins. I stepped back
to admire myself, when the door was flung open and the mistress stood
there, resplendent in purple satin, leaning heavily on her cane. She
stared at me, speechless for a moment, and I wondered if she would
refuse to let me come to the ball—so outrageous must she think my
appearance.

Finally she spoke. "You surprise me, girl. I never knew you could
be such a beauty." Before I could stammer relieved thanks she sailed
onward. "You're to keep an eye on things tonight. There's something
in the air—I can feel it."

"Yes, ma'am," I murmured, uneasily aware of the truth of her
strange precognition. I had felt the same wildness in the night, and its
inevitability frightened me.

"Well, come along, then," she snapped. "Give me your arm. You
have the doubtful honor of escorting an old lady down to meet her
guests."

It seemed a very long way into the ballroom that night. Long
flights of stairs, long hallways stuffy with the unusual heat. And then
we were poised at the top of the long winding stairs, the same stairs
that had almost seen my death the night before, with a blurred
crowd of people below us, watching us as we descended with slow,
stately grace. The old lady was enjoying the drama of her entrance to
the fullest, and I tried to concentrate on getting down those murderous stairs, doing my best to ignore the buzz of comment on my presence there at her side.

"The governess," I heard one high-pitched voice say. My hand
tightened convulsively on the heavy oak banister, and then for not
the first time I reflected what a marvelous sliding pole it would make.
Particularly with nice slippery satin skirts. I laughed to myself, at
ease again by the time we reached the foot of the stairs, and then the
crowd of people forced the old lady away from me, into her own
milieu, and I was free.

"Lorna!" A firm hand grabbed me and I spun around, my heart in
my mouth. It was all I could do to hide the disappointment that filled
me when I faced Charles. "I've been looking everywhere for you."
His eager boyishness would have warmed most girls' hearts. But not
mine. Not then.

I smiled at him. "What can I do for you, Mr. Cameron?"

"Charles," he corrected, smiling in a tender way that left me sadly unmoved. "You must promise me at least half your dances. Particularly the supper waltz."

"Oh?" I replied absently, my eyes searching the crowds of glittering people. "Why, certainly, Charles. Now, if you'll excuse me for a moment . . ." I tried to break away but he held me even more firmly.

"You look so beautiful tonight," he said in a husky voice. "Who but you would have dared to sit out in the sun on a day like this? And it only adds to your loveliness."

I like compliments as well as the next girl, but this was getting a little overdone. "Thank you, Charles, you're very kind. Now I must check on your mother." I pulled away and disappeared through the people as quickly as I could, painfully aware of the interested eyes that had watched our encounter, that had noted my fast escape. I wanted to find a corner of the brightly lit room where I could stay quietly while I searched for Alex. But that was to be denied me. The orchestra struck up, and before I knew it I was in the arms of a strange middle-aged gentleman, being whirled in a lively fashion around the highly polished floor.

And one strange man followed upon another, leaving me no time to think of a reasonable refusal. And as I was sped around the floor it made it impossible for me to ignore the devoted couple, Alex and Miss Sutton, wrapped in each other's arms for each dance, his dark face bent over hers with seeming attentiveness, her perfect features alight with an animation I wouldn't have thought possible. He looked in my direction once, and his eyes passed over me without a change in his expression.

I danced with Charles twice. Once early in the evening and then at the promised supper waltz. For that one he had to outwit several fervent admirers, and his expression as he led me in to supper was smug and self-satisfied. "You're the belle of the ball, my dear," he praised me in a proprietary manner as he filled a plate for me with distressingly lady-like portions. He filled a more generous one for himself and led me to a table. Too late I realized that it was the family table, and I would have to sit at close range and watch Alex and his future wife flirt. I wanted to run in the opposite direction, and I steeled myself against such weakness, determined to be gay and charming at all costs.

"Oh, hello, Lorna." Allison looked up and greeted me absently. Although she observed her state of mourning enough to eschew dancing, she hadn't lacked for attentive males, and a pale and very pretty young man a number of years her junior was paying devoted court to her, speaking in low, impassioned tones. She seemed not the slightest bit concerned over Alex's desertion of her, and I decided that none of her emotions went very deeply. She needed a man, any attractive man, and she would fight for the best available. I think she was secretly relieved to be finished with Alex. He certainly wasn't my idea of the sort of man one could toy with.

"Are you enjoying yourself, Lorna?" Lady Margaret questioned me from the opposite side of the table. "You've taken the place by storm, hasn't she, Alex? She must be quite worn out from all that dancing."

Unwillingly my eyes sought him out. He turned from Miss Sutton absently and glanced in my direction. "What? Oh yes, certainly. You look very nice, Miss MacDougall." He turned back and it was all I could do to keep myself from flinging my plate of lobster salad at his head. His preoccupation with the simpering young lady was so absolute it was slightly unbelievable. My doubts about his sincerity didn't lessen the slight ache beneath my corsets, and I took solace in my food, eating with a boorish concentration rather than having to make polite conversation around the oblivious young lovers. And I flirted, oh so gaily, with a delighted and receptive Charles, who took advantage of my sudden capitulation to squeeze my hand meaningfully right under his disapproving stepmother's nose. Alex didn't even notice.

When the orchestra started again I was claimed before I rose from my seat. Senator Goodridge, who had ignored me completely before this evening, was awaiting my hand for the fourth time. His compliments were even more flowery than Charles's had been, and his hints of a large, mistress-less mansion in Bangor filled me with more apprehension than delight. I escaped from him into the arms of Allison's poetic young man, and then to Charles again, and then to several others, whose faces were a blur to me. And then the night was coming to an end, the night I had longed for and dreaded, over, leaving me with a hollow feeling inside. The introduction to the final waltz was heard, and I felt tears of some emotion I refused to recognize well up in my eyes. I turned blindly for the door, when I felt a pair of strong arms around me and I was swept onto the highly polished dance floor before I could break away.

I never danced like that before or have I since. I looked up into Alex's rather grim face above me, and I didn't care. We danced perfectly, as if we were made for each other, our bodies completely in tune. I was in a cloud, a happy, stupid cloud, through which I saw only two things. Pamela Sutton standing unpartnered, her face a mask of polite disinterest, her hands clenched in rage, and Charles, to whom I had promised the last dance, an inscrutable look on his ruddy, handsome face. And then nothing but the feel of Alex's body a few inches from mine, his hand pressing the small of my back, seeming to press me closer and closer so that I had to fight him as we danced.

And then it was over before it had even begun. The music ended, his arms went away from me, and he bowed and left me there, abandoned in the middle of the dance floor, to join the discreetly fuming figure of his lady.

I stood alone, deserted in the midst of the curious. With amazing aplomb, I marched over to the refreshment tables. The superior hired butler had just opened a fresh bottle of champagne, and, with a great show of authority, I took the bottle from him. Passing close to the tables on my way out of that hated ballroom, I scooped up a heavy-laden plate of hors d'oeuvres and an extra champagne glass before I sailed from the room.

No one tried to stop me, or even noticed me for that matter, and I arrived in my room all set for an orgy of food, wine, and tears. All of which I enjoyed immensely, until I fell into a dazed sleep that was little more (I must confess) than a weepy and intoxicated stupor.

Chapter XIX

I don't know how much later it was when I awoke with the strong moonlight streaming through my open windows. I lay still on the bed, my head a bit fuzzy, trying to will myself back to sleep. The night was hot and incredibly airless, my stays were digging into my sides, and the heavy satin of my ball dress smothered me. My eyes refused to stay shut, so, sighing, I rose from my bed and began disrobing. There wasn't a hint of breeze from across the ocean, and, even clad in my thin cotton shift, I felt stuffy. The empty champagne bottle lay on its side next to the empty plate; telltale signs of the night's debauchery.

I looked out the windows over the deserted lawn toward the ocean. Not a sound, not a light came from the house as far as I could see. Now is the time, I told myself. If there ever was a night made for a moonlight swim, tonight was the night. The entire household would be sleeping off the effects of too much champagne, good food, and dance; no one would peer out their window at four o'clock in the morning (said my watch) to see the scantily clad governess-companion go flitting across the lawn toward the sea. And the person I wanted least to see would be passed out in his own bedroom, or perhaps asleep in Miss Sutton's arms. Or Allison's, for that matter, I reflected, slipping out my door with nary a sound.

My ability to be perfectly silent (and my love of midnight swims) derived from the nights when I would have to sneak from the farmhouse without my mother or father hearing. All of us had done so in our time, for swimming in public was considered indecent, particularly in broad daylight when all the neighbors could see you in less than twelve pounds of clothing if they had a mind to. My brothers and sisters had accepted our parents' dictum, and had swum without their knowing it in our thin cotton chemises. (The boys, I suspect, wore nothing at all.)

I still must have been a bit the worse for wine. Not much more than twenty-four hours earlier someone had tried to murder me, and off I went, alone and unprotected, into the darkness. Surely such foolhardiness must have been alcohol-induced, for I even sang softly as I went.

I scampered down the back stairs lightly in my bare feet, reveling in the complete freedom I had with so little encumbering my body. I would have loved to join one of those Utopian societies I had read about, and danced half naked in the grass. The stone steps were pleasantly cool against my feet, and so pleased was I with myself that I wasn't aware of another presence until I ran into it halfway across the kitchen.

I heard a small feminine shriek, and I swore explosively, partly from surprise, partly from the pain of having my foot trampled upon by someone's not too delicate hobnailed boot.

"Who is it?" I demanded in a hoarse whisper.

"It's me, Katie," she answered, moving away from me in the darkness. A moment later a match was struck to relieve the gloom and I could make out her figure over by the stove.

"What in the world are you doing up so late?" I demanded somewhat rudely, oblivious to the fact that she had just as much right to be roaming about as I had.

A look of pained guilt and furtiveness swept across her expressive features as she stammered, "I . . . I . . . I'm meeting someone," she finished in a rush.

"Oh?" I said mildly enough. "And would it be impolite of me to inquire why you're wearing my dress?" For she had squeezed her ample torso into my apple-green cotton dress. She jumped guiltily and I noticed in dismay that a good three inches of hem trailed on the kitchen floor.

"Oh, I'm so sorry, miss," she choked out. "I know I shouldn't have done such a thing, but I couldn't help it, truly I couldn't. I just wanted my . . . my friend to see me in it. I wanted to look more like . . . I wanted to look pretty," she finished lamely, yet I knew perfectly well what she had almost said. She had wanted to look like me for the man she was meeting, and I wondered who it could possibly be. As far as I could tell no young man around the place was consumed with a hopeless passion for me.

"You won't tell the old lady, will you?" Katie begged. "She'll turn me off without notice if she hears what's been going on, I know she will. She sets such a store by the family name and all." She clapped a hand over her rouged lips, aghast at her own indiscretion. "Forget I said that, oh, please, miss. I should never have said a word; he'll kill me! Oh, please, miss."

"All right," I agreed uneasily. "But do you think you ought to be doing this? He doesn't care for you, you know. He cares for no one except himself." This was tactless but necessary, I felt. Alexander Cameron would give her nothing but sleepless nights and illegitimate babies, and underneath my frightening upsurge of jealousy I felt sorry for her.

"You don't know nothing about it." Katie drew herself up with dignity. "And I don't know why you're jumping to conclusions about who I'm meeting, either." She shook her (or I should say my) skirts out lightly with a carefully careless hand. "I bet it's not who you think it is."

This drew me back for a moment. "I hope it isn't," I said wearily. "For your sake."

She laughed then, without humor. "For your sake too, miss."

I shook my head. "I'm going for a walk," I told her then, still ashamed of my aquatic activities. "If I see your friend I'll send him to you."

"Never you mind, miss. I'll take care of my own business in my own way."

"All right," I agreed, going to the door. "Bring my dress back in the morning, will you? And mind you don't trip on the hem."

She smiled gratefully through the gloom. "Thank you, miss. I'll be careful with it."

I was troubled. Whoever Katie was meeting, she was going to regret it. It's none of your concern, my girl, I admonished myself sternly. Your morals are your own business and hers are hers.

But still I felt a heavy weight around me, one I couldn't define. I walked slowly down the moon-drenched lawn, humming softly to myself, then singing the melody that wouldn't leave me. And stopped myself abruptly when I realized it was the popular waltz of the day, the waltz I had danced with Alex.

But I couldn't be moody for long. The soft summer air, the starry night, the call of the water, whispering to me, the feel of the dew-spangled grass beneath my feet, all conspired to bring a furtive and strangely savage joy to my heart. I ran the rest of the way to the water, a curiously exultant feeling in my breast.

When I reached the edge of the cliffs I stopped for a minute, listening intently. Had I heard someone following? Or, to be more exact, had I "seen" someone? I turned and looked out over the moon-bathed landscape, the manicured lawn with the Chinese lanterns still hung crazily about, the huge stone mansion that held its secrets of death deep within it. All was silent, all were asleep.

Shrugging my shoulders, I scampered down the wooden steps and into the soft sand. As my bare toes touched the beach a surge of wild joy ran through me, alone in the warm night with the ocean and the moon and the stars around me. I wanted to throw myself into the sand, roll in it, toss it in the air. And once more I felt a presence, one I couldn't see, and I sobered quickly. Once more I turned and no one was in sight, and I shook my head as if to clear away the dusty cobwebs of too much champagne.

I dashed into the water and dove under chill and icy waves. To be borne aloft by the ocean was the most exhilarating feeling I had ever known, and I laughed out loud with the joy of it. Tirelessly, over and over I dove and swam, feeling free and untrammeled for the first time in months. The water swirled around my body, pulling my shift halfway off, and I felt alive for once. I could have stayed forever in the inky blackness of the ocean, but against my will I began to tire. Slowly, reluctantly, I swam back to the shore, fighting easily against the undertow, until I collapsed in happy exhaustion on the beach. I lay there for a few moments, letting the water lick my toes, staring out at the endless expanse, and suddenly I was filled with longings so intense I could have cried out with the pain of them. Longings I could scarcely identify, longings that were somehow all wrapped up in the seas and the captain who had mastered them.

I was aware of his presence in pieces. The feeling, a certainty this time, that someone was there, the faint whiff of cigar smoke floating to my nostrils, the small sound of sand being scuffed.

"It affects you that way too, does it?" Alex's voice came low and sure across the sand. He was nearer than I had realized.

"What does?" I questioned obtusely, not turning.

"The ocean. The call of it. Like a siren, day and night, calling you to come to her." His voice was hypnotic, and I found myself staring dreamily out at the water.

"Then why are you here?" I couldn't help but ask, gently, so that I wouldn't break the spell. I was having a hard time remembering that this was the Alexander Cameron who smiled at me and then turned his back on me, who had strange, dark rages, who wanted to get rid of me one way or another. Who may be a murderer. "You could be out there on your ship; why do you stay bound by the land for months and months?"

"One year, two months, and seventeen days," he said quietly. "And I have to stay for reasons I'm not about to divulge to a foolish little girl like you. Suffice it to say I'm staying here because I have to." His voice was softly enticing in the mood-washed night, and a sudden uneasiness filled me. I rose from the sand with what I hoped was a casual air.

"Tell me, did you drink all that champagne yourself?" His voice held a lazy amusement.

"Certainly," I answered calmly.

"What a shame. I was tempted to join you when I saw you making off with all that delicious food." This odd excitement in him worried me. By now I was cold sober and just a little bit frightened by his sudden change of manner. For the past week he had seemed to hate me. No, that was too extreme. He simply hadn't noticed me. "You were very beautiful tonight," he said, and my casual air fell by the wayside.

"I'm surprised you noticed," I snapped.

He laughed then, and it struck me that I had seldom heard such a pleasant sound. "Are you by any chance jealous, my dear Lorna? But you must understand, I could scarcely disappoint my mother and Pamela. After hatching up such a scheme it was the least I could do to go along with it."

"Don't . . . don't you care for Miss Sutton?" I found myself asking, wishing I had the will-power to be coolly silent.

"Not a bit," he said cheerfully. "I thought I had already made my feelings clear to you on that subject."

"You told me to leave." I turned and faced him in the moonlight, my sopping hair plastered to my back, the thin, knee-length cotton shift clinging to my body, leaving, in the bright moonlight, nothing to the imagination. I didn't care. He stood a few feet away, his fancy white shirt rolled up at the elbows, his cigar tip aglow. I could feel his eyes running over my body, and my knees trembled.

There was a sudden, sharp intake of breath, and then he moved. I felt his hands reach out and take me by the shoulders. Very gently he turned me around to face him, very gently he brushed his lips against mine. I stood there, numb with surprise, and he kissed me again, just as lightly. I still didn't move, and, laughing quietly, he pulled me into his arms and his mouth met mine with a fierce hunger that seemed to paralyze me. And then suddenly his hunger was mine, his passion was mine, until I was trembling with the strength of it. His mouth traveled over my face, my eyes, my neck, and his body, his lovely lean body, was shaking as his strong, capable hands grew more demanding. And then, just as I was ready to sink into the whirlwind of passion Alex was stirring up within me, sheer, idiotic virgin terror engulfed me, and I tore myself out of his arms.

"How dare you?" I whispered, shivering with fear and rage and frustrated passion.

"How dare I what?" he said coolly, reaching for me again.

I knew if he kissed me again I would be lost. In desperation I reached out and slapped him across the face. His eyes narrowed in sudden anger, and without hesitation he slapped me back, hard.

"You should know by now I'm no gentleman," he said slowly as I stared at him in shock, tears slipping down my cheeks. Consternation replaced the anger after a moment, and he reached out gently. "Lorna . . . I . . ."

I ran past him up the winding wooden steps to the top of the cliff without waiting to hear another word. No one had dared strike me since I was twelve years old and had beaten my older and larger brother soundly. That he would *dare,* would actually dare to do such a thing! I ran silently across the lawn, rage and hatred and misery welling up and threatening to spill over into a loud, infuriated scream. I saw a figure move across the east lawn, and I wondered if Katie were on her way to meet Alex. If so she was going in the wrong direction. But then, maybe she was meeting someone else entirely. At that point I no longer cared.

I let myself in the kitchen door and made my way silently up the back stairs. I went to my room and threw off my wet and clinging shift. Wrapping myself in my old cotton bathrobe, I sat down at my windows and looked out across the lawn. There was no sight of anyone, neither Katie nor Alex nor Katie's lover. I stared down dazedly, until the sun rose over the ocean, and still there was no one. In another hour or two the children would be climbing all over me, begging me for expeditions and stories of the party last night. I wasn't up to facing anything, not even able to make an excuse. Picking up one of the soft feather pillows and a fluffy comforter, I crept out of my room and down the back hallway to the sewing room. Shutting the door behind me, I curled up on the little daybed and fell asleep.

Chapter XX

I awoke the next morning with a dry taste in my mouth from too much champagne, a sticky feeling on my skin from the salt water, and a heavy feeling of dread. The sun was shining brightly through the window, and I lay there on the lumpy daybed in a stupor for a moment before I realized what the streaming sunlight meant. I jumped out of bed and rushed to the window, and, sure enough, the sun was directly overhead. It must have been at least twelve o'clock, and quite possibly later. There was a strange silence about the house, an odd, unearthly silence. Why hadn't Katie awakened me? Surely she would have had enough sense to look for me in the sewing room? Or would she perhaps have thought I was in Alex's bed, and dared not disturb me? She had jumped to so many conclusions about him and me, I would not have put it past her.

Furtively I opened the door, peering this way and that for a sign of one of Lady Margaret's oh-so-elegant guests. The hall was deserted, and, pulling my thin bathrobe more tightly around my slender body, I scurried down the stone passageway and into my room without encountering anyone.

I dressed swiftly but carefully, willing my mind not to think about those kisses and the painful aftermath. I reached up and touched my cheek where he had slapped me. It was still tender, and I moved to the mirror. There was a small bruise on one cheekbone, underneath the violet shadows that circled my eyes. I certainly wasn't in my best looks today—I was worn out and depressed and more than a little frightened by the unnatural silence that seemed to hold the house in its thrall. I didn't feel like facing it right now—more than anything I wanted to crawl away and hide. Sighing resignedly, I searched through my top drawer for my bag of delicately scented soaps and pulled out the box of dusting powder my younger sisters had given me last Christmas. I smoothed some across the bruise, and the effect made it even worse against my tanned face. Sighing, I brushed and braided my hair, wrapping it around my head in the severest manner possible. I laced myself so tightly that it hurt to breathe, and each bit of pain pleased me. I won't think of last night, I won't, I told myself grimly. I put on every single petticoat I possessed, as some sort of guard against who knows what. The more clothing encasing my thighs the safer I felt. Before leaving I took one last look in the mirror at my tired face with the shadowed eyes, the tremulous mouth. Something was wrong in this house this morning, something was terribly wrong. And I dreaded having to find out.

I descended the great stairs slowly, once more wondering at the total absence of servants and guests. When I reached the main hall I heard the quiet buzz of voices from the green drawing room. Sighing inwardly, I moved to the door and opened it silently, in time to hear the tail end of the conversation.

"I don't know what to do," Lady Margaret was saying piteously. "Such an awful, hideous thing to have happened. And it wasn't an accident; no one can tell me that it was!" Her lined old face was wet with tears, and impulsively I moved forward to comfort her.

"Lady Margaret" was as far as I got. She took one look at me and screamed like a banshee, with a force surprising in one so feeble, and then collapsed in her chair in a dead faint. Allison shrieked also and collapsed on the floor, and the remaining occupant of the room, Charles, looked at me with such horror that I was even more shaken. We stared at each other across the prostrate bodies of his female relations, and neither of us spoke for a moment.

"What's . . . ?" My voice came out in a croak, and hastily I cleared it. "What's going on?"

He rose then, slowly, like someone in a daze, and moved to his stepmother's side. He began chafing her thin, blue-veined hands, not looking at me as he spoke. "We thought you were dead." Slowly, Lady Margaret began to rouse herself. Her head shook slightly, and her wrinkled eyelids opened. She focused on me and began to tremble all over.

I was at her side. "It's all right," I reassured her. "Nothing's happened to me. I just slept late."

"You weren't in your room," she complained fretfully.

"I was in the sewing room," I answered patiently, ignoring the melodramatic sounds issuing from Allison as she lay unattended by the marble fireplace. "I wanted to be somewhere away from the noise of the guests."

"But then, who was it they found?" the old lady questioned. Before I could ask her what she meant, Allison moaned even more loudly and sat up. She stared at me from out of her slightly bulging eyes.

"You're alive," she stated, and I was surprised to see the relief on her spoiled, pretty face. All this time Charles had said nothing, but now he moved to her side as if to comfort her.

"Get away from me," she screamed suddenly, and cowered in the corner. "Don't you touch me!" He moved back, shrugging his broad shoulders helplessly as if to say, Deliver me from all women.

"Pull yourself together, Allison," Lady Margaret snapped. "Get up from the floor and seat yourself over there in the corner and just be quiet. All of you," she turned to Charles and me, "sit down so that we can discuss this matter like calm adults instead of hysterical children."

I seated myself quickly in the nearest thing at hand. "Speaking of which, where are the children?" I asked as the other two obeyed the old lady's autocratic instructions.

"I have sent them out with Nancy on a picnic to the opposite end of the island."

"Opposite to what?"

"To the body of a young woman lying at the bottom of the east cliffs," she said brutally. "Wearing your green dress and apparently with red hair."

Now it was my turn to be numb with shock. Lady Margaret continued on, watching my pained expression carefully. "My son Alex found her. He stormed into the house while we were having breakfast and announced that you were lying dead at the bottom of the cliffs—right in front of the guests, too! I've never seen him so distraught." In retrospect she looked rather shocked at such a display of bad manners. "You can be sure they all left as soon as they could. John and some of the hired men are down there now trying to bring the body up. God only knows where Alex has disappeared to." She stared at me with sudden curiosity. "Who do you think it could be? Surely not one of the guests; their absence would have been noticed."

I roused myself from my pained stupor. "I don't think, I *know* who it is," I answered her sharp-tongued questions slowly. "It's Katie." And then, as if by saying the words out loud I had made it come true, the tears began sliding down my face.

"Aye, ma'am, that it is," John said from the terrace door. "We've brought her up now and we was wondering where you'd like us to put her."

After a speechless moment or two the mistress snapped at him,

"For God's sake, I don't know. Put her in her bedroom until you can get in touch with her parents or something."

"Excuse me, ma'am, but she has no parents. No relatives at all, save an aunt that died last year," John broke in. "It looks like the Camerons are responsible for her now, poor thing."

"Well, then, put her in her bedroom and summon whoever takes care of such things. She can be buried in the family plot, I suppose. Just don't bother me anymore with it!"

I thought of gay, lively Katie, who had served the Camerons all her short life, and I wanted to slap the heartless old witch.

"Yes, ma'am," John said woodenly. He made as if to go, then held out something bright orange, splattered with darker, rust-colored stains. "She was wearing this on her head, ma'am. That's why she was mistook for Miss Lorna."

I shuddered at the sight of the pitiful, bloodstained scarf. With an oath Charles jumped up and grabbed the scarf from John's trembling old hand and ran out into the hot afternoon sun as if a thousand furies were after him.

"I didn't know there was anything of that kind between Charles and a servant," the old lady sniffed. "Perhaps it's all for the best that she tripped."

I stared at her with absolute horror at her heartlessness. Without another word I followed John outside, ignoring Lady Margaret's calls.

"Is there anything I can do, John?" I asked when we were out of earshot from the house. I felt somehow responsible for Katie's death, and I needed to atone in some way.

"Nay, miss. I'll take care of everything; no need to bother your pretty head about it. I knew it couldn't be you, miss. I just knew it couldn't." There were tears in his rheumy old eyes, and I remembered that he had lived through all this before, when his pregnant young sister had been driven by the Camerons to throw herself off the same cliffs that Katie had died on. There was no way I could comfort him.

As I turned to leave him, he reached out and caught my arm. "There's one thing you can do, miss. One thing that it's your duty to do."

"Certainly," I agreed lightly, trying to hold back the tears.

"Go and tell Master Alex that you're all right. I saw his face when he came to get me, miss, and it's a face I wouldn't like to see again in my life, however long I might live."

I shied away nervously. "Oh no, John. Let someone else tell him. I really don't want to . . ."

"It's your bounden duty to tell him," he insisted sternly. "He's down in his workshop. Go to him, lassie."

I could think of no excuse, no reason other than my own cowardice. Nodding slowly, I walked across the lawn, heart pounding against my breath-constricting stays. Obviously, it hadn't occurred to Old John that Alex's grief might be a belated remorse for committing one more murder. Unfortunately, it had occurred to me.

No sound came from within the workshop, no sign of life. I paused a moment, telling myself he'd gone, there was no need for me to knock on the door. I could turn and go back to the house with the smell of death heavy in it. I reached up and knocked loudly.

Silence emanated from the small workshop. He's not there, I told myself, and turned to go. But then I heard something being knocked over in the room, heard slow steps near the door.

"Who is it?" Alex's voice was rough, unfriendly. I opened my mouth to answer but the sound choked in my throat. "Who is it, damn you!" he demanded again, and the door was flung open to expose him standing there, tall and black and furious.

"I . . . I . . . ." I quailed before the fury in his face. "I just wanted to tell you that it's Katie who's dead. Not me." This was rather lame, I confess, but I didn't have time to balance the merits of my speech. As his eyes and mind focused on my angular form he let out a whoop of wild, joyous laughter. He grabbed me in his arms and swung me around, my feet leaving the ground, and then held me to him fiercely. A moment later, before I could catch my breath or comprehend the near-miraculous thing that had happened, he thrust me away, his face black with fury once more.

"What do you mean by frightening me like that?" he shouted, shaking me so that my teeth rattled. "What the hell did you think you were doing, chasing around in the middle of the night . . . ?"

It had all been too much for me, the long sleepless night, the shock and pain of Katie's death, the riotous emotions stemming from the man shaking me, the tightness of my stays. I heard a great roaring sound that I knew was Alex's voice, shouting at me, and, try as I could to fight it, I fainted.

I regained consciousness lying stretched out on one of the elegant sofas in the green drawing room with Lady Margaret hovering solicitously over me, chafing my hands. Charles stood at the foot of the couch, looking gravely concerned, obviously recovered from the emotions that had rocked him earlier.

"You're better, dear Lorna," he said soothingly, his handsome face troubled. He turned to a corner of the room that I could not see from my prone position. "No thanks to you, Brother." His voice was like cold steel. "You must have frightened her half to death."

"I had no idea she was so delicate," Alex drawled, moving into my range of vision. "I trust I didn't upset you." He spoke to me, his voice and words coldly polite, his blue eyes burning brightly into mine.

I shook my head mutely, unable to trust myself to speak. I wanted him to knock Charles away, to take my hands from Lady Margaret's and hold them in his strong, tanned ones. But he did no such thing. He nodded and moved back with all his old apparent unconcern, and I wondered if I had dreamed those last few moments before I fainted.

"I think it might be about time for you to leave, Alex," Charles said sternly, and uncontrollably I stiffened.

"I think it might be time, also," he replied coolly. "The figurehead is completed, and word from the foreman came that the ship should be ready for her christening in two weeks' time. So perhaps I'll travel down to the yard with you, my dear brother. There seems to be no further need of my services around here." With that he strolled out of the room.

"Allison will help you upstairs, Lorna," Lady Margaret said in a slow, sad voice. "You need rest—I'm sure this has been as great a shock to you as it has been to all of us."

Accepting my dismissal, I rose slowly from the couch. Allison moved silently to my side, and together we left the room. We exchanged not a single word until I reached my bedroom door. I turned to thank her, and was horrified by the look of abject terror on her face.

"He's going to kill me, you know," she whispered, her control suddenly breaking. "And there's nothing I can do about it." Her face had aged incredibly since last night. The skin was pulled taut over her cheekbones, the lines running along her forehead and from her nose to her mouth were etched deeply, ineradicably.

"Who?" I whispered also.

She shook her head, looking older than her thirty-one years. "It's no use," she said sadly, turning from me. "It's no use." She stumbled down the hall, her shoulders sagging under her elegant dress. As I watched her go my mind went into a haze, and suddenly I saw her in that very same black silk dress, the elegant lines splattered with blood, her small pretty face cold and still. I ran into my room and slammed the door shut against the horror of such visions.

Chapter XXI

Alex and Charles left that afternoon, waiting only long enough for Charles to manage all the formalities over Katie's death with the local minions of the law, and for Alex to have wrapped up and packaged his mysterious figurehead. I watched them leave from the sewing-room window, both brothers tall and stately in the saddle. I noted without emotion that Charles had chosen Ladybird for his mount, placid, gentle soul that she was, and that Alex seemed to be enjoying his fight for mastery with Samantha. The figurehead, wrapped in what appeared to be an old sail and tied to the wagon that John trundled along behind them, looked curiously, horribly like a corpse, and my mind flew back to Katie, wondering what she felt as she was falling down those steep cliffs, wondering if she knew whose hands had pushed her.

For someone's hands had pushed her, of that I was sure. The third murder in a little over a year on Cameron's Landing left me frightened and very wary. I wasn't about to confide my beliefs in the constable. Charles the lawyer had spoken with them, and the verdict was clear. Death by misadventure. The young lady was taking a romantic walk in the early morning hours in a borrowed dress that was far too long for her. She had tripped on the overlong hem and met her death. Unfortunate that an accidental, violent death should occur on the very spot of a murder a little more than twelve months previously, but then, these things could happen. Coincidence, of course, but what a shame for the poor beleaguered Camerons. And with Mr. Stephen so recently dead, too!

I knew better. My long skirts hadn't tripped Katie, who had been the most graceful creature imaginable, putting my lanky height to shame with her lithe delicacy. No one had wanted to kill poor Katie, whose only fault was perhaps a flirtation with one of Lady Margaret's upper-class sons. No, no one had planned to kill a slightly wanton maid as she wandered out to meet her lover; they had wanted to kill a snooping, romantic governess-companion, who was just the sort of fool to go for moonlit walks. Whoever had tried two nights ago had tried once more. He or she had seen my bright green dress wandering across the lawn, had seen a bright red scarf and mistaken it in the moonlight for my unfortunate red hair, and he had acted, swiftly and violently. And God help me for a helpless, love-struck fool if it was Alex.

Katie was buried early that week after a routine inquiry. No one came forward with new evidence. Charles had left his deposition and Alex had offered a pack of lies with no fear of contradiction from me. His statement said that he had retired at about one o'clock, as soon as the ball had ended, and hadn't risen from his bed till ten the following morning. No one came forward with contrary information, no one mentioned meeting Katie in the deserted kitchen on her way to a midnight swim. And so the case was closed, and Katie's poor battered body was laid to rest in a small grave in the lower, unused corner of the family plot on the west side of the island, as far from the spot where she had met her death as could be managed.

We all left little nosegays made from the wild flowers that bloomed with such carefree abundance all over the island. They were pathetic next to the family's elegant hothouse wreath made from the best orchids to be found in New England. As I left mine I murmured a word of apology to her cold, still body. I couldn't begin to justify my silence to myself, much less to her remains. I wept silently on the ride back to the house, from guilt as well as sorrow.

Fortunately the children didn't quite comprehend what had happened. For them death (the word I had insisted on using) meant no more than a long vacation. "Will she be with my father?" Jenny questioned when I had finished explaining.

"Yes, she will," I answered, hoping to give them some comfort.

"That's good." Jenny nodded complacently. "Mama says she was always very fond of my father. She liked all the Cameron sons, Mama says."

This was an interesting thought, and I wondered if Katie had met her death at the hands of her favored Camerons. It seemed likely, and I pitied her all the more, as I pitied Allison, who remained a shadow of her former self, thin, incredibly nervous, jumping at the slightest untoward sound.

Time passed in a dream. Allison remained with us, eating little, sleeping less, if I could judge from the increasing shadows under her pale brown eyes. She would snap at her children, given the least excuse, and I took care not to give her one. The days passed.

It was almost a week after Katie's poor remains were placed in the little family plot that I finally found myself with some free time. It had taken that long to procure another maid to assist Nancy—the mainland girls being naturally loath to accept live-in work in such a doom-ridden household. The new girl was slow, quite fat, and practically dull-witted, and it was through her grudging offices that Nancy finally had time enough to spare to take care of the little ones.

And I was free. The children were finishing their lunch when Nancy appeared, divesting herself of her apron as she came. There was a new shadowed look beneath her eyes, as if she'd been weeping excessively. As I expected she had. "I'm ready for them now, Miss Lorna, if you want to leave," she greeted me cheerfully enough.

"Gladly." I jumped up, kissing the children heartily on their food-stained cheeks. I left the room in unseemly haste, stopping by my bedroom long enough to collect a light shawl. I escaped from the house unseen and in a few minutes found myself free at last, alone on the wide stretch of lawn to the sea, the sun blazing overhead, a light breeze tossing my heavy skirts, tugging at my severely entwined auburn curls. I wanted to shout, to dance, to sing at the top of my lungs. For once I was free of the burden of guilt and fear that Katie's "accidental" death had hung over the household. I ran down the lawn to the cliffs, to the sea, like a bird in flight. When I reached the edge of the water I sank down in the sand and was silent, dreaming.

Somehow the thing I must know still eluded me. Try as I would to entice visions from my inner mind, I remained blind. I could no more tell if Alexander Cameron had willfully murdered his father and brother and a young, blameless girl than I could fly out across the ocean. And the dreadful uncertainty of it was slowly gnawing away at me, threatening to turn me into a distraught, nerve-racked creature like Allison.

"Well, it seems as if Alex is finally leaving us," Lady Margaret had announced gloomily from the breakfast table that morning. "Charles writes me that the *Sea Witch the Second* is finally ready, the figurehead is in place (and a huge, mysterious fuss Alex appears to be making over it) and the christening plans only await my approval." She put down the elegant blue note paper (a little too elegant, I thought) and sighed. "Well, once Alex sets his mind to a thing he certainly wastes no time in accomplishing it. I wonder that it took him so long to make up his mind." For a moment her faded eyes met mine, and there was more than wonder in them. There was a very real fear.

"So we're all to take the early train down on Thursday for the christening," she continued, as if that split second of apprehension had never happened. "Your presence, Lorna, is specifically requested, you'll be pleased to know."

"By whom?" Allison demanded with a touch of her old malice. Then she sank back into her plush chair apathetically. "Not that it matters."

"Lord!" Lady Margaret exploded. "I don't know what ails you, girl, with all these die-away airs. I liked you better with a bit of spirit. Cheer up, for heaven's sake, we're going to a party!" Allison, however, refused to be comforted. The same bleak look remained on her face; the look that had descended upon her at Katie's death and had not left her for more than a few seconds since that dreadful time. With an exasperated snort Lady Margaret turned her attention to me.

"You'll have a marvelous time, my dear. Just the thing to get us over our doldrums since Katie's unfortunate accident. There'll be hundreds of people there—all the very best people, of course. The mayor usually arrives, drunk, of course, but then, everyone knew about his little weakness when he was elected, so who are we to complain? Lord, it will be so good to get off this blasted island!" She eyed me speculatively. "Perhaps Senator Goodridge will be there. He was quite taken with you, if I remember correctly. How would you like to be a senator's lady, my dear? I doubt you'd set your sights that high, eh?"

"No, ma'am," I murmured docilely.

Sitting in the damp sand, I went over the conversation in my mind, remembering well that brief look of fear on Lady Margaret's face. I stared out at the glistening ocean and wondered how a place that had seen three murders could be so peaceful.

Who could have done such horrible things? Who was capable of murdering a woman in cold blood? And what possible reason could they have? Thora could want revenge for having been spurned by her long-time lover; Nancy and her countless half brothers and sisters might want some sort of retribution from the high and mighty Camerons for their besmirched birth and comparatively poor upbringing. Both Allison and Lady Margaret were unstable and vindictive enough to kill, if only their reasons were strong enough. But I didn't think they had the strength to plunge a knife through the tough layer of bone and flesh that had covered Josiah Cameron's flinty old heart.

And what about the men? Old John certainly had reason enough—

the Camerons had used him very ill, and then seduced and murdered his sister as an afterthought. But Old John, beneath his crusty exterior, was too gentle, and too philosophical about life. No, I couldn't see him as a murderer, anymore than I could see Charles as one.

Charles was too decent a man, too strong and upstanding and perhaps too unimaginative, unemotional. He had the strength and the determination necessary, but no motive that I could see at all. And I hated to say it, but he was just too *bland* to be a killer.

Which left me with one suspect, one person who was neither bland, unemotional, nor terribly decent and upstanding. As I watched the sea gulls soar and dive, I thought back to all the meager clues Lady Margaret had let fall. She knew who did it. And some last vestige of maternal instinct was allowing her to let him escape, to board his beautiful new boat and sail away, perhaps to drown in the vast blue of the sparkling ocean.

It couldn't happen, I told myself, I wouldn't let it happen. Voices and visions, far too vague for me to decipher, convinced me that he could not leave. But that was a foolish dream on my part. Sea captains were always leaving. And suddenly the frothing waves in front of me no longer seemed so lovely—now they were my enemy, conspiring to steal Alexander Cameron, who was never mine and never would be, from me. I could no longer bear it, and I leapt to my feet and ran from it as if the hounds of hell were at my heels.

I didn't stop until I reached the kitchen, the safe, warm haven of Thora's fiercely run domain. The new kitchen maid stared at me numbly as I leaned against the table, panting heavily. Thora took one look at my overwrought face and shooed the new slave out.

"You look as if you need a good strong cup of tea," was all she said, and set about brewing it. I collapsed gratefully on the rough bench and sat there, silent and brooding, until Thora brought the pot, cream, and sugar and sat down across from me. We drank in silence, the silence soothing me as much as the tea. It wasn't until I had finished one cup and begun another that Thora spoke.

"You've taken all this too much to heart, Lorna," she said sadly. "Not that we all haven't. Katie was a dear thing; not the best of workers, mind you, nor the best of girls morally speaking, but a sweeter, kinder girl you'd have a hard time finding." She sighed gustily and I nodded. "Ah, but this house has seen many a tragedy, that it has. A lot before my time and a lot more since I've been here, these past thirty-five years."

She caught my interest. "I didn't know you'd been here that long, Thora," I encouraged her, but she needed no encouragement.

"Really, my dear? I would have thought someone would have told you all about the old scandals first chance they got.

"I was Josiah Cameron's mistress for over twenty-nine years. He brought me here from Boston a few years before he married her ladyship." Thora's tone of voice was contemptuous. "That woman! But Josiah had ever an eye for the ladies, it's true enough. He always came back to me, though, every time. Until the last." I wondered if those were tears in her hardened eyes.

"I had heard something about you and Josiah," I admitted, sipping on the strong, sweet tea. I could see she was dying to share some indiscreet gossip, to brag of her past position of doubtful honor in this household, and I was nothing loath. I sat there expectantly, encouragingly, willing for anything to take my mind off the thing I couldn't forget.

"Yes, many sad things this house has seen. Starting with poor Mr. Charles's mother."

"Yes, that must have been very sad," I murmured. "Dying in childbirth at such an early age."

Thora was amazed. "Why, whoever gave you that idea? For one thing she was older than Josiah—she'd already shed one husband and would have gone through the master if it hadn't been for her sins catching up with her. Oh, she was a bad woman, that one. Always flirting with the young lads from the village, and some of them only half her age!" Thora's brow glistened from the heat of the kitchen and righteous moral indignation. "She bewitched them all, everyone, including Josiah until he was half mad with love and jealousy. Until Charles was born there was some question of whose child it was."

I clucked in appropriately shocked tones, inwardly amused at an old sinner like Thora passing moral judgments. Already my fears had vanished. Old scandals were capturing my imagination. "And then she died giving birth, with him thinking so poorly of her."

"She did no such thing!" exclaimed Thora stoutly. "That's just the story the family likes to give out. She died a full two years after Mr. Charles was born, mad as a hatter."

"No!" I cried in disbelief.

"It's the gospel truth, so help me God." Thora looked heavenward, as if seeking confirmation. "Have you ever been up in the attic? Seen that giant cradle up there? That's where she ended her days, crooning and babbling like the witless thing she was. Not until after she tried to murder her poor innocent wee babe. It's no wonder her ladyship felt sorry for the little tyke, cosseted him a bit more than was good for the lad."

"But that's awful! I had no idea anything of the sort had happened."

"It's over forty years ago," she said philosophically. "It turned out there was madness in the family, and chances were she'd killed her first husband. Of course, there's no knowing the truth of that, so long in the past it was."

"I suppose not." I took another sip of the now lukewarm tea.

"And now, with all this new trouble, I get to thinking the Camerons are a cursed breed," she said, leaning across the table toward me. "And I've got to wondering, miss, whether Master Stephen died of entirely natural causes, or whether he was helped along. If a person's killed once, he's likely to kill again. And it wouldn't make much difference if it was a father or a brother."

"My God," I whispered in horror, sick at the sound of those words, finally speaking out loud the thing I had feared.

"Me, I take life as it comes." Thora shrugged. "Evidence points clearly in one direction, and you know all too well what direction that is. I can see it in the misery in your face every time you think of him sailing off in that fine new boat of his." I didn't bother to try and deny it; it would have been useless. "Dearie, it's all for the best. Forget about him, as he's no doubt forgotten about you already. With any luck the sea will claim him as it ought, for there's no greater sin than a patricide and a fratricide." She sighed. " 'Cain rose up against Abel, his brother, and slew him.' Surely you must see that's an evil no decent God-fearing person can forgive?"

"There's no proof!" I cried out futilely, desperately.

Thora shook her iron-gray head sadly. "No proof's needed in a case like this one," she pronounced, and I wanted to slap her thin, condemning face. Unable to control myself any longer, I ran from the room and her pitying gaze, to hide my doubts and misery in my bedroom walls.

Chapter XXII

That Thursday in late July dawned hot and muggy. The air weighed on my skin like a wet and sticky cloth, and the atmosphere was so thick with moisture and heat and haze that I could scarcely breathe. I awoke slowly that morning, fighting against full awareness on such a humid, miserable day. Slowly I opened my eyes, and a feeling of doom settled on me. For a moment I considered slipping away from the house before anyone else arose—the last thing in the world I wanted was to smile casually and bravely as Alexander Cameron sailed out of my life. But common sense told me I couldn't hide from the unpleasant things in life, and that hearts don't break all that easily. I climbed out of my rumpled bed and went to the windows, searching in vain for a stray breath of air, a single cloud. There was none to be found. Just a smoky gray haze that matched my state of gloom.

"Are you up yet, Lorna?" There was a rapping at my door, and Lady Margaret's imperious voice calling me. "It's quite a ways to the train station, and the christening's set for half-past noon. Hurry up, my girl."

"Yes, ma'am," I answered docilely. "Would you like any help, or should I get the children ready?"

"The children aren't coming today," she snapped back through the heavy oak door. "We'll have too much to keep us busy as it is, without two little ones getting under our feet. Stephen would be sure to lose himself, just as his father did before him. No, they'll stay with Thora and Nancy. You will be expected in the breakfast room in exactly fifteen minutes! Allison's been up and preparing herself for hours."

Typical, I thought in a disgruntled mood. Allison's natural sloth deserted her when it was a matter of devotion to her beauty. As of late she had even begun to neglect her appearance, and I was contrarily pleased to see a spark of life in her. Her brooding listlessness bothered me more than I cared to admit, leaving me without an enemy to take my mind off my troubles. I would welcome a touch of her malicious tongue.

Fifteen minutes barely allowed me enough time to array myself properly, and for this I was grateful. With a spurt of bravery I discarded the stifling confines of my corset—on such a humid day I would surely swoon, and that was the last thing I wished to do. I had my self-image as a strong, self-reliant woman, and swoonings didn't fit in with it.

Clad only in one light cotton petticoat and bloomers, I searched through my meager belongings in the heavy wardrobe for the coolest thing I owned. My green dress had been burned; my navy ones would kill me before we were halfway there. Disconsolately I put on the pale blue dress I had made, and winced at the demure picture in the mirror.

"It's all for the best," I told myself severely. "You'll fare much better if you fade into the background. Everyone in the household seems to know what's ailing you—you needn't disgrace yourself in public as well."

"Yes, Miss Lorna?" Nancy's blond head poked through the door as I stood surveying myself. "Did you call me?"

I flushed with embarrassment. "No, thank you, Nancy. I was just . . . talking to myself."

She cocked her head to one side to stare at me oddly, and for a brief second I could see her resemblance to Jenny. But that was only natural—the girl was her niece, even if it was on the wrong side of the blanket. When it came right down to it, there were a great many people on this island with cause to hate the Camerons, and I would have given several years of my life to have Nancy's face form into a murderous rage, to have her attack me, confessing her murderous activities.

This fantasy lasted for only a second. Placid, gentle Nancy had never had a murderous thought in her life.

"All right," said my late suspect. "Well, let me know if you need help. Is *that* what you're wearing?" Her tone implied contempt.

"Yes," I replied defensively. "It's a very proper dress."

"A bit too proper, if you ask me," she muttered under her breath, shutting the door behind her.

"And that's what you get for talking to yourself, my girl," I whispered, pulling my hair out of its braids and brushing the flaming tresses ruthlessly. I rebraided it and arranged it in two minutes flat, in an appallingly severe style that made my head ache. I swept from the room before I could change my mind.

When I entered the dining room I looked to neither the right nor left, going straight to the sideboard and heaping my plate to forestall the inevitable comments from Allison and her sharp-tongued mother-in-law. I seated myself and began shoveling the food in, determined not to behave as if anything were out of the ordinary. When I had finally devoured a mound of scrambled eggs, three blueberry muffins, and twelve sausages, my empty stomach felt a little bit better, even if my heart still ached. I looked up challengingly.

Lady Margaret was eying me calmly enough, having had time to assimilate all the nondescript details of my costume. Allison was staring out the windows, dressed to the teeth in flowing black crepe.

"You needn't have worried, Lorna, my dear," Lady Margaret broke the silence with some asperity. "Pamela Sutton is christening the ship—we're expecting an announcement momentarily. He wouldn't have noticed no matter how attractively you dressed."

I flushed, and a new wave of misery swept over me at the thought of having to face that supercilious female once more. If he was fool enough and bastard enough to marry her when he swore he didn't care for her, then I hoped the *Sea Witch the Second* would sink, with both of them on it.

"Well, at least you two won't disgrace me, though heaven knows why Allison chose such funereal garb," she continued. "A little lavender or pale gray might help the general atmosphere, my dear." Allison turned her curiously dead gaze from the windows to her mother-in-law.

"I felt it appropriate," she answered in a small, lifeless voice, and turned back to the open window.

Lady Margaret opened her mouth to speak, then snapped it shut again. We finished our meal in silence, then rose to leave at Lady Margaret's signal. And I knew something was very wrong. I knew that when I returned to this house it would be changed forever. The end was near, and suddenly I no longer wanted to know the truth. I was frightened, terribly frightened of what I knew I would find out this day.

"What's ailing you, girl?" Lady Margaret demanded as she stood before the hall mirror, adjusting the stiff plumes of her elegant purple hat.

For a brief moment I wanted to plead a sick headache, wanted to run and hide in my bedroom and await the denouement I knew was coming. I stiffened my back. I may be a poor, lovelorn creature but I certainly am not a coward. "Not a thing, Lady Margaret," I answered calmly, offering her my arm to assist her frail old body down the wide stone steps of the front entrance. "Not a thing."

It took us a full three hours to make our way to town, and we completed the journey in several stages. First the wagon from the main house to the dock, then the dory taking us to the mainland. There we were met by a more elegant equipage, driven by Nancy's uncle, who apparently didn't bear grudges for his sister's fall from grace.

This carried us the four miles to the train depot. From there we took a private coach to the outskirts of town and disembarked to meet Charles's affable grin.

"Well met, beautiful ladies," he greeted us. Everything about him was perfect; his tan wool suit perfectly tailored, his shirt starched to the nth degree, not a strand of brown hair out of place. He looked cool and calm and oddly exhilarated as he helped us off the train, and I wondered how he could bear the heat. I knew my forehead glistened, and the back of my dress clung damply to my uncorseted skin. Charles's expression, however, seemed to imply that I was the loveliest thing he had ever set his eyes on, for he held my waist just a little bit longer than was necessary, and when he let go he took my hand for a brief instant and pressed it meaningfully, and I knew I wouldn't be able to forestall a declaration much longer.

Before I had time to respond (or even decide how I wanted to respond), he moved to assist his mother, and I was left to ponder why such a charming, gentle man should be attracted to a gawky virgin like me. And why was I unable to respond with nothing more than polite uneasiness at his ardor?

To the latter question I knew the answer. He was waiting at the shipyards with the revered Cameron name emblazoned all over them, his coat unpressed, his tie awry, his black curls tangled above his tanned forehead. He looked as if he had been drinking, yet his greeting was perfectly sober.

He was dressed all in black, like Allison's mournful garb, from his long slim legs to his rumpled coat. I shivered in foreboding, and his piercing blue eyes met mine.

"How are you, Lorna?" he greeted me in a quiet, formal tone of voice. "I'm pleased you were able to come."

"Oh, I'm sure she wouldn't have missed it for the world." Pamela Sutton fluttered up, placing a slim, possessive hand on his black-clad arm. "After all, we want to make sure she sees all the various parts of Maine culture so that she can tell all her agricultural friends about

it when she returns." Her use of the term agricultural was laden with
contempt, and I longed to rip her pretty black hair out by the roots. I
smiled frostily.

In no time at all we were surrounded by a milling crowd of people,
and I was separated from all the Camerons. I searched around hopelessly for a familiar face, and then wished I hadn't. I was rewarded
with the overbearing presence of Senator Goodridge.

"Well, if it isn't pretty little Miss MacDougall!" he cried heartily,
grasping my unwilling hand in his plump, be-ringed one and gazing
into my eyes. As I was neither little nor particularly pretty, I realized the man was seriously smitten, and I tried to remember if he was
the politician Lady Margaret said drank. I greeted him uneasily, trying in vain to loosen my hand from his impassioned grip.

"You must allow me, my dear Miss MacDougall, to escort you
into the reception room and procure a glass of champagne for you on
this hot day. Wonderful crowd, isn't it? These Camerons certainly
know how to entertain royally." He continued a steady stream of
chatter as he steered me firmly through the crowds of people and into
the equally crowded reception room of Cameron Bros., Inc. "I'm
glad to see Alex is finally settling down—Pamela Sutton will do very
nicely for him. She has money and family and looks. Of course, she
has a wicked temper, but a wild un like Alex should be able to keep a
filly like her in hand, don't you know? About time for him to be setting out again—if there's one thing I don't hold with it's a shiftless
younger generation. That's what first caught my eye about you. Goodridge, I told myself, there's a damned handsome girl, not afraid to
go out and work for a living. There's a girl with spirit, I told myself.
If you don't watch yourself some young sprig is going to snap her up
before you have a chance. Get in there, boy, I told myself." I was
paying little attention to this, and unfortunately the poor man took
this for compliance and youthful shyness.

"Lorna," he said huskily, "Miss MacDougall, I . . ."

"Senator Goodridge." A polite young man appeared at our elbows
and I breathed a sigh of relief. "Mr. Charles Cameron wishes to
speak with you." He gestured to Charles's waiting figure.

"What does he want?" the senator demanded testily, his romantic
ardor dimming slightly.

"I believe he wishes to ask if you'd address a few words to the
crowd," the young man murmured deferentially, his eyes lowered.

"Oh well, in that case." Senator Goodridge did a complete about-
face. "You'll excuse me, my dear," he said to me hastily. "My public,
you know."

"Certainly," I murmured shyly, trying to keep the look of relief from my expressive face. His stuffy little figure moved off across the room and the young man turned and followed, pausing only long enough to give me a conspiratorial wink.

For some reason this cheered me as nothing else had done, and I wandered around the outskirts of the crowd almost lightheartedly. Someone thrust a glass of champagne into my hand, and I drank it swiftly, grateful for anything cool and liquid on such a hot, stuffy day. The Cameron family were all surrounded by well-wishers and family friends, and I felt an irrational moment of anger that Katie's death could have been glossed over so easily and forgotten by these very same people. I kept drinking the champagne that filled my glass each time I had finished, and soon lost count. I felt hot and dizzy and angry as I searched the crowd for a view of Alex. And there he was, dancing attendance on that smooth little bitch, I thought truculently. Well, I wished him happy, and his eyes met my unhappy ones across the room.

In a dream I watched him detach himself from Pamela's clinging hands and move through the crowd with a surprising swiftness and grace. In a moment he was by my side. Without a word he took my hand in his cool strong one and pulled me gently, inexorably through a door and into an elegantly appointed office.

Chapter XXIII

"This is Charles's office," he said briefly, closing the door behind us and moving to the window. "I thought you might need some fresh air after all that stuffiness. You weren't looking too well." After a short struggle with the latch he opened the window and a waft of salt air blew in, ruffling the neatly arranged papers on Charles's desk, ruffling my tightly braided hair, catching any loose strands. Alex turned and faced me across the room, an inexplicable tension filling us both.

"Senator Goodridge looked as if he was about to offer a proposition to you," he said, a trace of amusement in his dark blue eyes. "I sent Danny over to save you; I trust I did the right thing?"

"Yes, thank you," I murmured politely, staring out the window over his shoulder. "When will the christening be? I'm longing to see your figurehead. It must be something of rare beauty to have filled your time like that." I sounded like a debutante, and I hated myself.

"Don't chatter," he said. "Whatever did you do to your hair?" He moved closer to me, and the tension rose.

"Nothing," I muttered nervously, longing for escape, dreading it. "Shouldn't you be with your guests?"

"No." He came even closer, standing directly in front of me, looking down on my not too petite frame from his superior height, dwarfing me. I was finding it a little difficult to breathe, and he was well aware of it, as a man is always aware of the effect he has on a woman.

I stared up at him, suddenly frightened. He wasn't a bit drunk, as I had first imagined. He was in a strange, wild, reckless mood, and I knew that anything might happen. His iron control had finally snapped. Without thinking I reached up and smoothed his rumpled collar, and he caught my hand in a cruel grasp.

I let out a gasp of pain, and he laughed. It was not a pleasant sound. "Why are you afraid of me all of a sudden?" he demanded, his hand like a vise on my wrist. "Do you think I'm going to strangle you, or toss you out of my dear brother's window into the sea?" He was so close I could feel the heat from his body penetrate mine.

"Let go of me," I demanded hoarsely, dizzy with fright and other emotions, foremost among them a desire to throw myself into his arms.

"I'm not some poor orphan like my niece and nephew," he said harshly. "I don't need an itinerant mother."

"Then what do you need?" I cried helplessly, and, twisting my wrist, he pulled me into his arms and kissed me, hard.

We were both surprised at the swiftness of my response. I no longer had time to think, to weigh, to condemn. I flung my arms around his neck and answered him with a passion equal to his own. He kissed my mouth, my face, my neck, and when he tried to draw away I brazenly put my mouth on his once more, unwilling to let it stop. For who knew when it would ever be repeated? I was lost in his body, and he in mine, so lost we didn't hear the door open to our private haven.

"So this is where you are, Alex." Charles's voice was cold as ice. We jumped apart guiltily, I with an irrational nervousness. "I might have known you'd be seducing servants in your spare time, leaving your future wife for the family to take care of. You never had any sense of family, any sense of consideration. You never really belonged with us, you know. With your twisted habits, just like our father . . ." His voice was getting shriller by the moment. Alex merely stared at him expressionlessly, his blue eyes remote and bored. "It's not as if you cared for Lorna at all, is it?" demanded Charles. "You knew I . . . I was fond of her and you went out of your way to prove that even though I couldn't have her all you had to do was snap your fingers. And it worked, Brother mine. You used her as you used Allison; she means nothing to you, isn't that true? Isn't it?" He was almost screaming now, his ruddy face redder than ever, the veins bulging in his temples.

I turned to Alex, waiting for the denial I knew must come. How could I be mistaken in him?

He smiled slowly then, refusing to meet my pleading eyes. "You're right, of course, Brother Charles. You've always been so right, haven't you? I always was a bastard, in every sense of the word but one." And with those few words, so very few words to destroy a human being, he nodded coolly and strolled from the room.

We stood there in deathly silence, Charles and I. He spoke first. "Lorna, I'm sorry. You had to know. He's . . ."

I left the room before I had to hear another word. I could stand no more of the Camerons. The reception room was emptying of people, and, blinded by tears, I felt myself pulled along in their wake. Without realizing where I was going I found myself at the front of the crowd, a few feet away from Pamela Sutton and the glorious Camerons. Charles's assistant made a hasty appearance, the senator in tow, and the crowd grew quiet, awaiting the formalities. Of Charles himself there was no sign. The prow of the ship stood above us, tall and majestic, the figurehead shrouded as a work of art about to be unveiled. From my limited view the *Sea Witch the Second* was the most beautiful ship I had ever seen, and sincerely I hoped it would end on the bottom of the ocean floor with as many Camerons aboard as could fit.

"Where's Allison?" Lady Margaret spied me from her place of honor.

"I haven't seen her," I answered in a loud whisper, averting my eyes from her two sons.

"Thoughtless creature," Lady Margaret sniffed, leaning back in her chair.

"I'll go look for her," I offered, desperate to escape from the withdrawn look on Alexander Cameron's face, Pamela Sutton's beaming smile.

"No, you don't," her ladyship snapped. "You stay right there where you belong. If Allison misses the christening then it's her problem."

I stood there, shifting uneasily, as the senator's mellifluous tones flowed on and on over what was obviously a carefully written speech. My mind was in a daze, I was barely aware when the senator stopped and Lady Margaret started. And then a bottle of champagne was placed in Pamela's delicate hand.

"I christen thee *Sea Witch the Second,*" she called out, and, as she smashed the champagne over the prow the protecting sheet was pulled away from the figurehead.

A hush fell over the crowd, and I thought Pamela Sutton might faint. For there, larger than life for all to see, was Lorna MacDougall in wood, naked to the waist with coils of hair like snakes around her shoulders and slightly exaggerated breasts. And then I saw the face, my face that Alex had carved. And it was a far more beautiful face than I had ever seen in a mirror, the forehead broad and compassionate, the face sweet and yet full of a devilish humor. And I knew that he loved me, and I laughed out loud for the joy of it.

And then a shrill scream shattered the afternoon, and all was chaos. Alex leapt from the platform, ignoring the furiously blushing

Miss Sutton and myself, and ran in the direction of the scream. I was shoved out of the way by the milling crowd, and unwillingly I found myself face to face with Pamela.

"You slut!" she hissed at me. "You shameless hussy!" She spat at me, and without thinking I hauled off and slapped her as hard as I could. She shrieked and ran to Senator Goodridge's side, and I was forced to meet the grim amusement on Lady Margaret's face.

"I had no idea anything of this sort was going on," she stated. "I thought I'd scotched such a complication. Help me to Charles's office, girl. I have a dreadful feeling the worst is yet to come on this Godforsaken day. Someone will bring us news of this latest disaster."

I took her arm and we moved slowly past the startled spectators. Please, let me be wrong, I prayed silently. Let it not be Allison.

But it was. As we moved toward the office I saw the cluster of men: Alex, the senator, several ominous uniforms, standing over the body draped on the stretcher, the body with Allison's voluminous black skirts.

A woman was standing to one side, weeping audibly, telling her tale to avid listeners.

"I found her lying there in the corner," she was saying. "With blood all over her, pouring out. I was late, you see, and I thought I'd take a short-cut . . ." Her plump form shuddered dramatically and her audience pressed closer in sympathy.

"Oh, my Lord," Lady Margaret breathed. "Help me to the office." There were tears on the old lady's face, and tears on my own, I knew. It was slow going, and when we finally reached the inner sanctum Lady Margaret sank down gratefully, the weight of the world on her shoulders.

"I was afraid of this," she murmured brokenly. "So afraid." It was piteous, to see the indomitable old lady break down, and my heart spared a moment's pain for her.

She turned her grief-ravaged face to me. "Leave," she ordered suddenly. "Get back to the children. We were fools to leave them alone."

A cold feeling of dread washed over me. "What do you mean?" I demanded fiercely. "Are they in any sort of danger?"

"Of course they are! Isn't this all obvious to you?" she screeched back, then shook her head in despair. "No, perhaps it isn't. Just get back to them. There's a train leaving in half an hour . . . if you hurry you can make it." I stood still, staring at her in amazement. "Stop dawdling, girl. Their lives may depend on you!"

I turned to leave, stopping only for a moment. "If anything happens to the children that you could have prevented," I said coldly, "I swear to God I'll . . . I'll . . ."

"Nothing will happen if you hurry," she snapped, desperation in her eyes. "If I could possibly leave I would, but I'll only slow you down. They'll try to hold us up and question me—this is one death too many. For God's sake, child, run!"

Chapter XXIV

And run I did. I collared a passing hansom and sped to the train station with barely a second to spare. There I handed out almost all of my remaining money for a ticket, then settled myself as best I could into the scratchy blue velvet seat to await my destination.

The train was almost deserted at that hour. It was a bit before three o'clock, too early for the tired workingmen to make their way homeward. I sat there, fidgeting, wondering, going back over the monstrous, incredible happenings of the days as I fought against the headache that pounded behind my eyes. Surreptitiously I loosened the bone hairpins, then sighed with blessed relief, able to concentrate for the first time that day.

A fog was rolling in; I could barely see ten feet beyond the grime-specked window of the slow-moving train. My hands were restless in my lap, stripping off my serviceable white cotton gloves and putting them on again. How could this have happened? I thought desperately. How could it?

By this time Alex would be in custody. There would be no chance for him to take the easy way out, to sail off into the blue and never return. And he would have taken me with him, and I would have gone, willingly, knowing full well that a man who has killed once, twice, even three or four times will certainly kill again. Because he loved me—there was no denying that. The proof was in that indecent carving of me, proof that only decades of salt spray could begin to obliterate. And then I remembered his words to me. "Do you think I'm going to strangle you, or toss you out of my dear brother's window into the sea?" For that was what had happened to poor Allison, who knew she was going to die. She had been stabbed and her body dumped out of the office window like so much refuse. But her body hadn't been claimed by the sea, it had become wedged in the dock pilings. I had heard them talking of it as I ran by; the conductor had been full of news. So they would take my lovely Alex and hang him. If they caught him before he harmed the children.

But that did not make sense, I thought stubbornly. Alex loved the children, loved them dearly. He could no more hurt them than he could have walked on water. Something was wrong with this whole thing, something was missing. Or perhaps I was just grasping at straws, searching for an escape from Alex's inevitable guilt. Something was missing from the puzzle, and try as I would to force my poor head to see it, the vision stubbornly, infuriatingly eluded me.

I must have run from the train station to the Camerons' private dock. It was after five by the time we arrived, and the fog had settled in with all its Maine denseness. I had worried about how I would make it to the island; that problem was solved. The boat was tied up, waiting conveniently, too conveniently, I would have thought if my wits had been about me. As it was I was too muddled with terror and haste to even grasp the significance. Someone was expecting me on Cameron's Landing.

It seemed to take forever to make my way through the fog. I was haunted by hideous imaginings—that I drifted out to sea and they found my body weeks or months later. Or perhaps not at all, and my sun-bleached bones would drift forever around the Maine coast. The denseness frightened me more than anything had so far, and it was with amazed relief that a patch of visibility showed me the island dock directly ahead. I jumped out onto the damp sand, barely remembering to tie up the dory. I paused for a moment, trying to decide which would be the fastest route to the house, by the beach or by the road, when I heard a familiar whinny.

"Samantha?" I called softly, and her ghostly figure loomed out of the darkness. She was saddleless and nervous, and I wondered briefly at her timely appearance.

"Come, girl," I murmured quietly, soothingly. "Come here." She recognized my voice, and her dancing stopped. I reached out and stroked her muzzle, whispering all the time.

"You're going to take me home, girl," I said, soothing her, grasping her reins loosely so as not to frighten her. "You're going to take me back to my children." I jumped up on her back, and she reared in sudden fright, nearly throwing me. I calmed her as best I could, but she was fear-maddened. Like a crazed creature she took off down the road, and I could only hold tight and thank God it was in the right direction.

She didn't stop until she reached the courtyard, and I jumped from her quickly, before she could decide to take off in another direction. I stood there for a moment, my hands trembling with sudden terror.

The house looked strange to me through the mist, and then I realized why. There were no lights burning, no sounds of activity.

Almost hysterical with fear and dread, I slammed open the back door and ran into the kitchen. The dying fire gave out only a fitful light in the deserted room usually filled with servants at that hour of the day.

Suddenly through the gloom I could see Old John's still form sitting by the fire.

"John!" I called out gratefully. "Why didn't you answer me? I was . . ." I stopped within a few feet of him, silenced by sheer horror. A knife protruded from his scarcely moving chest.

Slowly, very slowly I backed away. I had to find help. Turning, I ran out into the great hallway, searching through the gloom, calling the children's names in desperation.

"But they're gone, my dear Lorna," a quiet voice said, and I whirled around in terror to face Charles, his face wreathed in an attractive smile, the oil lamp in his still hand spreading gloomy shadows on the walls. And suddenly I knew, the simple, obvious truth that had eluded me for so long. The cradle, where Charles's mother had lived out her mad life before passing on the taint to her son, was my warning, and I had chosen to ignore it; too besotted with the murderer's half brother to recognize his innocence. I hadn't even noticed Charles's damning absence at the unveiling a few short hours earlier.

I drew a deep, shuddering breath. "Where have they gone, Charles?" I asked him gently.

His smile broadened. "You don't fool me, Lorna. I could read it in your face when you saw me here. You know perfectly well that Alex didn't kill Allison. Nor Katie nor Josiah nor Stephen nor Old John."

Pretended ignorance would have availed me nothing. "Old John's not dead yet," I said flatly. "You killed them."

"If he's not dead yet he will be soon enough." He smiled his charming smile. "Of course I killed them, Lorna. It was unpleasant but necessary." He held out a hand to me, which I studiously ignored. "I'd like you to come with me, please, Lorna," he said in a sterner voice. "I want to try and explain it to you, so that you might not judge me too harshly." He gestured toward the terrace. "Please. There's nothing to harm you out there." He waited for me to precede him, and like a mesmerized being I did. The cool sea breeze hit me as I stepped onto the flagstones, and some bit of rationality came back to me. I must escape from him, I thought. I must find the children.

Smiling then, I turned to him with courteous interest. "Tell me, Charles."

He paused, flattered by my attention. "It was necessary, you see," he began. "Each death begat the next one, just as my poor mad mother begat me. Some people would say I'm mad, you know."

"Yes, Charles, some would," I agreed recklessly, but my honesty seemed to please him.

"That's what drew me to you at first," he said eagerly, his brown eyes shining. "Your outspokenness. In this house no one ever spoke the truth. It's just as well, I suppose." His eyes were glazed with sadness.

"You killed Josiah."

Charles's handsome face grew sad at the thought. "My father began to suspect something was wrong with me. He feared my mother's madness, and all my life he looked for signs of it in me. Until he finally thought he had found some. He told me he was taking the charge of the company out of my hands. He said that I was . . . unfit to handle it."

"So you killed him," I prompted.

Charles began to pace the terrace like a caged animal. "And then Stephen. He suspected that I might have something to do with Father's death. He knew my mother was mad, and that I had inherited the family weakness. He knew I used to . . . to hurt things when we were younger. He told me I was getting worse and worse, that he no longer could keep silent about it. But that wasn't true!" he cried. "He only wanted my part of the inheritance, for himself and his stupid, greedy wife. I saw through him. And disposed of him. You do understand it was necessary, don't you?" he pleaded of me. "He was trying to steal my birthright. A man can't let his birthright be stolen."

"Of course not," I said softly, not wanting to break his concentration.

His mad eyes narrowed. "Ah, but then I was clever. I thought if Alex could be convicted of it, then I would never have to worry about my inheritance again."

"But not so clever," I said quietly. "No one realized that Stephen was murdered. No one but me."

"You found that burr." It was a statement, not a question. "Really, Lorna, you've certainly been a lot of trouble. If you had only shown the burr to someone it would have been traced directly to Alex, and all this would have been over with." He kicked at the terrace, a spoiled, fretful child. "That was when things began going wrong. Allison knew I killed my father. She saw me walking away from his body that afternoon, and she blackmailed me." His outrage was almost touching. "She never realized that I was responsible for her husband's death too. Despite her shallowness, I think that would have been too much for her."

"The poor, stupid creature," I murmured in disgust. She had almost deserved to die for her abysmal, stupid greed. "But why did you kill Katie?"

"Oh," he said sadly. "Katie. That was a mistake."

"You meant to kill Allison then?"

"No, my dear. I meant to kill you." The words were so prosaic, so mundane, and the meaning so hideous that I could say nothing. Apparently I was not expected to reply. "You had betrayed me, my dear. I could see my brother Alex was totally overcome by you, and you; you were another one of his many conquests. I would have thought he'd learned from his childhood that he couldn't thwart me, couldn't take what I wanted, but apparently not. All that business with Pamela Sutton never fooled me for a moment. I thought Katie was you that night, running out to meet her lover. I threw her down the cliff before she had a chance to utter a word." He was staring at his highly polished shoes, mumbling slightly, like a small boy confessing some minor naughtiness.

He looked up and smiled his beguiling smile. "But this time there'll be no mistake. Alex has been taken into custody by now for Allison's death, and everyone will believe that you walked into the sea after stabbing poor Old John in a frenzy, driven mad by the thought of a life without Alex. That will be easy enough to believe, after that shameless figurehead he carved."

"Charles, where are the children?" I broke in. I wasn't sure how I could escape from his murderous intent, but I would scarcely try until I knew the children were safe.

"The children?" he questioned vaguely. "Oh, they're gone."

"Gone where, Charles?" I demanded, a note of hysteria in my voice.

He smiled maliciously. "I took them down to the beach and left them there. The tide should be almost in by now."

"Oh, my God," I breathed. Without a second thought I leapt from the terrace and raced across the lawn, praying all the while that it wouldn't be too late. I could hear his laughter following me, and the sound sped me on even faster.

I took the beach stairs two at a time, tripping and falling down the last flight. My dress caught on a nail and I ripped it free savagely to run across the beach, calling them.

There was no sign of them. I felt horror and a pain so hideous I couldn't even begin to bear it welling up inside of me. They were gone, without a trace.

And then I realized that there would have been a trace. The tide wasn't in yet—they would have stayed as far away from the water as possible. I could have wept with relief and rage, murder in my heart that I should have been so frightened. Had I been wise I would have run along the beach—Charles never could have found me in that pea-soup fog. But he knew and I knew that I could never run when the fate of the children was uncertain. With barely a second's hesitation I went back up the wooden stairs, knowing full well I would find my murderer waiting for me.

He smiled blandly, blocking my way. "You didn't find them," he said gently.

"Of course I didn't." My voice was cold with a rage that drove out all fear of him. "Where are they?"

"Gone with Thora and Nancy, my dear. I would have liked to keep them here and finish the whole business tonight, but, alas, that wasn't to be." He sighed. "Have no fear, they'll join you in whatever lies beyond death soon enough."

"They won't harm you," I protested irrationally, knowing full well the insanity of using logic with a madman.

"They inherit their father's money. Money which should be mine." He took a step closer, smiling all the time, and I thought with a detached wonder, How very handsome he still is. None of this touches his perfect face.

"If only you'd realized I loved you, Lorna," he said sadly. "I would have shared everything with you. But instead you were bewitched by my brother." He sighed. "You've chosen your own punishment. I'm truly sorry, my dear. But think of it this way—you and Alex and the children will be together throughout eternity." His hands grabbed my shoulders in a vise-like grip, and I was curiously helpless to resist. I watched him out of numbed eyes, awaiting my death stoically. I felt the fingers tighten, and I shut my eyes.

"Let her go, Charles!" Alex's voice rang out in the fog. "Let her go or I'll shoot you in the back without another thought."

Charles's face twisted with rage. "But then I'll take her down with me, Brother mine. She'll be dead all the same."

"Let her go." His voice was filled with a cold, implacable rage, and I wondered that he could be so calm.

"Charles!" It was Lady Margaret's voice, autocratic and unflagging, and for the first time I saw the murderous determination in Charles's face waver.

"Yes, Mother?" His voice held a plaintive note.

Lady Margaret recognized it and exploited it ruthlessly. "You have been a very naughty boy, Charles. Very naughty."

Charles's shoulders sank. "I know." His voice was curiously younger, child-like even.

"You've been playing too roughly. You've hurt too many people," his stepmother continued, and each harsh word was like a blow. "You let Lorna go right now, and then I want you to go to your room and stay there until I say you can come out. You'll have to be punished. You know that."

To my amazed relief I felt his large hands loosen and let go of me. It took all the will-power I possessed to keep myself from collapsing and falling over the cliffs on my own volition. I stared with numb horror at Charles's unhappy, guilt-ridden figure.

"I'm sorry, Mother," he said sadly, moving away from me. "I'm sorry," he sobbed, then broke and ran off into the fog back toward the house.

Alex's tall form moved out of the darkness and caught me in his arms. I clung to him in desperation, somehow convinced that I should be safe if I simply never let go of his strong body.

Lady Margaret moved into sight, leaning heavily on her cane, her face the face of a destroyed woman. "I'm sorry, my dear, for what I've done to you."

"It's not your fault," I murmured from the shelter of Alex's arms. "You couldn't have known."

"I *should* have known," she overruled me. "Alex, stop crushing the poor child and help her back to the house. The constable should be here by now—we ought to be there to receive him properly."

I felt a burst of hysterical laughter well up in me at the thought of Lady Margaret's insane etiquette, and grimly I forced it down. I moved a bit in Alex's arms, and immediately he let go of me, which wasn't what I had wanted at all. His tanned, handsome face was absolutely expressionless.

We were an odd trio, making our way up the lawn to the Cameron mansion. As we neared the terrace I noticed through the fog that it was ablaze with lights.

"How did you get here?" I questioned briefly. "I took the dory."

"Alex stole a boat," answered Lady Margaret for him, and for the first time I detected a note of motherly pride, of maternal warmth that had heretofore been reserved for her beloved murderer. I cast a quick glance at Alex's impassive face, and wondered what he was thinking.

A stout, red-faced man in a blue uniform met us at the door. "We can't find a trace of him, ma'am. He ran up the back stairs and as far as my men can tell he hasn't come down yet. We searched all the rooms up there but so far nothing's turned up."

"I know where he is," I said quietly.

"Where?" the constable rapped sharply.

"I'll show you," I answered, starting toward the door. For a moment I thought Alex would say something, but when I turned to him he was still cold and impassive. Without another word I turned back, leading the way, up the main staircase, past the rows of silent and deserted bedrooms, to the attic door.

Silently, stealthily I opened it and started up. Someone passed me an oil lamp, and fearlessly I held it high as we crossed the dusty attic floor. A steady creaking filled the room, and, as we neared the discarded furniture a strange little noise floated to our ears. It was, or seemed to be, the sound of a baby humming to itself. And there, in the cradle, lay Charles, rocking quietly back and forth, gazing at us with unseeing eyes as he drifted back into childhood forever.

Epilogue

I made my way down the quiet hallways, my bare feet making scarcely a sound on the carpeted floors. Lady Margaret was safely in her bed, a warm fire making some dent in the damp chill that had followed the incredible heat of the day. The constable and his minions were watching Charles—I had brought them coffee and cakes from Thora's vast supply. They'd been able to get Old John to the mainland before the smothering fog made travel impossible. There was a good chance he'd survive, they told me. But they didn't dare try to take the poor blubbering baby from his cradle in the inky, soupy darkness. Tomorrow would be time enough. God knows, he was harmless at last.

I wondered where Alex was. Not a word had he spoken after we found Charles in the attic. He had turned from us all in silence and disappeared, and I was too shy and uncertain to go after him. Besides, a now fretful Lady Margaret needed me more right then. He would come back if he wanted to, he would go if he wanted to. I was past wondering, I told myself wearily.

I pulled my night robe closer around my slender body, trying to ignore the frightened pounding of my heart against my ribs. I could only hope I wouldn't run into one of the constable's men, with me traipsing around the old house with my hair a heavy curtain down my back, dressed in my night clothes. We'd have enough gossip as it was.

Alex's bedroom door was open. A fire was crackling with indecent merriment in the hearth, and it lit the room with a fitful glow. Enough light to see him standing in front of the window, staring out into the fog.

I must have made some sound, some movement. He turned and watched me across the wide expanse of the room. We stood there for a breathless eternity, not saying a word.

"Come here, Horace," he said softly. And I came into the room, shutting the heavy oak door behind me.

There was a scandal that couldn't be hushed up, of course, and for months the Cameron name and the ghastly murders figured prominently in the scandalmongering journals of this country and Europe. After all, the Cameron ships were known all over the world—such a juicy piece of gossip could hardly be passed over lightly.

Alex and I were married a few days after they took poor witless Charles away. I had no intention of spending another night alone in that house, nor did Alex have any intention of letting me. So we were lawfully joined in holy matrimony three days after the consummation of our marriage—a fact which bothered everyone but my husband and me.

Starting out a marriage with two children might not seem the ideal situation to most, but it suited us very well. We loved Jenny and Stephen very much, and in a reasonable amount of time we presented them with seven little cousins to keep them company while I sailed off with my husband, leaving them all in the capable hands of their Aunt Nancy and their tyrannical grandmother.

Poor mad Charles died only a few years ago at the advanced age of eighty-seven. His mind was still that of an infant, but his body had unfortunately been a strong, healthy one. He was buried in the old graveyard in between his blood mother and his stepmother, a few feet away from his victims.

And dear Miss Pamela Sutton! She married Senator Goodridge and spurred him on to greater things, eventually ending up as a Cabinet member's wife. Alex and I went to their wedding, and perhaps only I noticed the rueful, longing expression in the bride's fine eyes whenever she glanced at Captain Cameron and his pregnant wife.

And now years and years have passed, and our lives have been turbulent and productive. Our children and grandchildren visit us often on our tiny island, safe haven among the suddenly crowded Maine coastline. And whenever they ask me, I tell them once more of the time when I was a lovelorn governess-companion and their tall, stately grandfather was a handsome sea captain.